SENTENCED TO TROLL

S.L. ROWLAND

ALSO BY S.L. ROWLAND

Pangea Online

Pangea Online: Death and Axes

Pangea Online 2: Magic and Mayhem

Pangea Online 3: Vials and Tribulations

Sentenced to Troll

Sentenced to Troll

Sentenced to Troll 2

Sentenced to Troll 3

Sentenced to Troll 4

Sentenced to Troll 5

Path to Villainy: An NPC Kobold's Tale

Vestiges: Portal to the Apocalypse

Collected Editions

Pangea Online: The Complete Trilogy

Sentenced to Troll Compendium: Books 1-3

Sentenced to Troll Copyright © 2018 by S.L. Rowland

SLRowland.com

All Rights Reserved. This book may not be reproduced or used in any manner without the permission of the author.

This is a work of fiction. Names, characters, places, and incidents either are the products of the author's imagination or are used fictitiously. Any resemblance to actual persons, living or dead, businesses, companies, events, or locales is entirely coincidental.

Editing by LKJ Bookmakers (lkjbooks.com)

Sign up for S.L. Rowland's Newsletter

Support S.L. Rowland on Patreon at patreon.com/slrowland

❀ Created with Vellum

To JKR, for showing the world that anything is possible.

PROLOGUE

"Died to the trolls again, did you, Glenn?" asked Randy. The dark skinned man emerged from the shadowy corner of The Dancing Donkey, his boiled leather armor and long black cape making him almost invisible in the dimly lit inn. His sword hung from his waist opposite a dagger the length of his forearm. Glenn wondered if he could grab the dagger and shove the pointy end through Randy's eye before anyone noticed.

Maybe later, thought Glenn.

"They're tougher than they look." Glenn patted Randy on the shoulder and forced a smile. "They nearly destroyed this world once. They could do it again."

"Most of these people have never even seen a troll." Randy laughed, pushing his thumbs against his belt. "From what I've heard, they're on the verge of extinction. I don't know how you keep convincing so many NPCs to follow you to your death, but you can have your trolls, Glenn. I'll stick to the dungeons and keep all the good loot for myself."

Glenn found a table in the corner of the room, taking in the other players who were settling in for the night. To them, this was a game, but to Glenn, this was everything he had ever dreamed of—an island where he could be anything he wanted to be and do anything he wanted to do. Sure, it was prison, but it was also paradise.

Glenn didn't care about dungeons. They were only useful in replenishing the gear he had lost each time he died to the trolls, along with a hard-earned level. He was interested in survival. If he wanted to become anything in this world, he needed to make sure the trolls wouldn't hold him back. He could influence people, bend them to his will even. He knew his Charisma was higher than most players and more than that, he knew how to use it to get things done. It didn't work on trolls, though. Somehow, they resisted his charm. In the end, it didn't matter. With every death, he took more trolls with him. And they didn't respawn.

He'd read the stories of old and talked to the townspeople. If there was anyone that would inhibit his rise to power, it would be the trolls.

The trolls were the problem, and they had to be destroyed.

CHAPTER ONE

1. Sentenced to Troll

My heart races. I sit behind the table. Its dark cherry wood is polished and pristine, unlike my reputation. To my right, my lawyer shuffles papers in a bored manner. He doesn't give two shits about this case. I'm sure he's ready to be out of here so he can meet his cronies for a beer or a game of golf. The swish of the paper is like a thousand papercuts to my eardrums. This must be how teachers feel when the whir of zippers crashes through their lecture like a tidal wave and there are still five minutes left in class. Except this is much worse. This is my future on the line.

I shouldn't be here. I should be at home logged into my computer, slaying orcs, trolls, and every other manner of foul creature.

The clock ticks by slowly on the wall. Tick. Tick. Tick. Who knew a second could be so long?

Sitting back in my chair, I straighten my tie. My hands shake slightly as I align it with the buttons on my shirt. It always seems to go askew, no matter how many times I fix it. The action doesn't waste nearly as much time as I want it to.

Any minute now, the judge should be coming out to announce my sentence.

I know I'm toast. I screwed up big time. Being a professional streamer, I'm supposed to set the example. Set the culture. I'm known for my clever taunting and never-say-die attitude; it's the main reason people follow me. I'm not a phenomenal gamer. If I were, I'd be a pro gamer and not just a glorified commentator. I screwed up, and I lost my temper. If it had been the first time, I probably wouldn't be here, but I'm a repeat offender. The sad thing is that I learned my lesson. Finally. I regretted what I said as soon as the match was over.

When they cuffed me and brought me into the station, that's when I knew that I had really screwed the pooch. The city wants to make an example out of me. If one of the top streamers in *League of Mythos* can be punished, it'll set a precedent for those below me. They hope to stamp this behavior out of esports entirely. Honestly, I don't blame them. I've dealt with my fair share of bullying and name-calling. I get trolls every time I stream. A lot of people would say I brought it on myself. The way the system works, it's almost like you're set up to fail. An entire community that hides behind a keyboard or an avatar. Some would call me a troll, but that's not true. Not really. I'm a rager. Not that it's any better. At least by punishing me, they'll finally show the world that no one is safe.

Sweat runs down the back of my shirt. I don't know what they have planned. The maximum sentence for online griefing is one year in prison, though I don't know anyone who has ever served that much time. Even though it's a crime, it's often ignored. Much like jaywalking. Those that are brought to trial, they get community service, a fine, and a slap on the wrist, but ever since the mayor's son offed himself because of online bullying by a rival guild, the city has been on a witch hunt.

I just happen to be the unlucky son of a bitch who lost his cool on a nationally-televised event. I had been invited to participate in a 'celebrity match' with other popular streamers before the championship.

Apparently, telling your teammates they are worthless cockroaches who only have one brain cell between them and that they probably have to pass it back and forth in the middle of the fight is frowned upon. If I had stopped there, I'd probably be fine. But I didn't stop there. I definitely should not have told Jordan to go kill herself for healing our DPS instead of the tank. Multiple times. I yelled at her so much that she had a mental breakdown right in the middle of the match. That was a dick move. I realize that now. And yes, using racial slurs is never a good idea. I had been breathing fire by the end of that match.

I lost my temper, plain and simple, and now I'm about to pay for it.

Just please don't send me to prison. I'm too pretty and too skinny to survive the ogres that are in there for real crimes, like murder and assault. I am not made for that type of environment.

The click of the doorknob announces the judge's return. Her face is stern, giving nothing away. The black robe she wears swishes when she walks, like some wizard of doom. The long black sleeves conceal a small envelope in her hand. I imagine that is the sentence she will be giving me. It's almost like winning an award, except for the part where it's not. There will be no afterparty once she reads its contents.

Anything but prison. I repeat the mantra in my mind like it will make a difference.

She takes a seat and bangs her gavel, bringing the courtroom to order. My lawyer sets down the papers he has been torturously shuffling and smiles. I want to punch him. Of course I was guilty, but he never even seemed interested in fighting for me or letting the judge know that I was remorseful. I bet the sorry sack of shit already has one foot out the door.

She clears her throat before reading the sentence that may change my life forever.

"In the case of New York vs Chadwick Bryan Johnson, based on video and audio evidence presented in court, I find the defendant guilty of online griefing." She sets the envelope down and looks at me directly. "Mister Johnson, this is not your first time being accused of griefing. Hell, this isn't even your fifth. You are widely known as a toxic player throughout your community, and I'm surprised it has taken this long for charges to be brought against you. Telling someone to kill themselves, hate speech, those are things that are no longer tolerated in League of Mythos or anywhere in society."

The entire time she is talking, the only thing I can think is 'please not prison.' I repeat it over and over. Anything but prison. Anything but prison.

"Is there anything you would like to say before I sentence you, Mister Johnson?" she asks.

I had a speech planned before we came in today, but now that the moment is here, all I can think of is the mantra running through my mind. My throat is suddenly parched. I open my mouth to speak but only a croak comes out.

"Mister Johnson?" she asks again.

"I-I'm sorry," is all I'm able to get out. This was my moment to at least show some remorse and maybe convince the judge to give me a lighter sentence, and all I can do is croak like a frog.

"Very well. The law states that one year in prison is the maximum allowed for offenses such as yours. Prison may very well be where you end up if you don't change your ways, but in your case, I feel it may do more harm than good."

I let out a sigh of relief. I'm not going to prison. I have to fight to keep the smile that dances at the edge of my lips from taking over entirely.

"It is not my goal to punish you, Mister Johnson, but to make you better understand the seriousness of your actions. Yes, they may just be words in an online game, but let me assure you, words do have power. If Miss Jordan had indeed acted on your words, you would be being sentenced for far more than online griefing right now. Let that sink in for a minute." She pauses and looks back down at the envelope. I'm on the edge of my seat, wondering what is in store for me. Prison is off the table, but I can tell by the look in her eyes that she has something bigger planned than community service. "Mister Johnson, you have been, for lack of a better word, a troll. A bully. Miss Jordan, the victim of your tirade, doesn't wish to hurt you or your ability to play online games. She wishes that you treat her and other players with respect, both your teammates and players on the other team. To help you learn what it feels like to be constantly attacked and berated, I think it is only fitting that you become the very thing you already are. You have therefore been sentenced to one month of full-immersion rehabilitation in Mythos Games' newest development, *Isle of Mythos.* You will be forced to play as a troll, the most hated faction on the island. For the next month, you will experience the same degree of verbal assault and backlash you have dealt out on so many occasions. I hope you are able to learn from this experience."

I let out a breath I didn't know I was holding. That's it? My punishment is to play a game for a month? Piece of cake. If I'd known that was an option, I wouldn't have been so worried.

"Guards, please take Mister Johnson to his holding cell while he awaits transport to Mythos Games Headquarters."

The guards grab me by the arms, and my lawyer is already out of the courtroom before they even have my hands cuffed.

As they walk me out the back of the courtroom, I scan the room, hoping to see my mother or father. They were in Japan on business. Business that was more important than seeing their only child before he was potentially shipped off to prison. That's the story of my life, though.

Their business was always their favorite baby. I honestly don't even know why they had a child. Maybe it saved their marriage by giving them something to ignore together.

"You got this!" a voice shouts. I turn to see Taryn, with his giant billowing afro, giving me a thumbs up. He's the only person I consider a true friend, as well as my queue partner in most games. The one person I can count on to have my back when things go south.

The guards lead me to the holding cell where a man in a black suit waits inside. He looks like some kind of special agent with the way the suit fits him perfectly at every angle. You can tell he's well-built underneath and could probably kick my ass in a hundred different ways. I wonder if he's here to make sure I don't escape. Not that I could.

I step inside and take a seat on one of the metal benches. It's cold and hard against my backside, a far cry from the ergonomic gaming chair I use when playing games.

"Feeling sorry yet, kid?" he asks. His voice is deep and gravelly. There's more manliness in those four words than I have in my entire body.

I nod. Now that I'm out of the courtroom, I wonder what kind of game I'm about to be logged into. I know full immersion has existed for a few years now, but it's so expensive to produce that it hasn't been marketed on a mass level yet. With Mythos Games being the biggest name in virtual reality gaming, it only makes sense that they would have something running on the down low.

Thirty days of full immersion. How is that even possible? It can't be healthy for a human to be still for so long.

We sit in silence. Mr. Secret Agent is content to let me sit and brood with my own thoughts. A few minutes later, his cell phone rings. He answers it, but doesn't say a word. When the call ends, he taps on the bar of the jail cell and a guard comes over to unlock the door.

"Our ride is here. Don't try anything stupid, and I won't have to hurt you," he says. He nods to the guards as we exit through a door into an alley where a black SUV waits with one door open.

My hands are still cuffed, so Mr. Secret Agent guides me into the SUV and takes a seat next to me. Two other men, both dressed in similar black suits, sit up front. As soon as the door shuts, we're on the move.

All of this makes me feel more important than I am.

"Where are we going?" I ask.

"Mythos Games Headquarters." Mr. Secret Agent pulls out his phone and sends a quick message to someone. "They take their security very seriously."

"What, do you think I'm going to escape?" I ask.

"Don't flatter yourself. This isn't for you. We're here to make sure you aren't followed. There are a lot of people who would love to get their hands on the technology you are about to experience."

Consider me intrigued. Mr. Secret Agent reaches into his jacket pocket and pulls out a fabric bag.

"This is for you, though." He puts the bag over my head and everything goes black.

The driver takes turn after turn, jostling me against the door, and I wonder if it's necessary or if it's all an attempt to lose anyone who might be trailing us. I don't understand what the big deal is. Everyone knows where Mythos Games Headquarters is. It's the biggest building downtown, dwarfing all the others. The architecture makes the building look like a giant wizard's tower and at night, it glows and smoke billows out the top. I've done several press events there with my team.

The SUV makes a sharp turn, slamming me into the wall. Mr. Secret Agent removes my blindfold and I see we are in an underground parking garage. A metal gate closes behind us and we go down three levels before stopping in front of another gate. The driver rolls down his window and scans his badge. The gate opens, and we speed through. This far down, all the levels are empty. We descend three more levels before coming to a stop in a parking space far against the back wall in a dimly-lit parking deck. There are only a handful of cars parked here, along with a few more black vans. We're so far down that this is practically a dungeon.

I can see an elevator tucked into the wall near where we park.

Mr. Secret Agent opens his door, and I attempt to do the same. It doesn't budge. They child-proofed me.

"This way," he orders.

Surrounded by the three men, I feel like someone important, a president or a celebrity. For a moment, I'm not a criminal.

They guide me towards the elevator, but when I stop in front of it, Mr. Secret Agent nudges me in the back to keep walking. There is nothing ahead of us but a brick wall and a flickering light attached to it.

A thought runs across my mind, and I stiffen. Are they going to kill me?

Mr. Secret Agent must sense my nervousness, because

he says, "Relax, kid. Nobody is going to kill you today. Now get moving."

For whatever reason, I believe him.

I do as I'm told, and we walk to the corner of the parking deck. One of the other men faces the brick wall, searching for something. I try to see what he is staring at but can't see anything other than brick and mortar.

His fingers run along the bricks before abruptly stopping. He presses against a single brick and it slides deeper into the wall.

A secret entrance!

The brick recedes and a door seems to form in the wall, opening into another dimly-lit cavern. The hidden entrance closes behind us as we step through.

Old Edison bulbs dangle from the ceiling, their light bathing the tunnel in an eerie glow. I follow the two men in suits through a labyrinth of brick tunnels for what seems like forever. We could be anywhere under the city by now. Eventually, the dungeon-like atmosphere morphs into something more industrial. The concrete floors smooth out, the old bulbs are replaced by white neon lights, and the aged brick walls become painted cinder blocks. At the end of the hall, a metal staircase winds upwards next to an elevator.

The two men stop in front of it. It looks like we might actually be able to use this one. One of the men flashes his ID card in front of a proximity reader next to the elevator and the doors whoosh open.

What could possibly be so important that we have to go through this much secrecy?

The doors close rapidly after we step into the elevator. There are no floor numbers for the men to press, but the elevator begins to move all the same. My legs give way slightly as we ascend at a rapid pace, and then just as suddenly, we stop moving.

The doors open, and I find myself looking into a pristine laboratory, whiteness engulfing the room. The floors, the lighting, and even the walls are white. The four of us are like specks of pepper in a salty landscape.

Men and women in white lab-coats shuffle about the room. They carry digital pads, making notes and checking figures. One lady bends down, inspecting one of several pods in the center of the lab.

I suddenly notice that there are people inside the pods. Full immersion.

Ignoring the three men who brought me here, I step further into the lab. They don't say anything or try to stop me. There must be two dozen pods, each one occupied. Those inside are completely submerged in a blue liquid. They look peaceful, asleep almost. Video feeds display their movements in the game.

"Mister Johnson," says a silky-smooth female voice. A brunette woman in a tight high-necked blue dress appears to my right. It's modest, but clings so tightly to her body that it leaves nothing to the imagination. She can't be older than thirty. Much too young to be running an operation like this. "Welcome to Mythos Games, the part we don't show the public." She looks oddly familiar, but I can't quite place where I've seen her. She winks at me, then turns to the men who brought me here. "Adams, Franklin, Roosevelt, I think I can handle it from here."

The men nod and leave. I wonder which one is Mr. Secret Agent.

"What is this place?" I ask.

She flashes me a smile. I'm sure her pearly-white teeth have been the downfall of many men.

"This is R and D." She waves her hand through the air, putting the laboratory on display. "Research and Development. The next wave of Mythos Games."

"And why exactly am I here?" It doesn't make sense why I am in some highly secret technohub for a crime that would land me a year in prison max. There has to be more to it.

"Follow me," she instructs, taking me across the lab to a white desk near the wall. It's oddly neat for a research department, with only a computer and keyboard. "Have a seat."

I take a seat, and she sits across from me.

"You're here because you were a bad boy." The way she says it has me feeling like she is toying with me. She bites her lip, and I feel blood rushing to my face. "And because your parents happen to know some very influential people."

So my parents can call in a favor, but they don't have the decency to call me. Typical. I could have spent a lot less time over the toilet if I knew this was an option.

"And them?" I point to the other pods in the center of the lab.

"They're even worse than you."

"Worse than me?" Who is this woman?

She leans forward, her dark brown eyes gazing into me. "Each of those men, all twenty-four of them, are in prison for violent crimes. We have an agreement with the state of New York that allows us to use prisoners to test out the effects of rehabilitative gameplay while in full immersion. Each of them volunteered to play *Isle of*

Mythos as a hero to see if it would cure their violent tendencies."

"Has it?" Nobody mentioned anything about other prisoners. I mean, it's not like they could actually hurt me, could they?

Her smirk has me on edge.

"It looks like you're about to find out."

CHAPTER TWO

2. Into the Pod

"Why me?" I lean against the hard back of the chair. Even if my parents did manage to call in a favor to someone, this is next-level technology. There are twenty-four pods, maybe a few more I haven't seen. How am I being punished but also lucky enough to be able to test out the next wave of gaming at the same time? There have to be people who would volunteer, no questions asked, for this type of experience.

"The simple answer is that we wanted a gamer in the mix," says the beautiful brunette who still hasn't told me her name. "Someone to test the boundaries of our creation. We knew from the get-go that your case would be found guilty. Not that many gamers wind up in prison."

"So, what, am I not actually being rehabilitated?" I

mean, I'm perfectly fine playing a game for a month with no consequences. What I really want to know, though, is why prisoners?

She leans forward and flashes me a dangerous smile.

"Oh, everything the judge said is true. You will most certainly experience what it feels like to be attacked, to be bullied, to be persecuted for simply being what you are. We have embedded a deep history in *Isle of Mythos*, and trolls are hated like no other. In time, you will find out why. But that is not to say you won't have any fun. This is a game after all. There will be quests and crafting and all the adventure of a traditional RPG, but it will be more real than you have ever experienced. You will feel pain, but you will also smell, taste, and experience everything as if you were actually there."

"Pain?" I interrupt. How in the hell is it legal to put criminals in a simulation where they can be hurt? Isn't that torture?

"Absolutely. That is one of the things that separates full immersion from traditional VR. If you get stabbed, you feel it. Luckily for you, trolls have a thick hide and a higher tolerance for pain. Plus, we set the pain settings at fifty percent to make things more bearable."

"What if I don't want to do it?" I challenge. Maybe being an outcast that everyone hates isn't something I want to partake in.

"You go to prison," she says matter-of-factly, as if that solves everything. "Now, unless you wish to go to prison, I suggest we get started."

I don't want to go to prison. She stares at me, waiting for a response. Her smile never falters, and her vibrant white teeth mesmerize me. They are almost too white.

Unnatural. What other choice do I have? I know people who would pay good money to be in this testing phase, pain included.

"What's your name?"

"Valery Barrett. Anything else?"

I shake my head. All that's left is to see what this is actually about.

"Now if you don't mind, please follow me. The next several hours will be spent gathering your vitals and running tests to make sure your body can handle thirty days of immersion. You look like a healthy kid, so I don't foresee any problems." She leads me through a door at the other end of the room, down a hallway, and into a waiting room. It's really no different than one I might see at a doctor's office, minus the posters for erectile dysfunction and heart disease. The walls here are white and bare. Just like everything else in the lab.

Barrett. That's the last name of the owner of Mythos Games. I suddenly remember where I have seen her before. It was at a ceremony after the last season of *League of Mythos*. She was sitting next to John Barrett at the head table. Is she his daughter? Niece?

Valery disappears, and over the next several hours, I have my vitals taken. They draw blood, take my temperature, and stick me with an assortment of cold medical instruments in places I wouldn't let my mother touch me. I run on a treadmill, sit quietly, look at ink splotches on a piece of paper. It all makes me feel more like a lab rat than a prisoner.

I'm pretty healthy, except for asthma and acne. Part of me wonders if I would still be approved even if they found something that disqualified me? It's like she said, though, gamers aren't just lining up to go to prison. Maybe if they knew this was the punishment, they would. Even if I'm not a professional gamer, I still make my living playing games, so I'm probably a hell of a lot more useful than some of the players they have now.

It definitely makes me wonder why only convicted criminals are in this stage of the testing. Maybe because they know we won't be able to talk about it?

After my visit with the doctor, Valery shows up and takes me back to the lab. "Are you excited to see what you're going to be getting into?"

I nod.

"Well, first, we need you to sign the non-disclosure agreement. Once you get out, we can't have you talking about everything you've seen in here."

I flick through the legal jargon on the tablet and sign my name before being led back to the pods.

There's a new pod added to the end of one line, except it is black and the others are all white. It's sleek and beautiful, looking more like a spaceship than a gaming machine. The glassy surface reflects a distorted picture of my face back at me. My greasy black hair and obnoxiously large nose seem comical. In my peripheral, Valery's curves are only more emphasized in the glass. I still can't comprehend why she is here. Maybe she has some expertise, but at that age, it seems unlikely. She presses a button on the side, and there's a hiss as the pressure equalizes and the lid to the pod slowly rises.

"We've added a few updates to the newest model," she says.

Inside, a translucent blue liquid fills the pod.

"What's in the liquid?" I ask. There's an almost radioactive glow to the substance.

"That is what makes all of this possible. There are millions of tiny nanites that report feedback from every inch of your body, inside and out. This will be the most realistic gaming you will ever experience. They will clean you, feed you, and caress you ever-so-gently. They'll take better care of you than your mom or girlfriend ever could. Go ahead, touch it." She motions to the liquid.

I'm hesitant, but I do it anyway. Reaching my hand into the pod, I expect the liquid to part around my fingers like water, but when I submerge my fingers, it's like it molds to my skin, changing density in an instant. Then suddenly, it's like I'm touching nothing at all. The temperature of the liquid has mirrored my own perfectly. I pull my hand back and the nanites release as if they have no viscosity whatsoever.

"Pretty amazing, huh?" She gives me those seductive eyes. Dark brown and full of mystery. "The nanites are like a second layer of skin. They form to your body, mimicking the resistance you feel in the game. They can contract and expand in a fraction of a second. They will allow you to taste, to smell, to feel. Essentially, they will replicate the gameworld around your body. The difference between the game and reality will be indistinguishable."

"And what if I have to go to the bathroom?" It's a silly question, but I don't want to be swimming in my own filth for a month.

"There is a state-of-the-art filtration system. As soon as the nanites detect a change in their habitat, they attack the invader and flush it out of the system. Sweat, dead skin cells—" She pauses. "—other forms of waste. It's all filtered out immediately. The environment in the nanite gel is a thousand times cleaner than most hospitals. They will also be responsible for your breathing and nutrient intake while immersed."

"So, what now?" I ask.

She closes the lid to the pod and it locks into place. "Now, we get you in the game."

One of the technicians brings her a package and she hands it to me.

"I'll need you to change into this," she says, handing me the package.

I open it and find a pair of silky white underwear inside. They remind me of the tighty-whities I wore as a child. I guess she senses my consternation at stripping down to my underwear, because she comments on them.

"Apparently, no one likes getting naked in front of so many people, so we had these made. They are constructed from a special material that doesn't interfere with the nanites. There's a bathroom over there where you can change. Leave your clothes by the sink and we will have them put away and waiting for you when your immersion is over."

"Don't I get to look through the game manual or anything?" I ask.

"Where's the fun in that? You'll find out everything you need to know as you play the game."

In the bathroom, I take off my gray suit jacket and lay it delicately on the counter. So much has happened today that I've hardly had a chance to process it. As I take off each article of clothing, it almost feels as if I am shedding my old skin. The skin of a streamer who lost his cool one too many times. For a moment, I just stare at myself in the mirror. In real life, I'm a skinny nobody, but online, I've always been a giant among men. With quicker reflexes and a better understanding of game mechanics than most, I never had a problem excelling at whatever games I played. I take a deep breath. This will be no different. Prisoners or not, this is my element. I've always enjoyed playing the characters no one else touches—the ones labeled weak and ineffective—and using them to wipe the floor with my opponents. It doesn't matter what they throw at me, I'll be just fine.

I put on the tighty-whities. My new skin. I have no idea what my new skin will become in the aftermath of my sentencing. It's much too soon to tell, but I have a feeling the next thirty days will be the basis.

If I want to continue to play games at a professional level, then I have to be able to control my emotions, even under stress. If what they say is true about *Isle of Mythos*, then this'll be a very real test.

I leave my clothes on the marble counter and meet Valery back out in the lab. The chill of the room nips at me and goosebumps prickle along my body.

Truth be told, I'm nervous. Who wouldn't be at least a little nervous knowing they are about to be trapped inside a game for thirty days with felons convicted of violent crimes? Yes, the whole purpose of the game is to let them play the hero in the hopes of rehabilitating them, but when I'm their sworn enemy...I don't know what to expect.

"Ready?" Valery asks, her voice as seductive as ever.

It's time to quit stalling and either nut up or shut up.

"Let's do it."

As the technicians prep the pod, I get into my normal pre-game routine. I tune out the outside world and drift inside my head. I can see them working, but I'm not watching them, not really. Heavy metal blares inside my head. A montage of some of my greatest battles plays out before me. I sling fireballs as a wizard at an oncoming goblin mage. Our spells collide in a maelstrom of ethereal energy. As a stealthy rogue, I teleport behind an elven archer and slit her throat. One of my personal favorites was when I played as a damage-based support and cast an ultimate healing spell on a vampire, exploding him into red mist.

A peacefulness washes over me as the chaos replays in my mind. The only thing I'm missing is an energy drink and a bag of chips.

"Mister Johnson." Valery motions toward my home for the next thirty days. "Please step into the pod."

Some of my confidence has returned and I wink at her as I slide into the nanite gel.

"Please, call me Chad."

She laughs. I don't know if it's because of my sudden boldness or the absurdity of it, but it doesn't faze me. I submerge into the blue liquid. It's only cold for a split-second before the nanites mimic my body temperature. The door to the pod closes with a hiss, and more nanites begin to flood in. I can see Valery leaning over the pod, her features clouded by a blue haze as the nanite gel covers my face.

When I can no longer hold my breath, I give in and the nanite gel flows into my lungs. I'm not sure what I expect, choking maybe, but it's not this. The nanites coat my lungs and it's like I'm breathing on a misty day where the rain is so thick that you can't help but take it in with every breath.

Valery waves at me, and suddenly everything goes black.

I don't know how long I sit in the blackness, seconds or minutes, I'm not sure. My heart beats in my eardrums and the rasp of my own breathing are all that I know.

Gradually, the blackness fades. A tiny dot appears far away in my vision and begins to grow. It grows and grows until I realize it's a planet. A planet with blue oceans and green continents. Not that different from Earth except that the landmasses are all the wrong shapes. I zoom through the atmosphere and the green continents develop different hues. There are sandy deserts, snowcapped mountains, lush dense forests. My vision focuses on a particular continent floating all alone.

It's longer than it is wide, and a rocky mountain range separates the continent in two. The camera halts and the words *Isle of Mythos* appear atop the continent in letters carved from stone.

CHAPTER THREE

3. Character Creation

The logo fades away and is replaced by something I know all too well. A character creation screen. Epic instrumental music has me ready to click randomize and hit the ground running. Except there is no randomize button. I'm also not playing this entirely for fun. The judge wants me to play to better myself. Valery and Mythos Games have their own unknown reasons. Personally, I don't want to be tortured by a bunch of murder hobos just because someone told them they should hate me. I'm going to make the strongest character I can right from the start.

A forest green, lumbering troll rotates in the center of my vision. A flat face with two gigantic tusks jutting upwards stares back at me. Blue freckles adorn its wide nose. Pointy ears protrude from both sides of his head, where two long, black braids dangle down each side and drape over his massive shoulders. Each shoulder is covered in patches of rough walnut skin, almost rock-like in appearance. He holds a wooden club in one giant hand tipped with razor-sharp black claws that it occasionally lifts, sending ripples through its thick, bulging muscles. A loincloth is the only clothing he wears.

These aren't the fat lovable trolls from children's TV shows. These are beasts. Warriors.

Awesome!

Enter Name.

"Chad," I say.

Chod pops up above the troll's head.

"No. Chad," I say again.

The name doesn't change.

"CH-AD," I do my best to enunciate my single syllable name.

Nothing.

According to Valery, all of my in-game icons will be activated simply by focusing on them, so I try to mentally click on the name to see if I can change it, but it doesn't work. Nothing I do changes the name.

It seems I'm already being trolled by the game. Great. At least it didn't call me Chode. I'll take that as a win.

Choose Race.

I cycle through several races, but they are all grayed out and unavailable. There seems to be a wide variety for players to choose from in the future. Or maybe if you're not being punished by a court of law. There are dwarves, elves, humans, gnomes, halflings, minotaurs, wereraces, and many more. There are even a few shadows that must be for special races they aren't showing yet.

Troll. *Trolls are barbaric creatures, gifted with physical* *prowess but not much else. Very rarely are trolls able to learn magic, and those that do are not of much renown. Most of their lives are spent trying to fill their insatiable appetite. Trolls have the ability to blend in with their surroundings when not moving.*

Bonus Abilities: Night Vision, Increased Regeneration, Thick Skin, Camouflage, Savage.

I focus on troll and a new category appears.

Choose Subspecies.

Several subspecies of trolls now appear before me with their stats displayed to the side—mountain, desert, and forest. Arctic and seaside are grayed out for some reason. Each one is uniquely different from the others.

The forest troll is my current selection.

Forest Troll. *Forest trolls dwell in the depths of the forest. They can usually be found in a wide clearing, having uprooted the surrounding trees in boredom. Forest trolls are big and strong, but they are also the fastest of the subspecies of trolls.*

Strength: 18
Dexterity: 15
Constitution: 19
Intelligence: 7
Wisdom: 10
Charisma: 6

Next, I cycle to the mountain troll. His light plum-colored skin is dotted with speckles of gray. A short gray mohawk runs down the center of his head. A hawk nose nearly touches his lips, and the tusks are shorter but more girthy. He is stockier than the forest troll, built for strength and not speed. A large fur shawl is tossed over his shoulders.

Mountain Troll. *Mountain trolls are most commonly found* *tucked away in the depths of caves. The strongest of all trolls, they find entertainment in tossing boulders from great heights and watching them tumble into the depths below.*

Strength: 20
Dexterity: 12
Constitution: 20
Intelligence: 7
Wisdom: 10
Charisma: 6

The final option available to me is the desert troll. Its skin is a dull tan with patches of hazelnut and toffee around the shoulders. Shaggy orange hair is pulled into a ponytail that falls down his back. He is less muscular than the other two, but far wider.

Desert Troll. *The largest of the troll subspecies, the desert troll can survive for days at a time without food or water due to extra fatty tissue stored in their backs and midsection.*

Strength: 18
Dexterity: 13
Constitution: 21
Intelligence: 7
Wisdom: 10
Charisma: 6

The last two subspecies of troll are grayed out to me. I can't see their stats or descriptions, but the arctic troll has black skin and is covered with long white fur everywhere except for its belly. The seaside troll, with baby blue skin, is the smallest of them all, and it appears to have webbed fingers and toes.

I take a moment to look over the three available subspecies, weighing the pros and cons of each. I quickly disregard the desert troll. While the higher Constitution and the ability to travel without food and water is nice, I want to be more than just a walking tank. Especially considering I might be going at this alone.

That leaves the mountain and forest trolls. The mountain troll definitely looks the coolest with his purple skin and bulging muscles, but the trade-off of Dexterity for Strength just isn't worth it for me. I want to be able to move quickly and hit hard.

I guess I'm going to be a forest troll.

I select him, and a new category appears.

Select a Class.

Only four classes are available to me, most likely based on my low Intelligence, Wisdom, and Charisma. They are barbarian, fighter, ranger, and rogue.

It would be cool to be a wizard or paladin troll, maybe even a bard. Had the choices actually been there, I might have even taken one just to stick it to the man. But then I remember the pain settings and the other players. If I'm going to do this, I'm going to play to my strengths.

Ranger. *Masters of both close-combat and ranged weapons, rangers are in tune with nature and use natural magic in conjunction with physical attacks to tackle quests across the realm.*

Ranger is a no-go. Trolls aren't really known for their ranged attacks and my low Intelligence means I would have a hard time mastering any of the magic usually associated with the class.

Rogue. *Known for their seedy antics and untrustworthiness, rogues are masters of stealth and trickery. Experts in bladed weapons and poisons, these scoundrels thrive in their nighttime escapades.*

Rogue is also not a good choice. While my Dexterity is

on the higher side, I'm too large to be sneaky. My night vision would be an asset, but I'd essentially be wasting my Strength and Constitution on sneak attacks and subterfuge. Plus, I doubt I would be a very good poison-maker with my Intelligence. My Charisma is basically nonexistent, and who has ever met a rogue that wasn't a quick talker? Like I need another reason for society to hate me.

Fighter. *Masters of a multitude of weapons and fighting styles, fighters are able to learn to use any weapon or martial art with ease.*

Barbarian. *Savage warriors capable of using basic weapons and entering into a berserker rage.*

So, it looks like I'm either a fighter or a barbarian. Being a fighter would be easy with the ability to master weapons and fighting techniques. Being a troll, though, I think I should rely on my natural abilities. Brutal strength with basic weapons. Barbarians are capable of going into berserker rages, which considering why I'm here to begin with, seems fitting.

I select barbarian and my character locks into place.

Chod, the Barbarian Forest Troll appears above my avatar.

I'm not going to lie, I look like a badass. I'd like to see somebody take a swing at me.

The next thing I know, the screen fades to black and I open my eyes in the middle of a forest.

CHAPTER FOUR

4. They See Me Trolling

The smell of cedar washes over me. I stand in a clearing, a beam of light breaking through the canopy and bathing me in warm sunshine. A brook murmurs somewhere nearby and I can hear the scuffle of insects and birds chirping all around. This is by far the most peaceful place I have ever been. Maybe I'll just chill here for the next thirty days.

I take a step forward, my legs stumble, and I fall straight on my face. My chin slams against a rock and even though my tough troll skin keeps me from feeling more than a bump, stars dance in my vision.

Attempting to rise to my feet, I stumble and sway back and forth. My body slams into a tree, causing a flock of birds to take flight and several exotic fruits to fall to the ground. I wrap my hands around the tree to stop the world from spinning and dig my sharp black nails into the bark. It holds me steady.

It takes me several minutes to acclimate to my new troll body. Being eight feet tall, I didn't take into account that it might be like a toddler trying to walk for the first time as I stumble through the forest.

Eventually, I adjust to my new body and feel its power coursing through me. Once I get the hang of it, this is going to be fun. I must weigh several hundred pounds, because every step I take leaves deep impressions in the earth.

Slowly, I begin to jog and then run. Each step rumbles the nearby earth, sending anything foolish enough to be in my path scurrying into the forest's depths. I move faster than I thought possible, faster than any human.

Now that I know my speed, I want to test my strength. I grab a nearby tree and its bark crumples beneath my grip. With a heave, I uproot it almost effortlessly. I lift it over my shoulder and toss the tree like a javelin. It soars through the air and lands with a violent crash.

"This is awesome!" I yell. My voice is deep and cavernous. Terrifying, really; it sounds more like the roar of a lion than anything.

Wanting to test my strength some more, I cock my fist and unload into a nearby pine. Wood splinters at the impact and sawdust rains down all around me like the fallout from an atomic bomb.

"Chod smash!" I hit the tree again and another large chunk of timber explodes into sawdust and splinters. It takes five more hits before I hear a loud crack and the pine falls. It crashes through the canopy, clearing a wide path before smacking against the earth and disheveling everything that isn't rooted in place. Pine needles fall like confetti on New Year's Eve.

I am one powerful motherfucker.

But there is always a bigger beast.

Something rumbles in the depths of the forest. Whatever it is causes the remaining birds to take flight. Several deer run by me, escaping what is coming from the other direction. I stand tall, awaiting my challenger. The crunch of trees announces its arrival and a moment later, I am face to face with my first opponent.

Ogre. *Level 5. Big, strong, and ugly. Ogres are quick-tempered, powerful brawlers.*

Standing a good two feet taller than me, the ogre has pasty yellow skin and crooked brown teeth, all dull except for the row of jagged, sharp teeth at the front of his lower jaw. He's draped in an assortment of furs with a bone necklace dangling from his neck. In one hand, he holds a wooden club, crudely fashioned from a broken tree, and in the other, the bloody remains of a deer. I guess I interrupted his dinner.

Large, bloodshot eyes stare at me with fury. The top of his head ends above his eyebrows, showcasing what little brains he has. Ogres have never really been known for their smarts. He tosses the carcass of the deer to the ground and unleashes a deafening roar. Spittle flies from his mouth and hot breath permeates the air in my direction.

He yells something at me, but I don't speak fucking ogre, so I just stand there and wait for the showdown that is inevitably about to happen. Yeah, he's big and ugly, but so am I.

The ogre obviously takes offense to me not responding, because he swings his club at me. Luckily, I am expecting it and dodge the attack. While he recovers his balance from the swing, I jab him in the ribs and his HP drops by ten percent.

I really should have taken a moment to look through my abilities before I got in a fight, but here we are and there is no time like the present. The ogre swings again, and I step back and to the side. His club collides with a tree and cleaves it in two.

I finally take stock of the icons floating in the edge of my vision. They're translucent except for when I focus on them. One looks like a notebook. That should be where my abilities are listed.

The ogre swings again, and I sidestep, dodging the attack as he falls past me. I kick him in the back, and he stumbles forward. I use the momentary distraction to check my abilities.

The book opens across my vision, obscuring my sight completely. I'm looking through, searching for my skill list, when a sharp pain erupts in the side of my head. My vision goes dark around the edges and the words become unreadable as my vision wavers. I try to close the notebook and focus on the fight at hand, but I can't do anything until my head stops spinning.

The spinning stops, and I close the notebook just in time to catch another club to the side of my face. Again, my head spins and I notice I'm down to a third of my health. No wonder. He's level five and I'm still level one.

The world moves back and forth like a crashing wave. My head is throbbing, and I want to throw up. I blindly throw a punch, hoping against hope I connect with something. The action throws me off balance and I feel two large, powerful arms grasp me around the neck. Hot breath and heavy breathing assault my ears. The ogre says something, but it only sounds like grunts to me. A moment later, my neck goes tight, I hear my vertebrae crunch, and everything goes black.

CHAPTER FIVE

5. Let's Try This Again

Alert! You have died. All items on your person have been lost. Items can be retrieved at the site of death in the event they have not been looted. One level and any stat points associated with it have been removed.

I respawn in the same clearing as before, fuming. Man, that was so stupid of me. The middle of a fight is not the time to study up on my abilities. I know better. I've been playing games for years, for crying out loud. Just because this feels like I am actually here, it doesn't mean I can just forget everything I know about gaming. I uproot a tree, breaking it in half in my frustration and tossing the remains deep into the forest. Not to mention taking on an ogre five levels higher than me. Of course he could kill me in three hits. If I wasn't a level one scrub, I would have lost everything I had on me, including a level.

If I want to be the best, then I need to play smarter. I need to know what I'm working with here.

I pull up the notebook and look at my abilities.

Abilities: *You have three starter ability points to use. A new ability point is unlocked at every odd level. New abilities may be learned from completing quests, equipping new items, and various achievements.*

Bite. *Using your massive tusks and powerful jaw, you take a bite out of an opponent, dealing immense damage. Cost: 10 rage. Level 2.* ***Massive Bite.*** *Deals double damage. Cost: 20 rage.*

Claw. *You attack with sharp claws, swiping at an opponent and dealing extra damage. Cost: 5 rage. Level 2.* ***Claws.*** *Swipe at an opponent with both hands, dealing extra damage. Cost: 10 rage.*

Multi-Attack. *Bite and Claw at the same time. Cost: 20 rage.*

Iron Will. *Immune to slows and stuns for 15 seconds. Cost: 50 rage. Cooldown: 180 seconds.*

Intimidation. *You let out a roar at your opponent, freezing them in place so that they are unable to attack for two seconds. Cost: 10 rage.*

Berserker Rage. *(Ultimate. Available at level 5.) Attacks and physical damage build your rage meter. 5 rage per attack. Rage meter deteriorates over time when out of combat at a rate of 5 rage per second. When Berserker Rage is activated, for 30 seconds, rage meter is full, deal increased damage, increased attack speed, health regenerates at 5x the normal rate, cannot be stunned, slowed or otherwise affected. Cooldown: 60 minutes.*

I'm Always Angry. *(Available at level 10). Once rage meter is at 50%, it will not deteriorate below 50% when out of combat.*

Beneath those, there also five bonus abilities for picking troll as my race.

Increased Regeneration. *(Passive) Regenerate health at a faster rate. Level 2.* ***Rapid Regeneration.*** *(Passive) When below 10% health, regeneration is doubled.*

Night Vision. *(Passive) Increased vision in darkness and low light.*

Thick Skin. *(Passive) Take 10% less damage from physical attacks.*

Camouflage. *(Passive) When out of combat and not moving for 20 seconds, trolls blend in with their surroundings.*

Savage. *(Passive) Ability to eat uncooked meat without consequences.*

Not a bad list of starter abilities. The five racial abilities are already unlocked, so I'll need to pick three more from the list above them. The low cost on Claw will boost my basic attacks significantly. The fact that they all rely on rage instead of mana is nice, because I can always replenish it by simply attacking. Bite and Claw are easy choices, because they play off my already high Strength. Multi-Attack seems like a luxury at my current level, so the choice for my final ability is between Iron Will and Intimidation. I elect to go with Intimidation because of the low rage cost and its ability to be used for offense and defense.

In the top right corner of my vision, an avatar of my character's face looks down at me. Beside it, there are bars detailing my Health, Mana, Rage, and Experience Points.

Chod, Level 1 Barbarian Forest Troll
HP: 475/475
Mana: 0/0
Rage: 0/100

XP: 0/300

It's interesting that I don't have any mana, but seeing as how all of my abilities feed off of rage, it makes sense. The creation screen did say that trolls were not known for their magical aptitude. I wonder if it means I can't learn magic or if I just need to find a way to unlock it. At least I won't have to waste my money on mana potions until I know for sure.

In the bottom right corner of my vision, there is a map. I focus on it and it enlarges, displaying the *Isle of Mythos*. I am currently smack dab in the middle of a giant forest on the southern half of the island. An enormous mountain range separates the northern and southern halves of the island near the center. Several towns are marked on the map with question marks. The map will probably fill itself in as I travel.

Above the map, there is an icon of a backpack. I focus on it and it opens my inventory. Between my Strength and Constitution, I bet I can carry a massive amount of loot. The only item I have right now is the ragged loincloth that drapes over my trollberries. I pick up one half of the broken tree and it shows in my inventory as a wooden club.

Item. *Wooden Club. +1 Strength.*

I'd like to replace it with something made of stone or metal once I have the chance, but first I'll need to earn gold or find something worthy of a trade.

First things first, though. I need to find a town and see what this game really has to offer. Looking at the map, the closest town is on the outskirts of the forest to the west. That's where I'll go and maybe find out a little more about what makes this world tick. If I'm lucky, I might even run into another player.

On the way, I can farm and test out my abilities.

The first animal I come across is a tiny bunny. One smash of my club kills the poor creature. It drops a rabbit pelt, and my XP goes up by five. I tuck the rabbit pelt into the strap of my loincloth. I need to find some better monsters. At the current rate, it'll take sixty rabbits for me to get to level two.

Remembering my Camouflage passive, I stop moving. When the twenty seconds is up, I don't notice any difference in my appearance, but nature explodes to life around me. Birds tweet from the trees above, insects rattle and buzz in a violent cacophony. It's like I completely vanished from the forest. Then I notice an icon flashing next to my avatar. It's a small picture of a more animated version of me hiding between two large bushes. It pulses slowly. I move and the icon disappears. The forest goes quiet once again.

That'll be useful.

I freeze my movements again. When the timer is up and the icon appears, the forest roars back to life. I sit and wait, letting the animals grow comfortable. Several more bunnies appear around me, hopping and frolicking as if all is good in the world. They're not even worth my time at this point. I'm way too strong to be wasting my time killing bunnies and rats. I need bigger game.

So I sit. Patience is a virtue for a reason. Five minutes later, my patience is rewarded by several fox-looking creatures walking in my direction.

Jackal. *Level 2. Ranging in size from as small as foxes to as* *large as wolves, jackals are known for being sly and for their high perception.*

They are about ten feet away when one of them senses something isn't right. It lifts its nose in the air, smelling my scent.

Not wanting the creatures to run away, I end Camouflage and leap towards the small pack of canines. I smash one with my club, dropping its health by a third and claw at another. The three jackals turn to face me, teeth bared and ready to fight.

With my ten rage, I use Bite and attack the first jackal again. The bonus damage is enough to kill the creature in one attack. The biggest of the remaining two lunges at me, taking a bite out of my leg. A dull pain runs up my leg, and I smack the jackal to the side. I kick the other before it has a chance to attack. Using the newly acquired rage, I activate Intimidation and let out a roar that freezes both jackals in fear, unable to attack for two seconds.

By the time the effect wears off, I've killed another jackal and use Bite to finish off the third.

Congratulations! You have reached level 2. +1 stat point to distribute. +1 Strength and Constitution racial bonus.

Not bad at all. I elect to save my stat point until I have more and can decide the best way to allocate them. Without an in-depth tutorial, I'm kind of learning this as I go and don't want to do anything I might regret so early in the game.

I gather the jackal pelts and tuck them in my loincloth, setting off toward the town marked on the map. I really need to find a satchel of some sort to carry my items in. My little loincloth is only going to be able to carry so much.

For a moment, I contemplate going in search of the ogre. To prove to him and myself that I'm not really as big of a chump as I was in that first fight. I think better of it and realize that maybe that's why I raged so much online. Because as long as I've been playing, I've had a chip on my shoulder. Something to prove. Deep down, I wanted to be a professional gamer. If I could somehow show the world what I'm capable of, then maybe my parents might actually notice me. The fact that the mistakes of other people kept that from happening was the trigger that set me off each time.

I flip a calloused green middle finger into the air and wonder if Valery and her team are watching me as I contemplate my life's work while walking as a monster through a lush forest in a video game.

Along the way, I cross paths with a wild boar, which gets me almost to level three. Not wanting to let a good opportunity go to waste, I kill a few more bunnies and go the distance. I use my new ability point to unlock Iron Will.

Between the tusks from the boar and all the pelts, I've run out of places to store items unless I want to carry everything in my hands. That just won't do.

The boar hide is the largest, so I lay it flat on the ground and then fold it in half. Using my razor-sharp claws, I poke several holes along each side of the hide and a couple along the top. I search a nearby tree and find exactly what I'm looking for: thin, green vines. I pull several down and strip the leaves from them. Next, I run the vines through the holes on each side of the boar hide, creating a makeshift satchel. It's not the best work, but it should last me until I make it to town and can either buy some string or purchase an actual bag.

Now that I have the bag made, I loop the remaining vines through the holes I poked in the top to make a strap. I intertwine the vines together to make it sturdier and then tie off the loose ends on the other side.

I stuff the remaining pelts and the two boar tusks in the satchel and admire my work. Not bad. Not bad at all.

Congratulations! You have unlocked the skill 'Leatherworking.' You are now a level 1 Leatherworker (Novice). Increase your skill and learn advanced techniques for working leather by finding an advanced leatherworker (Apprentice or above). Crafting Ranks: Novice, Apprentice, Journeyman, Expert, Artisan, Master, Grandmaster.

Sweet! That means I'll be able to learn to make leather armor and as my skill goes up, the quality should increase. Since none of the animals have dropped gold, I'm guessing this is the type of game where you make gold from completing quests and selling the items you make. That's good. It means I won't spend all of my time fighting monsters. Not that that isn't fun, but it's nice to spice things up. I wonder what other types of crafting I can learn?

I toss the satchel over my shoulder and set off towards town. It's peaceful walking through the forest. New York City was never this calm. Walking down the street, even at three in the morning, car horns blared, lights flashed, and a thousand voices blended together in a raucous buzz as people talked on cell phones and ignored everyone else around them. Even at Central Park, it was hard to find a moment's quiet.

I take in a deep breath and just enjoy the sound of

nature around me. Sure, I'm here because I screwed up, but this is a once in a lifetime experience. I'm going to make the most of it.

CLINK.

My communing with nature is interrupted by a sound I know all too well.

A swordfight.

CHAPTER SIX

6. Ranger Danger

I follow the sound of clashing swords. As quietly as my troll body will allow, I do my best to find the source of the noise without being detected. There is something about the ringing of metal on metal that makes my blood pump. Probably the thousands of hours I've poured into games over the years. Magic is flashy, but nothing beats a good swordfight.

The clinking gets louder, and I'm finally able to see the source. Two men, both wearing brown leather armor and green cloaks, attack and parry on the bank of a gurgling stream.

Forest Ranger. Level 4.

The men are almost identical, except one has a brown beard and the other's is blond. The blond man attacks with a fierce slash, knocking his opponent off balance. He then follows up with another swift swing, but the one with the brown beard is able to deflect the blow, sending his attacker stumbling past him.

He turns to charge his opponent, but the blond man slips in the sand and falls to one knee, losing his sword. The brown beard raises his weapon overhead and swings, stopping an inch from the man's neck.

He says something I can't quite make out and they both laugh, then he extends his arm and helps the man to his feet.

That's when I notice their belongings piled neatly against a tree. Several bags, two bows, quivers full of arrows. They're traveling companions enjoying an afternoon spar. But are they players or are they NPCs?

If I had to put money on it, I would say the latter. As far as I know, there are only twenty-four actual players in *Isle of Mythos* right now. With this being a pretty large continent, not to mention the size of the planet, I would say that the majority of inhabitants are non-player characters. But which ones? And how do I tell?

It can't hurt to ask. Even if they are real players, convicts, they're supposed to be playing the hero. What do I have to lose?

"Hey," I shout, waving and poking my head over the embankment.

The two men immediately rise to their feet, swords drawn and pointed in my direction. They scowl at me as I approach.

"Whoa, no need for that." I toss my club to the ground and put my hands up in defense, showing them I mean no harm, but it does nothing to calm the men. They slowly back away towards their belongings. "I'm not going to hurt you. I'm on my way to town to get set up and maybe learn a few things."

Their faces are completely void of recognition to anything I am saying, their eyes wide in terror. I know Valery said trolls were hated, but this seems like an overreaction. They must not see too many trolls around these parts.

Brown-beard says something to Blondie, but once again, I can't make it out. Blondie sheathes his sword and grabs his bow. With shaky hands, he nocks an arrow and points it at me.

"Hey, man. What the actual fuck?" I stop my advance to give the little asshole an opportunity to calm down. His arm shakes as he holds the arrow pulled back against his neck.

Brown-beard says something else. Why in the hell can I not understand what they are saying? It all sounds like gibberish. Blondie shakes his head. What is this little twerp planning?

Sweat beads on his forehead and he starts speaking fast. I have no idea what he's saying, but it's coming out his mouth a mile a minute and he's shaking worse than ever. The man is having a full-on panic attack.

"Okay, guys. I'm just gonna leave you be. I'll find my own way to town."

I turn to leave and the next thing I know, I feel a dull pinch in my left shoulder. Reaching up to see what bit me, I find the shaft of an arrow sticking out of my forest green skin. Dark blue blood trickles down my back.

Not cool, little man. Not cool at all.

I pull the arrow out and toss it to the ground.

The two men are now yelling at each other while

Blondie attempts to nock another arrow. His hands shake so badly that he misses the string each time and the arrow falls from his grip.

He finally puts one in place and lets it fly. I swat it from the air like a fly and his eyes go wide. Brown-beard has obviously had enough, because he grabs his belongings and hightails it out of there. Blondie is not so smart.

I run at him full force while he tries to nock another arrow. When I'm a few steps away, he tosses his bow to the ground and draws his sword. He swings at me, but I step back and the blade whistles through the air, inches from my midsection.

Activating Claw, I attack his exposed side and rip through his leather armor with ease. He yells out in pain and slashes at me again, connecting with my shoulder. The blade cuts me, but not as deep as I expect. The wound is not much more than an inconvenient sting. Between the arrow and the cut, Blondie has only managed to drain ten percent of my health. Due to my increased regeneration, it's already recovering.

He, on the other hand, lost twenty percent from my single attack with the Claw bonus.

We stare at each other for a moment, sizing one another up. I'm stronger, faster, and tougher than this guy, and judging by the panicked expression on his face, he knows it. If his friend had stayed, I might have had a worthy match, but even though he is a level higher than me, I'm a warrior. He's a ranger. His strengths are in his quickness, and now that I've gashed his ribs, he's not going anywhere.

He attacks me again and I dodge his blow. I have just enough rage to activate Bite. Before Blondie can react, I bypass his guard and sink my tusks into his shoulder. The taste of blood surprises me and I let go. I didn't expect it to be so lifelike. Silky smooth iron coats my mouth and I attempt to spit it out. This is way too realistic for my taste.

Ow!

A sharp pain flares from my side and I look down to see a large gash running along my ribs. It's not deep, but it hurts a hell of a lot more than the other two attacks.

I've had just about enough of this guy.

"You picked the wrong day, asshole."

I uproot a nearby tree and swing it at Blondie with all my might. It crushes into him and I hear the crack of broken ribs and branches. He falls to the ground, stunned. It takes him a moment to come to, but when he does, the only thing I see in his eyes is fear.

Taking the tree, I break off the end to where it is the size of a club and walk over to Blondie.

"There's a saying where I come from," I say, but there isn't a hint of recognition on his face. "About picking on someone your own size. It's usually for when people pick on those smaller than them, but I think it works for you and me too. You should have left with your buddy."

Blondie doesn't understand me, but he knows he's about to die. He lets out a defeated sigh and drops his head. I send him swiftly into the next life.

Warning! *You have killed a human NPC. If word of this reaches a human settlement, your reputation among humans will be decreased by 100. Stop the ranger from reaching town before it is too late. Current reputation with humans: -1000. (-1000 Racial Penalty)*

You have got to be kidding me.

I quickly loot the belongings of the ranger. His pack is smaller than the satchel I created, but it is well made. I throw it in my satchel, along with the bow, arrows, and sword so that I can examine it better later and see what it holds inside.

Right now, I have a ranger to catch.

CHAPTER SEVEN

7. No Good Deed Goes Unpunished

After looting the body of anything useful and stuffing it in my satchel, I set off in search of the brown-bearded ranger. Due to my increased regeneration, my wounds are already healing at a rapid rate. The sting of the cuts were uncomfortable. I can only imagine what an injury might feel like on someone without my defenses and tough skin.

I scour the area behind the tree where their belongings were. The ranger is light on his feet and there are no traces of which direction he went.

Of course, it had to be a fucking ranger. Why couldn't it be a lumbering warrior and not this nimble-footed nutsucker? If his stupid friend had just kept his shaky fingers on the damn arrow, I'd be strolling through the forest now instead of worrying about further damaging my reputation with humans. I was expecting a little bit of racism, maybe paying more for goods and not being allowed into certain establishments, but I wasn't expecting to be attacked on sight for saying a friendly hello.

Really, though, can eleven hundred really be that much worse than one thousand when you're hated that much?

I'd rather not find out. If there is a chance I can stop him, I need to at least try.

Opening my map while I walk, the most logical location is the town on the edge of the forest. It's far closer than any of the others, and if he is looking to rat me out, that'll be his best bet. If I'm going to stop him, I don't have to track him, I just have to get there before he does.

Apparently, this is a big fucking forest, because, for the next two hours, I only move halfway towards the town. With my high starting stats in Strength, Constitution, and Dexterity, I don't need to stop for breaks often, but the rumble in my stomach tells me I am getting hungry.

Using Camouflage, I take a moment to blend into the surroundings. As soon as I disappear, the forest comes alive. It finally answers the age-old question, if a tree falls and no one is around to hear it, does it make a sound. The forest is full of sounds even when it assumes no one is around.

A rabbit hops out from a burrow beneath an old tree stump and nibbles on a nearby plant. A swift swing of my club and dinner is ready. I use my sharp claws to remove its fur.

What I have left is slimy, bloody, and not the least bit appetizing. Putting away my human inhibitions, I embrace the troll I am and take a bite. It's not as off-putting as the ranger's blood that had filled my mouth.

Maybe it's my new taste buds, but it actually doesn't taste that bad. It's more chewy than cooked meat and the tiny bones give it crunch every so often. Almost like eating a pretzel. Thanks to the passive from Savage, I don't have to worry about getting sick and it looks like I won't even need to invest in a cooking skill!

My hunger abates, and I feel like I have the energy to keep going for a while. With my stamina replenished, I take off through the forest at full speed.

It is truly amazing how fast and powerful I am. In real life, I was never that great of an athlete. The whole reason I got into esports was because I finally found something I was good at. I joined my school esports league and won the championship the first year I entered. After that, I joined the school team and we traveled for tournaments, playing whatever games were popular that year. It didn't matter what the games were, I could adapt. I had a natural affinity that most others didn't, and for once, I felt good about myself. Whatever the challenge was, I could master it. It turns out that the big leagues of esports are a lot different than being the best on your high school team. I tried out for a couple of pro teams, even got an interview, but never made it past that. I met Taryn at one of the tryouts. He was shy and quiet, but he was a damn good player. When he didn't make the team, I was shocked and asked him to join me as a streaming partner. We've been best friends ever since.

Even if I'm not a pro gamer, I'm still a gamer and that means I have a leg up on my competition.

I have to do a double-take when I see something swinging through the trees in the edge of my vision.

There is no way in hell I am this lucky. The ranger I've

been chasing dangles from a rope tied to a large pine. His dark silhouette swings back and forth several feet off the ground as he struggles to free himself.

I walk towards him and incoherent babbling flows from his mouth like a waterfall.

"I can't understand you," I say. I don't know if he understands the words or not, but he quits talking. He's a lot smarter than his partner.

Underneath him, I spot the wooden stake that was attached to the noose that is now cinched tightly around his boots. The ranger must not have been paying attention, because he somehow got himself snared. The ultimate irony would be if he'd laid the trap himself. But seeing as I can't speak anything but fucking troll, I'll never know how he got into this predicament.

His bow and sword both lay scattered on the ground next to his pack and a few other items. The cloak he wears dangles past his head, nearly touching the ground.

The ranger continuously tries to bend up and grab his feet, but time and again, he fails. Blood rushes to his head, making him look like a tomato.

I step closer and he stops struggling. There's fear in his eyes, but not the uncontrollable fear of Blondie. No, this is a fear built out of respect for what I can do. This ranger doesn't fear trolls simply because they are trolls. He fears us because we are predators. Because he is at my mercy.

Killing him would be so easy right now. He's practically served on a platter, dangling in front of me completely defenseless. One hit and my reputation remains the same.

Yet something stays my hand. I have a negative one thousand reputation. With the way things are, I'll never have a chance to better it. Trolls are hated and any humans I run into will try to kill me on sight. This could be an opportunity to change that.

I pick the ranger's sword up off the ground. It's light in my hand, almost like holding a paper sword. The ranger doesn't flinch, but his eyes follow my every movement. He knows I hold all the power in this situation.

Reaching up, I take the rope in my hand just above his boots. Using his sword, I make a swift slash and the ranger's full weight pulls against my hand. I gently let him to the ground and step back. He looks at me with wide eyes, like he doesn't understand what just happened. I point at his feet and he begins frantically untying the rope.

When he stands up, I don't move. I want him to know that I mean him no harm. He begins gathering his belongings, but never takes his eyes off me for more than a second. His hands shake as he gathers his bow, evidence that he doesn't truly believe I will let him live.

He tosses his satchel over his shoulder and stares at me for a moment. I imagine he is questioning if he is allowed to leave. I point a calloused green finger in the direction of the nearest town. He nods at me and turns to go.

"Wait," I say.

The ranger freezes in place and turns his head over his shoulder.

"You might need this." I take the blade of the sword in my hand and offer the hilt to the ranger. He doesn't have to speak my language to understand the gesture. He takes the sword and says something in return.

Then, he is gone.

Alert! You have spared the life of a human NPC. The

ranger knows you acted in self-defense and will no longer report you to the authorities. Instead, he will sing your praises for releasing him from a snare trap without harm. However, no one will believe him. Your reputation has increased by 1. Current reputation with humans: -999. (-1000 Racial Penalty)

My jaw hangs open once I finish reading the prompt. Are you kidding me? I spare the guy's life and get one measly point of reputation. Why would I ever want to be a good guy if that's the reward? I should have just killed him and taken his weapons.

I'm about ready to punch something when I hear movement behind me. I turn and see a giant green head towering over me. Two yellowed tusks jut into the air, one broken at the tip. A metal nose-ring gleams in the sun, and two dark black eyes bore into me. It opens its mouth and a deep, cavernous roar assaults my face.

"What have you done?" it asks.

CHAPTER EIGHT

8. The Well Runs Dry

The troll standing before me has skin darker and more scarred than my own, but there is no doubt he is a forest troll. He's at least a foot taller than I am with thick corded muscle running down his entire body. When I focus on him, the gamertag tells me he is level ten. Several furs are sewn into a vest and the tails of the dead creatures swish in the breeze against his massive tree trunk legs.

"What did you do?" he asks again.

His deep voice reverberates in my chest. His eyes don't blink as he waits for me to respond.

He's level ten, so I know better than to antagonize him.

"Uhm, I set him free."

The troll rubs his massive fingers over his eyes and lets out a sigh.

"You know the rules forbidding contact with humans, and the punishment for humans who wander into our tribal grounds. Come with me and the chief will decide your punishment. Try to resist, and I will take you by force." The nose ring that hangs from his septum moves with each word. I know better than to try and escape, so I follow the troll through the forest.

It seems that the fuck-up fairy has visited me once again.

This guy is no-nonsense as he leads me through the woods. He marches with purpose, intent on delivering me to some troll chief where I will undoubtedly be punished for breaking a rule I didn't know exists.

"What's your name, big guy?" I ask. I am thankful to actually speak to someone and have them understand what I am saying, even if he is a bit of an asshole.

"I am Gord, son of Guilda."

"Nice to meet you, Gord. What is it that you do out here? Besides bringing guys like me to the chief." Maybe a little sweetness will unsour his disposition.

"I am a guardian. One of many who watch the boundaries of our tribe and keep the humans away."

"So you placed the snare that caught the ranger?"

He grunts and nods in affirmation.

"Humans know the rules. The heart of the forest belongs to us. It is all we have and the penalty for trespassing is death."

Shit. I am so going to be in trouble. All for one sliver of reputation.

"Why do the humans hate us so much?" I ask.

Valery said that trolls were hated like no other and that in time, I would find out why. Maybe now is the time.

"Hmpf." Gord snorts. "Why does the sun rise in the east and set in the west? It is the way of life."

Really helpful. The first person I meet who speaks my language, and he talks like Confucius. What have I gotten myself into?

"What will my punishment be?" Maybe I can at least squeeze that much information out of him.

"That is for the chief to decide."

"Good talk." It's clear Gord isn't much of a talker. Hopefully, the chief will cut me some slack since I am new here and maybe I can be on my way to adventuring and not getting attacked by humans every time I turn my back.

I almost don't notice when we enter the troll village. It's rustic and earthy in a way that I have never seen. Almost elemental. It's like the village was formed out of the forest itself. Surrounding a large firepit are several wooden huts made out of living trees that seem almost like they were bent into the shape of the structures. The roofs of the huts are covered in vines and tree leaves still growing from the oddly-shaped trees. A large female troll sits on a throne constructed in the same way. A young troll nestles in her lap, no more than two feet tall, suckling at her teat. A half-dozen other female trolls sit in lesser chairs to her left and right. They seem to be discussing something and stop abruptly at our approach.

The woman on the throne is the same forest green as the other trolls I have seen, but her body type is starkly different from myself and Gord. Her arms are more lithe, less bulky, but still defined. A long, dark braid runs down her left shoulder. Where Gord and I have massive tusks, hers are smaller. Her chin is more pointed while ours are broad and square. Despite her slender physique, I am certain she is far more powerful than the rangers I met earlier. All of the female trolls that surround her are built in the same way. It's very sexy, in a barbaric sort of way.

Gord steps in front of the throne and bends a knee. The woman on the throne stares at him for a moment, and then her eyes fall upon me. They widen for a split-second before she resumes her stoic pose.

"Gord, what brings you into the tribal center?" she asks, her eyes still piercing into me.

"I found this one in the forest. He is not a member of our tribe. I witnessed him letting a human escape our lands. He helped him, even."

The child finishes feeding and unlatches. I find it hard to look away as the woman hides her breast beneath the fur shawl that covers her shoulders and chest. Those are some giant troll titties. Like watermelons. I don't mean it in a sexual way, just, wow.

"Is this true?" she asks.

"Technically, yes. But to be fair, I didn't know any better." It's not like I was dropped in the forest with a book of tribal laws at my disposal.

"Where do you come from?" She looks at me quizzically. "We are the last tribe of forest trolls on the island, and I know all who come and go within our land. You are not a member of our tribe, but there is no doubt that you are one of us." All eyes are upon me, except for Gord, who still kneels before her.

"I'm new to the area." That sounds better than saying, "I was sent here because I am a criminal."

"I see." She leans over and whispers something to the

woman sitting next to her. The woman is much older, but the only things that give away her age are the gray braid she wears draped over her shoulder and the crow's feet around her eyes. She nods and then their eyes are on me once again.

"There are stories, ancient stories, of those sent here from other realms. They look and talk like us, but they are not us. Sometimes they have special powers, often they are gifted in some way, and when they die, they do not pass on like the rest of us. There is word that these beings have begun appearing in the human settlements. Many of our guardians claim they have killed the same man on several occasions and that he continues to reappear. It seems the trolls may finally have found our own hero."

"I'm no hero, miss. I'm just trying to find my way."

There is a sudden gasp by the other women, and I know immediately I have violated some custom.

The troll on the far end stands and extends a long pointy finger in my direction. Her red braid seems to almost hiss at me when she shouts.

"Show respect when addressing the chief!"

"Easy, Tormara," says the chief. "It is clear he does not know our ways. Do not reprimand him for his ignorance, instead, educate him." Tormara is fuming, steam practically flowing out of her nostrils. "Now, you, what is your name?" she asks me.

"I am Chod." The eyes of all the women but the chief bore into me, telling me without words that I am not welcome here.

"Now, Chod, it is custom in our village to address those in power by their title. I am Chief Rizza. This is my council, and together we decide the fate of the forest trolls. We were discussing urgent business just as you arrived. However, it can wait, because if you truly are a hero, then we have great need of your assistance."

Whatever they need help with must be pretty bad if they're turning to me, someone who violated their customs and they know absolutely nothing about. Since I'm here to go on quests and hopefully better myself, I guess I owe it to them to help if I can. Judging by Gord, though, it looks like they have warriors much stronger than me already.

"What is it you would have me do?" I'm game for anything as long as it gets me the hell out of here.

"Gord, you are dismissed. Thank you for your service. We will handle it from here." Her eyes flicker to Gord before returning to me.

This feels like I'm in court all over again.

"Yes, Chief." Gord cuts his eyes at me as he disappears into the forest.

"Before I tell you of our needs, first you must understand the predicament that our people, *your people,* are in." The troll child has fallen asleep in her lap and snores softly. He's kind of cute to be so ugly. "Forest trolls are fading from this world. We have been for some time now. We do not have the luxury of inaccessible mountain passes like the mountain trolls or harsh environments like our desert or arctic sisters to keep our enemies at bay. Or the ocean's depths like the seaside trolls.

"We have the forest. It is a source of life, accessible to everyone, and the only protection it offers are its depths and our own fortifications." Her eyes don't break from mine while she speaks. I'm certain she is taking in my reaction to every word she says. "For thousands of years, we have been able to craft the magic that enters this forest and mold it to offer us protection. We have used it to hide our presence within its depths. To live our lives unmolested by the humans that spread out through the world like a parasite. For several years now, the magic that feeds the forest has been failing. Little by little, our presence had been discovered, the magic that hid us no longer working.

"To fight this, we reduced our borders, we made the magic cover less ground, we split into smaller tribes, but still it faltered." She turns to her council with a look of defeat. "Humans discovered us, they hunted us, until now we barely remain. The well that fed magic into the forest has been obstructed. We are no longer hidden from prying eyes. The guardians, like Gord, are the only defenses between us and the outside world that would have us dead."

"I'm sorry, Chief, but I thought trolls were unable to use magic." That's what the creation screen told me.

"For most, that is true. Very few of us have actual magical ability, only one in our village, but all trolls are gifted with the ability to craft magic if it is already there. Raw magic is powerful enough to burn most races if they touch it, but our tough skin allows us to craft it as we will. That is why we need your help, young Chod. Our well is dry."

"Why entrust this to me, though? Why haven't you tried to fix it already?" From what I've seen so far, I'm the runt of the litter.

"The journey is far and dangerous. We do not have the bodies to spare as it is. If we send our men away and they do not return, it will certainly spell our doom. It is no coincidence that you arrived when you did."

Great. I'm just an expendable piece of meat to these people.

"And why should I help you…Chief?" I add the last part when I see Tormara's nails digging into the bark of her chair. "What's in it for me?"

She smiles at me. It takes me by surprise how beautiful she looks when her face isn't stern and chiefly. Just as quickly, the smile is gone.

"As chief, it is my responsibility to look out for my people. My council guides me, they provide me with insight to help me make the tough choices, but at the end of the day, the decision is mine. Something must be done or my people will not survive. We need the magic returned to the forest. Take a day or two and explore our village, explore our tribal lands. If you bring magic back to the forest, you may have whichever reward you wish."

For the second time since I've been here, the women all gasp. They chatter in a dull roar at the chief. Tormara stands to her feet again and extends a hand in my direction.

"How could you? What if he would have your throne? You have offered too much, sister."

Chief Rizza responds calmly. "If my throne is the price of saving our people, then he shall have it. Nothing more will be said on the matter. Chod, do you accept my offer?"

Quest Alert. *You have been offered the quest 'Restore the Magical Well.' Something has blocked the magical stream that feeds into the forest. Find a way to clear the obstruction and return magic to the forest and tribal lands.*

Reward: Variable

It doesn't take me long to decide to help them. The fact that I can pick my own reward is amazing, and I'll make sure to do my due diligence before heading out. Becoming a troll chief right out of the gate wouldn't be such a bad thing. I need to complete the quest, but first, I want to know what I'm fighting for.

CHAPTER NINE

9. Party Hard

Chief Rizza instructs me to walk around the village while they finish up their council meeting. Honestly, there's not that much going on. Though the architecture is some of the most beautiful I have ever seen, their village doesn't offer much more than the most basic necessities. This is indeed a tribal village, not a town or city. Was it always this way or were they forced to live like this once their magic ran out? Most of the huts appear to be living quarters.

I pass a pergola where a woman boils leather and has an assortment of hides hanging from several branches. Underneath another one, a giant stew boils and several wild hogs roast over an open flame. A female troll slices meat off the roasting hogs with her sharp claws and stores it on a bed of waxy leaves in a wicker basket. She watches me warily as I pass.

I do my best to smile, but it comes off as a snarl.

The smell of the meat has my mouth watering. Based on my own experience with the rabbit, I would have expected a slew of uncooked red meat. Apparently just because we can eat raw meat doesn't mean that all trolls do.

Behind the huts, a troll sits fishing on the bank of a small lake. A line of large purple fish is displayed beside her.

One thing I notice as I walk the paths through their village is that aside from children, there are no male trolls around.

In the heart of the village, there is some kind of temple. It is constructed in the same way as the huts, with living trees forming the walls and roof, but smoke seeps out of a hole in the roof. A strong whiff of incense hits me as I come closer. The musky aroma reminds me of the cologne Taryn would wear anytime I saw him. I've told him a million times that it's not a good smell. And yet he wonders why girls don't sit near him. Next time I see him, I'll be sure to let him know it's reminiscent of a troll village.

I peek through the open door and spot a troll covered in furs sitting on the floor. He wears a mask that covers his eyes and a bright array of feathers stick out from it, making him look like some demonic bird. Dark dreadlocks with white tips hang across his back and shoulders. Both hands rest on his knees. He's smaller than I am, leaner, with painted white stripes running down his arms. He chants softly, and I swear there is a faint blue aura around him. When I focus on him, all it tells me is that he is level twelve.

A hand grasps my shoulder and I turn to see Chief Rizza. I was so focused I didn't even notice her approaching.

"Do not disturb the shaman while he is meditating," she says. Her eyes are like a golden wheat field.

"A shaman? What is he doing?" I ask.

He must be the only troll here with magic.

"Communing with his totem. The phoenix grants him great power and wisdom. Like I said, it is very rare for a troll to have natural magic. May we go for a walk?"

"Lead the way."

I follow the chief through the village, passing several other huts and a clearing where a half-dozen young trolls are training with wooden clubs. One of the children takes a club to the head and starts crying, throwing his own club to the ground and running to the instructor for comfort. The instructor gives the boy a stern talking to and sends him back out to battle.

There is no coddling around here.

"You have a very cute child," I say, remembering the baby that suckled at her breast earlier.

"He is not mine. Tormara is his mother, but we raise the children together here. If one is hungry, I will feed it like it is my own."

"That's…interesting." I can't imagine anyone whipping out a tit and just giving it to another child back in the real world. Maybe in some cultures but definitely not the US.

"We are raised to care for one another. That is the only way we will survive. When the rest of the world wants to destroy us, we only have one another to rely on."

"Do you have any children yourself?"

She smiles. "Not yet. In a way, the entire village is my child. While we are fighting for our very survival, I must focus on the task at hand."

The fact that she can feed the child, despite not having any of her own, is pretty incredible. The chief leads me through a dense patch of bushes to a bubbling stream and motions for me to take a seat on a large boulder on the bank.

"My grandmother used to tell me stories of the great heroes of the past. Long before our time, they would appear throughout the lands. They would go on quests, battle great monsters, and defeat powerful threats." Chief Rizza tugs at the tip of her braid and stares down into the stream. Minnows dart back and forth beneath the water. For a moment, she doesn't look like the stoic chief, but a young girl dwelling on old memories.

"I know that those times are returning. I can feel it in my bones. Great battles will come. Portals will reopen making it possible to travel to other continents in minutes, not days. Kingdoms will rise and fall with great heroes on all sides. It is my job to make sure that the forest trolls are still around when that time comes. To do that, we need your help."

She looks at me, all hints of the childhood stories gone. Rizza is a good leader. The leader I never have been on my own teams. She would do anything for her people.

"What makes you think I am the one who can help you do that? Gord is stronger than me. I mean, you have a shaman, for fuck's sake. I'm probably the least qualified person to take this mission." We sit in silence for a moment. The only sounds are the bubbling stream and the birds in the trees. Day one in *Isle of Mythos* and I'm already offered a grand quest. I just wanted to be able to stretch my legs for a bit before I took on the hard stuff. Just to make sure I don't screw anything up.

This is a once in a lifetime opportunity, though. I'd be a fool to turn down this chance.

Deep down, I know that I'm the man for the job. Solving problems is something I'm pretty good at. With the penalty trolls take just for being themselves, I know not many new players will choose that race even after the beta phase has ended. I may very well be the only shot they have at survival.

"I'll do it."

Chief Rizza wraps her arms around me in a firm embrace. She smells of spice, nothing like what I would imagine her to. I get the feeling that it is not very chiefly for her to hug me, but I don't fight it. She squeezes tight. I don't know if I have ever been hugged so hard in my life. Growing up, I was never hugged. Mom and Dad provided for me, they gave me everything I could possibly want, but were hesitant with affection. Whenever the newest video game system came out, I always had it first. When there were games that sold out day one, they could get me a copy. I drowned myself in my games, because the better I did in them, the more people followed me. They would comment on my streams, logging in simply for the entertainment of watching me. And the more trash I talked, the more they loved me.

When Taryn joined my stream, he didn't talk much, but damn was he good. It was a nice dynamic we had. He was the embodiment of the strong, silent type. No one would ever mistake him for a gamer, yet he was. And a damned good one. My viewers soared because not only did we entertain, we also won. His family didn't have a lot of money, so I always made sure I had an extra copy of any new game coming out.

"You will leave at dawn. Anything that we can provide for you on your journey, do not hesitate to ask. Tonight, we will celebrate finding our first hero in many generations!"

I'm not gonna lie, the prospect of a troll party has me excited.

"How will I know where to go?"

She raises her hand and places it against my temple. A tiny spark of energy flutters near my head and the next thing I know, the map in the corner of my vision has another layer over it. It looks like tiny cracks running along the map.

"What is that?"

"Those are magical currents. Ley lines. They travel underground. At certain locations, there are magical springs where raw magic filters into the air. These are usually the sites for temples and other magical buildings."

Looking at the ley lines around where my own location is marked, it's almost like looking at the central nervous system of the human body. Hundreds of veins branch out and break off, splitting from the main line that runs through the forest. I search the map and nowhere else on the island has such a concentration of ley lines. This place must have been something when they were active.

"Can I ask you something, Chief?"

"Of course."

"Why are there no male trolls inside the village?" It's been bothering me since I entered their lands.

"When our magic failed, we had to find ways to protect our way of life. The troll women have always held positions of power in our culture. We do not possess the ability to go into a rage like our male counterparts. We were blessed with something else, though: insight. For thousands of years, women would stay and raise the children and pass laws while the men were at war or off hunting. We each play to our strengths. For as long as our magical barriers have been down, our men have stood sentry at the perimeter, only coming back when it is absolutely necessary."

"That sounds terrible." I can't imagine being forced to guard a place indefinitely.

"We have all had to sacrifice, but tonight, we will toast to a new era. Perhaps even some of our brethren will join us."

I'm not quite prepared for what happens at the troll party. Before it begins, I spend most of the day roaming the forest and fighting what monsters I can find. The male trolls don't bother me this time. I guess word got out that I would be staying the night. They sit still as I pass by, statuesque guardians of the forest. When they are using Camouflage, I can still see them, perhaps because I am a troll as well, but they take on a translucent tone. Almost like looking at a ghost. When they move, their coloring returns. It's pretty wild to watch.

Slaying jackals and the occasional warthog, I manage

to squeeze out a level before dusk hits and I have to return to the village center. My muscles seem to increase slightly due to the bonus points to Strength and Constitution I get each level for being a troll. I wonder if I will look like Gord by the time I reach level ten?

Only one more level until I am level five and can unlock Berserker Rage. I'd like to grind it out tonight, but I am so looking forward to watching these trolls get down. I've never been to a real party, only press events and launch parties, unless you count a Saturday with energy drinks and snack food with Taryn a party, which I'm sure most people don't.

I pass Gord on the way back to the village and he watches me out of the corner of his eye. I don't know what his problem is, but I don't stay to find out.

The village is lively by the time I return. I am greeted with a wooden mug filled with a frothy liquid. The gray-haired troll from the council smiles as she hands me the drink.

"I am Guilda. My son is the one who brought you here. He and his brother have been great protectors of our people for a long time. You are also our protector now. You have the support of the council, even Tormara, though she may not admit it."

I don't know what to say so I chug the frothy liquid. It is sweet, yet it also burns like the fires of hell. The burning sensation starts at my throat and creeps along my body all the way to my hands and feet. My extremities tingle, like tiny strikes of lightning igniting inside my body.

"Wow!" is all I can say.

"Sweetwater. It's a gift of the gods." She clinks her mug against mine and disappears into the crowd.

The female trolls dance and drink, while giant drums echo through the air, reverberating against my chest. Children play amongst the chaos, chasing small horned animals that I assume are pets. The wary glances I experienced earlier are gone, replaced by welcoming smiles. Just like that, these people have embraced me as their own. Now that I have their support, I can't let them down.

Chief Rizza spots me and comes over.

"Aren't you worried about people hearing you?" I ask.

"Humans do not travel into the forest at night. Without night vision, they are fearful of what hides in its depths. Make yourself at home and enjoy yourself, there is no doubt your journey will be fraught with peril." She touches her mug to mine and we both take a drink. The sweetness washes over me, followed by the burn and tingling, but this time, it burns a little less. My head buzzes slightly, and I can't seem to fight the smile that tugs at my face.

I've never drank alcohol before, but I love the taste of sweetwater. The burn isn't so bad, either.

The chief returns to the crowd, dancing and singing and taking drink after drink. Trolls definitely know how to hold their alcohol. Even Guilda is chugging it down like a frat boy on Saturday night. I make my way through the crowd and can't help but let the rhythm flow through me. The beating drums remind me of a ceremonial performance we once watched in school about Native American tribes.

Darkness descends, and several pyres are set up throughout the village center. The flames flicker and dance, making the festivities seem even more alive.

Massive bugs the size of birds flutter through the air, their abdomens glowing and flashing like Christmas lights.

I find the shaman sitting on the steps of the same building where I saw him earlier. He watches the tribe intently, but doesn't seem to be having too much fun himself.

"Hi, I'm Chod. I saw you earlier, but you were meditating."

He looks up and our eyes meet. His pupils are a vibrant red and it's very unsettling to stare at them for long.

"I'm Jira. You witnessed me communing with my totem." He looks out into the crowd, watching their dancing bodies flutter through the night. "The closer I am to my totem, the more of its power I can channel."

"Why don't you go and restore the magic line then?" I ask.

He shrugs, his white-tipped dreads shuffling as he does. "What good would a ley line be if my people perished while I was away? Besides, magic does not clear an obstruction. Only brute force can do that."

"Then why not send Gord or any of the other male trolls?"

"Because we simply do not have the resources to spare. Our lives are hanging on by a thread as it is."

A young troll is running through the village and bumps into me, colliding with my leg and knocking herself to the ground. She giggles at me before standing up and running off into the night.

"Go and enjoy yourself, for I am old and need my rest."

He disappears into the hut, leaving me alone with my thoughts.

Several of the male trolls have returned from scouting. The women clear a space in the center and five of the males gather in a circle, Gord the largest among them. They let out a roar and the drum beats stop. Gord beats on his chest and a moment later, the other four do the same. They fall in line behind him, one beside the other. They bend their knees, slowly descending into a half-squat, their massive thighs displayed in all their glory. What happens next is a sight I will never forget.

In perfect unison, they all smack their legs at once, the sound echoing through the village. Then they smack the other leg, followed by a thunderous stomp and a deafening roar. They repeat this movement over and over, changing the sequence of stomps and slaps and roars. They roar like lions, and I see admiration in all who watch. The rhythm continues, musical madness composed of flesh and bone. It reminds me of a haka, the traditional war dance of the Maori people. I remember seeing it before a rugby game once on the television. But those players didn't have the same power as these trolls. As they dance, something in me resonates with it, wanting to join in.

With a final roar, the dance is over and there is clapping and cheering all around. The men are rewarded with sweetwater and slabs of warthog ribs.

Everyone is so excited by the performance that no one takes notice of the troll who stumbles through the crowd, blood dripping down his neck and shoulders, and collapses on the ground. He's covered in gashes and several arrows stick out of his back. One of his arms is charred up to the elbow.

I push through the crowd, making my way to the

injured troll. Several others finally notice him and bend down to help him up. Somehow, I'm the one he makes eye contact with. My head buzzes as I try to process his words.

"We're under attack," he says, as a flaming arrow soars across the reflection in his eyes.

CHAPTER TEN

10. Blood and Stone

A barrage of flaming arrows filters through the trees and shrubbery, igniting the night. The revelry is extinguished almost as quickly as it began, and nothing but sober faces surround me now. The panicked yells of women and children intermingle with the war cries of the few male trolls. Trees snap as trolls arm themselves with whatever weapons they can find.

In the depths of night, I hear the crack of branches and trees and wonder what chaos awaits.

"This is your fault," Gord roars at me. Caked earth falls from the tree trunk he holds.

"It can't be," argues Chief Rizza. Her eyes are wide with shock, taking in everything around us. "There is no way the ranger could have made it back in time for this to happen. This had to have already been planned. Regardless, there is no time to argue about it now. We must defend our homes. Guilda, gather the children. Everyone else, prepare for battle."

"Come on then, hero. Make yourself useful," Gord goads me.

I seriously don't understand what his problem is, but now is not the time.

I uproot a tree and take off into the battle behind him. Away from the pyres and burning huts, my night vision kicks into gear. In the depths of the forest, everything has a green hue to it. The occasional flaming arrow bursts through in a white blur. One hits me in the shoulder, and it burns like hell. Either it's coated with poison or I take extra damage from fire, because it hurts way more than the arrow that hit me earlier. I yank the arrow from my arm and toss it to the ground, leaving a wound which continues to sting long afterwards.

Battle rages all around me. Screams and grunts, along with the crunch of blunt force attacks, fill the air. I'm used to the clang of metal, not this. This is somehow worse. More brutal.

Whoever these men are, they came to wreak havoc. Most of them wear boiled leather armor, studded about the shoulders and chest. They carry bronze weapons, and most use wooden shields. Clearly, they are an organized militia, but more likely from a small town rather than a large keep. Dozens of torches glitter in the distance as they make their way forward. Many of the arrows have lodged high in the canopy of the surrounding trees, setting them ablaze and filling the night with the scent and crackling of the burning waxy leaves.

Gord rushes into the fight, not waiting a second to analyze the situation or formulate a game plan.

I survey the battlefield, seeing where I can be most useful. Dozens of mini skirmishes unfold all around me, one troll for every three or four humans. However you want to slice it, we're outnumbered. The trolls seem to be doing a good job of holding their own, even against such unfavorable odds.

The archers are peppering them with damage, though. There is the constant thwip of arrows sailing by and the occasional grunt when they make impact. Without shields, we only have our own tough skins for protection. Against normal arrows, we would be fine, but the fiery arrows are inflicting actual damage.

I need to find a way to get past the warriors and into the back lines. If I can somehow take out the archers, we might actually have a shot at saving the village.

I look for an opening to either side, but there's no way I can manage to sneak around with things as chaotic as they are. The rogue class is looking awfully good right about now.

Several men armed with spears and torches surround a troll to my right. An arrow shaft sticks out of his left bicep and he swings a club savagely at the spears closing in on him, brushing them aside. The spears offer the men a safe distance from the long reach of the troll. They scream words I can't understand and jab blazing torches more for effect than actual damage. Another arrow lodges in the troll's chest, and he shouts in pain. One of the spearmen jabs low, piercing the troll's calf and causing him to buckle at the knees. He tries to stand but can't put any weight on the leg.

I have to get in there and help him.

I take off running. At full speed, I collide with the offending spearman, knocking him to the ground and smashing the end of my club into his face. Notifications pop across my vision, but I ignore them and they fade into the background, barely noticeable.

The wounded troll is unable to stand, but scoots against a tree so that his back is protected. I toss him the dead man's spear and we make eye contact briefly. Anger burns in his eyes. At least with the spear, he can fight from the ground if he has to.

I'll do my best to make sure they pay. A spear jabs at my throat, but I smack it out of the way and unleash a powerful kick, sending my attacker to the ground. He gasps for air and I turn to face the final spearman, but he has already retreated. Turning back to the man on the ground, I don't listen to his cries for mercy as I stomp his head into the earth.

"Can you hold your own?" I kneel before the wounded troll.

"I will be fine. Help the others."

A sharp pain flares in my back and I turn to see a bloody sword about to pierce me again. I dodge at the last moment, leaving my opponent swiping at air.

"Big mistake."

He attacks again with a quick slash and the blade lodges against my club. I jerk hard and his weak human arms are unable to keep a grip on his weapon. A flick of my wrist and the sword comes free, sailing into the night.

He holds up his shield in defense and it splinters under the blow of my club, shattering the bones in his forearm.

His arm hangs limp, unable to let go of the rickety shield still strapped to it.

I'm up to twenty rage, but I don't need to use it. Not yet.

The man screams like a child, and then he screams no more.

So much of the forest is ablaze that I am worried the village may burn to the ground if we do not stop this carnage soon.

I spot Tormara in the distance, her red braid swishing through the air, almost alive. The female trolls fight much differently than the males. They attack with speed and grace, not power. She holds a stone dagger in each hand and sparks fly as it clashes, pieces of stone flaking off against the metal sword. She parries the sword to the side and slides the other dagger into the man's neck.

The chief must be somewhere among the madness, but I don't have time to search for her. I still need to stop the archers.

Ahead of me, a dozen men with swords and shields surround one of the trolls I saw earlier on my walk. He's level six and not much bigger than me. He keeps the warriors at bay by swinging a large club, but they are closing in.

Gord comes out of nowhere, his body covered in red blood. Human blood. He rushes to his comrade's defense, knocking two men to the ground with a single blow. The other troll takes action and the two are able to hold their ground, backs to back. The swordsmen move in, five on each side, but are unable to press any further.

The two sides are at a stalemate. The men are wary to move any closer, and the trolls are afraid to give up their position of strength. Their hand is forced when a volley of flaming arrows rain down upon the two trolls.

Gord and his partner cry out in pain, and the humans use the opportunity to attack. They land several blows before Gord swings out blindly, connecting his club with one man's head and dropping him instantly.

I can't just sit by. I need to help.

Using Intimidation, I release my battle cry and join the fray. The men look confused and sway back and forth for a moment, unable to attack. With our foes momentarily dazed, I help Gord and the other troll pull the arrows from their bodies just in time for our opponents to regain their senses.

"Keep our backs together," I say.

"I will give the orders here!" shouts Gord. He cracks his knuckles. "Keep our backs together."

I suppress the smile that I know will turn into laughter if I let it escape.

Three more men join and once again, twelve surround us. They range from level four to ten, but I can't really pick and choose who I want to fight. I'll take whoever attacks first.

"We need to end this before they attack with more arrows," I say.

"Arrows do not frighten me," Gord says, but I can tell he is favoring the side where I just removed six arrows.

"We can't stand here all day!"

"Fine, give me your club."

I don't know what he has planned, but I do as he says, mostly because I'd like to be fighting together and not with each other and the humans.

He takes it and hurls it like a boomerang at the men

closest to him. It collides with two of them, knocking them unconscious.

"Attack!" yells Gord.

The men are so surprised that we actually get in a few good hits before they react. I use Claw and rip out the throat of the man closest to me. He collapses while his heart continues to pump several streams of blood onto his fellow soldiers.

A sharp blade pierces my side and I kick out in that direction, feeling the crunch of bones beneath my foot. I don't have time to plan my attacks, so I flail and claw and kick anyone unlucky enough to step in my direction. It's not pretty, but it gets the job done. A moment later, it's only the three of us still standing.

"We need to get the archers," I try to tell Gord, but his eyes are fixed on something in the distance.

"Him." He points. "He brought this on us."

A man marches forward from the line of archers. There is nothing remarkable about him, but I can tell that he is a cut above the rest of the soldiers. For starters, he wears chainmail and carries a sword made of steel. A silver helm with a ruby set in the brow catches the light from the fires that rage around us. His armor is a hodgepodge, with no two pieces belonging together. Two separate bracers shield his forearms, one silver and one black. He carries a golden shield engraved with a raven.

Didn't anyone ever tell this clown you don't wear silver and gold together?

"Who is this guy?" I ask.

"He is the one they call a hero. Many times, he has come into our lands and many times, he has been slain." Gord growls. "Today will be no exception."

He shouts something as he walks, but it is all gibberish to me. There is no doubt in my mind that this man is a real player. No one else would ever dare to look so stupid on the battlefield.

I focus on him and his stats appear.

Glenn Orickson

Level 14

Warrior

Human

What's left of his men have retreated behind the archers. Many are injured, with only the archers coming through unscathed. At level fourteen, he is the highest level of anyone in the battle and would undoubtedly kick my ass. Gord seems anxious to have a go at him.

A large level nine troll charges at Glenn, stone club in hand. Glenn takes a battle stance and a yellow aura surrounds his body. The sword connects with the club and a violent arc of lightning lashes out, striking the troll and stunning him in place. The gasp from those surrounding me sounds like a thousand hissing snakes.

Glenn lets out a cruel laugh. It needs no translation. Then he pushes his sword into the troll's throat.

"Ramu!" cries Gord, mourning his fallen brother. "He has never attacked like that. The undying one has grown stronger since our last battle. I must avenge Ramu."

I grab him by the arm. As big of a dick as Gord has been, if he goes out there, Glenn will kill him.

"Unhand me!" He shakes his arm free.

"If you go out there, he will kill you."

"If I don't go, he will kill us all."

Gord is one of the strongest trolls I've met. The village needs him. I can't let him die.

"Let me go. If I die, I will return. You won't."

A fierce struggle rages behind Gord's eyes as he wrestles with his intelligence and his pride.

"Then I will die." He picks up a fallen club and sets out in search of Glenn, a loud roar erupting and setting his challenge in stone.

A smile flits across Glenn's face. There is history between these two.

The remaining skirmishes have all but dissolved and both sides now watch intently at the match before us. Several trolls lie dead, but far more humans. With the troll population shrinking as it is, this battle could prove to be catastrophic. I don't know how Gord can win this. If he dies, I fear his people die with him. I may very well be the last forest troll by the end of the night.

If only there was something I could do. I'm a hero, but I'm outclassed by the NPCs all around me.

Gord is almost to where Ramu died when Glenn takes a defensive stance. He sheathes his sword and holds firm behind his shield. What in the hell is he doing?

A silver sheen runs across the shield and when Gord attacks, there is an explosion like fireworks. It tosses Gord back nearly ten feet, sparks raining down around him.

All around us, the forest continues to burn.

Glenn pulls his sword and his laughter rings through the forest. It's almost maniacal. He's walking towards Gord, a yellow aura surrounding his sword, when I hear a flutter of wings pass by me.

Crimson wings, almost black in places, glide through the underbelly of the forest. As fast as it appeared, there is a puff of feathers and the giant bird morphs into Jira, the shaman.

Glenn takes notice and halts his approach towards Gord.

Jira stands proud, his white-tipped dreadlocks swaying around his shoulders.

Glenn raises his sword and charges Jira. I sure hope he knows what he is doing.

Jira stretches his arms wide and the forest goes silent. Even the crackle of fire disappears. His hands connect with a thunderous clap and flames spark from inside. The fiery tips of the archer's arrows and the flames that dance in the trees disappear, causing red streams of light to streak across the battlefield towards Jira. A flaming bird rushes out of the shaman's chest, screeching. It dives for Glenn, pecking and clawing and scorching. He screams in agony, the fiery phoenix burning him alive.

The archers abandon ranks and run.

"After them!" Chief Rizza's voice cuts through the chaos.

Gord is on his feet, club in hand, running at Glenn. I take off after the fleeing archers and leave him and Jira to their vengeance.

CHAPTER ELEVEN

11. Peacemaker

There's no trace of the fires that raged through the forest only moments before. Whatever magic Jira used sucked every flame from the surrounding forest. I still can't believe the power of that attack. The fiery phoenix attacked Glenn like a bat out of hell. It makes me wish that magic among trolls wasn't so rare.

Speaking of Glenn, I return to find his gear stacked next to a larger pile of weapons and armor stripped from the humans. His body is nowhere to be found. The bodies of the fallen soldiers are being piled atop one another. Not a single human survived. Our night vision made the task of tracking them through the woods child's play.

Four trolls lay side by side on the scorched earth. Jira stands over their bodies, whispering silently.

Chief Rizza rubs ash across each of their foreheads, some ritual I have no knowledge of.

"The undying one will return. He grows stronger each time, but this is the first we have heard of him using magic," she says.

It won't be the last. I don't say it aloud, but I think they know it, too. There is no doubt that Glenn has been questing. His assortment of armor, his abilities, I'm going to need to hit the ground running if I'm going to have a chance at defending this village. He's already eleven levels ahead of me. Well, ten after his death. How can I be a hero if I can't even fight my own battles?

Jira finishes his chant and turns to the chief. There is a heaviness about his crimson eyes. A heaviness I'm sure the trolls have experienced far too often.

"I'm sorry I failed you," he says to the lifeless trolls. "I was deep in sleep when I heard the chaos. Old age has its pitfalls, but I never thought sleeping would lead to the death of my brothers and sisters."

"It is not your fault, brother," says Chief Rizza. "We were attacked unaware. We will have time before the undying one tries our village again, but it is all the more reason magic must be restored soon. The night benefited us this time. It may not be so kind again."

I look over the bodies, but I don't see Glenn's anywhere.

"Where is his body?" I ask.

"The only thing heroes leave behind when they die are their belongings." She tosses a bracer among the pile of looted armor. "We will add these to the stock from previous attacks. Perhaps we will have enough to work into weapons of our own."

"What now?"

Chief Rizza looks at the pile of bodies. "We will burn the dead enemies, and then we will mourn our own. You will leave first thing in the morning. Help where you can. I have business to attend to." With a flip of her braid, she is gone.

I suddenly remember all of the notifications I dismissed during the battle. I focus on recalling them and they appear in the left of my vision.

Congratulations! You have reached level 5. +1 stat point to distribute. +1 Strength and Constitution racial bonus. +1 ability point to distribute.

Congratulations! You have reached level 6. +1 stat point to distribute. +1 Strength and Constitution racial bonus.

Warning! *You have killed a human NPC. If word of this reaches a human settlement, your reputation among humans will be decreased by 100. Stop your enemies from reaching town before it is too late. Current reputation with humans: -999. (-1000 Racial Penalty)*

Warning! *You have killed a human NPC. If word of this reaches a human settlement, your reputation among humans will be decreased by 100. Stop your enemies from reaching town before it is too late. Current reputation with humans: -999. (-1000 Racial Penalty)*

Warning! *You have killed a human NPC. If word of this reaches a human settlement, your reputation among humans will be decreased by 100. Stop your enemies from reaching town before it is too late. Current reputation with humans: -999. (-1000 Racial Penalty)*

Warning! *You have killed a human NPC. If word of this reaches a human settlement, your reputation among humans will be decreased by 100. Stop your enemies from reaching town* *before it is too late. Current reputation with humans: -999. (-1000 Racial Penalty)*

***Alert!** You have failed to stop your enemies from reaching town. Your reputation has decreased by 400. Current reputation with humans: -1399. (-1000 Racial Penalty)*

What the hell!? We killed all of the soldiers. Not a single one escaped. There is no way I should have lost that reputation. Then, I remember.

Glenn.

Fucking Glenn has become a serious thorn in my side. One that I'm not likely to get rid of any time soon.

I pull up my stats and look them over.

Strength: 23
Dexterity: 15
Constitution: 24
Intelligence: 7
Wisdom: 10
Charisma: 6

My Strength and Constitution are really improving thanks to my racial bonus every level. I feel much stronger and healthier than I did earlier in the day. My loincloth even seems to fit a little tighter around my waist.

I now have five stat points to distribute, but I'm still unsure if I should put any into non-physical stats, so I hold off for now. What I'm really excited about is my new ability point. I don't even hesitate to use it on Berserker Rage.

***Berserker Rage.** (Ultimate.) Attacks and physical damage build your rage meter. 5 rage per attack. Rage meter deteriorates over time when out of combat at a rate of 5 rage per second. Once the meter is full, Berserker Rage becomes avail-*

able. For 30 seconds, rage meter is full, deal increased damage, health regenerates at 5x the normal rate, cannot be stunned, slowed or otherwise affected.

I can't wait to test out this bad boy in battle.

"Make yourself useful," says Gord. He scowls at me as he tosses a body onto the pile.

"What's your problem, asshole?" I challenge. He really makes me wish I had more than two middle fingers to point in his direction. I've had enough of this guy thinking he can boss me around. "You've been nothing but a giant dick to me since I got here. What gives?"

He's in my face quicker than I expect, saliva raining down on me as he yells, hot breath assaulting my face.

His voice is a growl when he speaks. "You come here and think just because you have green skin that it makes you one of us? You are no more one of us than the men who attacked. Ramu and I grew up together. We hunted and battled together. We have fought off countless attacks like today. Just because you can't die, do you think that makes you special? That I should respect you because the chief gives you a special mission?" He puts his finger against my chest and I feel his heated temperature radiating through it. "You are nothing."

"That's enough, Gord." Jira's raspy voice comes between us. "Leave the boy be. Chod, come with me."

I follow Jira back towards the village. Thoughts of pushing Gord off a high ledge run through my mind. He has the charm and charisma of a burning orphanage.

"You have to forgive Gord, he has always been spirited. He lost his father at a young age to an attack and has been distrusting of outsiders ever since."

That makes a lot of sense, but it still doesn't excuse his

dickish behavior.

"I would think he would be grateful for any help he could get." I don't owe anything to these people. I'm agreeing to help because they got a shitty lot, and if I don't help, no one else will. A little gratitude would be nice.

"Give it time. Chief Rizza knows we are lucky to have you. I do as well. Gord doesn't yet know the power of heroes. Besides, I think he may feel a bit threatened by you."

"By me? Gord is, like, ten times stronger than I am. Why would he possibly feel threatened by me?"

"Think about it. You come into our lands, commit a crime anyone else would be punished for, and end up receiving a quest and falling into the chief's good graces."

Damn. I hadn't even thought of it that way. Nobody likes a person who has everything handed to them. He doesn't know that I'm here as a punishment, that the very reason I am here is because I didn't have Mom and Dad bail me out. Or did I? I could be in prison right now, but instead, I'm playing a game for thirty days because of a favor they called in.

Back in the village, Guilda reunites the children with their parents. I'd like to think that something like that would frighten the young ones, but judging by the looks on their faces, they don't seem too upset. Is it their natural troll resilience or the fact that they have seen this type of thing way too often?

Many of the huts are charred in places, but for the most part, they are okay. The fact that they are living homes means that it wasn't just dried timber that caught fire. Living things are harder to burn.

"That's enough excitement for one night, children.

Everyone to bed." Guilda says it kindly, escorting children to and fro. She's like the nurturing grandmother who can bench press a truck.

I don't really know that there is too much more for me to help with. The funeral pyre has already begun for our attackers, and I'm not sure what will be done with the fallen trolls. I have a long day ahead of me tomorrow, so it's probably best if I rest for the night.

"You can stay in Ramu's hut for the night until we find you someplace more permanent," Guilda offers.

"Are you sure?" Something feels wrong about staying in the hut of a dead troll. I'm positive Gord will have something to say about it, but it's not like I can really argue. Guilda is on the council after all.

Stepping into the hut is a bit unsettling, like when people die in real life and they still leave behind their social media profiles. They're just there, forever, like nothing ever happened. Their pictures still smile, and the funny cat video still plays when you scroll over it. This room makes me feel like that.

A small wooden toy sits on a bedside table. I pick it up and notice it's a carving of a troll, very intricate and detailed. Heavier than I would have thought. The contours of its muscles and the loincloth are textured. He holds a tiny club in his hand. Whoever did this had skill.

A leather blanket covers a wooden pallet used as a bed. It's a step down from my pillowtop mattress, but I have a feeling that with my new body, I could sleep on a rock and not really notice. The room is all very rudimentary, but kind of endearing in a way.

I try not to think about Ramu, about what kind of troll he was. If he carved the troll or if it was a gift. Who he was giving it to or who had given it to him. I'll think of him as a video game character who died in a battle, not as someone who lived a life long before I ever got here.

Laying down on the pallet, I realize this is my first night sleeping in *Isle of Mythos*. My first night of full immersion. Somewhere out there, tiny nanites are cleaning my body and making me experience all of this like I'm really here. Whenever this game is ready to launch, it's going to be a worldwide hit. There's no doubt about it.

I don't recall falling asleep, but I wake up to the beating of drums. When I step outside, the bodies of the four dead trolls each have their own funeral pyre in the middle of the village.

The bodies are about three feet off the ground, covered in an assortment of brightly-colored flowers. Their fragrant aroma fills the air along with the musk of incense. Nobody says anything as Chief Rizza circles the pyres holding a torch.

"Ramu, son of Redma. Uhmi, daughter of Ezra. Hethe, son of Teja. Yavo, son of Zalma. You gave your lives for our village. For our people. We will see you in the next life."

There is a loud stomp that echoes from everyone, and they smack their fists against their hearts. I'm the only one who doesn't do it. Part of what Gord says rings true— I am an outsider. A foreigner to my own people. Chief Rizza ignites the kindling around the feet of each pyre and the bodies are engulfed in flame.

We all stand in silence as the fires crackle and burn, incinerating the bodies of the four trolls. They burn hot and bright, disguising what happens beneath the flames.

When the fires begin to die, trolls disperse to their everyday jobs. Gord cuts his eyes at me as he makes his way into the forest.

"I have a few parting gifts to help you with your journey before you go," says Chief Rizza.

She leads me into the temple where I first saw Jira. The smell of incense is as strong as ever and several wooden bowls send off blue and purple smoke that rises to the ceiling. Jira stands over a chest covered in furs.

"It has been too long since we have been able to craft with magic, but we still have a few items from the old days. I pray that they will help you on your quest." He moves the furs aside, revealing a dark chest complete with gold latches and studded with precious stones.

It's the most non-troll thing I've seen since I came here. Rizza pulls a key from her pocket and hands it to Jira. He opens the chest and the lid falls back with a thud.

He pulls out a dark crimson feather. It's almost black near the center and gradually fades into red tips. I focus on it and its stats display in the edge of my vision.

Item. Phoenix Feather. 10% resistance to fire-based attacks. *A very rare item, phoenix feathers can only be gathered if they are willingly given by the host. Feathers plucked from unwilling birds turn to ash.*

"As you know, trolls are very resilient, but we take more damage from fire than most races. I don't know what you will face on your journey, but this should prove helpful if you come across any humans. They have a strange fascination with fire." Jira hands the feather to Chief Rizza, and she ties it into the bottom of my braid.

Next, he pulls out a necklace. It is basically a long leather strap with a polished stone attached to it. The stone is a rusty brown with streaks of gold going through it.

Item. Tiger's Eye Pendant. Removes one debuff. Cooldown: 10 minutes. *A rare stone believed to ward off evil and bring balance to life.*

Chief Rizza takes the necklace and ties it around my neck.

"Trolls are not known as great metalworkers or weaponsmiths. Mostly, we use our own powerful bodies and sharp claws and they serve us well, but the time may come when you need a weapon. This one has been passed down for many generations." Jira reaches in the box and pulls out a glittering double-edged battle-axe. The handle has several engravings that run along its edges and three empty sockets where stones once sat. "Long ago, before the trolls were so despised, this axe was given to the great troll warrior, Gohma, by the dwarven weaponsmith, Kerrus Silverhammer. It has several sockets that can be set with enchanted stones to make the weapon stronger. It is a weapon fit for a hero. Its name is Peacemaker."

Item. Peacemaker. An enchanted battle-axe capable of taking on the properties of up to 3 attached stones. +3 Strength. *A relic from another age given as a symbol of peace and fortune among allies.*

From the bottom of the chest, Jira pulls out several green and red vials and places them in a small leather pouch.

"These should help if you fall into trouble."

Item. Health Potion. Restores 100 HP over 10 seconds. X5

Item. Potion of Greater Stamina. Increases stamina for 5 minutes. X3

Item. Potion of Greater Resilience. Increases total HP by

10% for 5 minutes. X3

He closes the lid and covers the chest. I have the feeling there are more items inside that I couldn't see.

"Oh, and one more thing." He hands me a large satchel. It's filled with pouches and compartments and has an actual leather strap for carrying. "The bag you were carrying looked like it was made by a child. Your leather skills definitely need some work. Perhaps when you return, Ahso can take you under her wing. Unfortunately, this is all we can offer you for now. Anything else you need you must find along the way."

"Now, come," says the chief. "I will walk you to our borders and see you off."

I'm not sure exactly where the village border ends or how to tell, but Chief Rizza comes to a stop and I know this is where we say our good-byes. In such a short time, I feel like I've already grown attached to the place and to the people. All except for Gord, he can sit on a pointy stick for all I care. It's going to be an adventure, but at least I feel like I have something worth fighting for.

"Good luck, Chod. You are our hero now. The fate of the village depends on you. Once you reach the obstruction and clear it, return here at once." With a quick turn, her braid whips through the air and I'm left watching as she walks away.

I thought she was supposed to be watching me go.

"Chief Rizza," I call out and she turns her head. "How will I know how to clear the obstruction?"

"I cannot answer that. We don't know what has stopped the flow of magic, but I have no doubt you will figure it out."

Looking at my map, my destination feels far away.

CHAPTER TWELVE

12. Muck it Up

Peacemaker is a massive axe, even by troll standards. So big that I can't imagine a human being able to lift it. It cuts through branches and vines with ease as I noisily make my way through the forest. Even after all these years, the blade has remained sharp.

The three sockets that run down the side of the handle are what really interest me. The item description says that it takes on the properties of whatever magical stones are inserted in them. The power of this axe is only limited by the enchanted stones I am able to find. My mind runs wild with possibilities of an axe that deals fire damage or increases my movement speed even further, making me a giant fucking ninja troll.

I need to find out where the stones are.

Unfortunately, I don't know anything about enchanted

stones or how to find them, and neither Jira nor the chief seemed too concerned about telling me. There could be a million different ways of getting them. Dungeons, quests, special monsters. If only I wasn't bound by my bad reputation and the ability to speak only one language, then I could ask one of the more magically inclined races.

As it is, I'm on my own.

I'm minding my own business, walking through the forest, when something hits me in the side of the face with a splat. My health drops by a tick and a cool gooey substance slowly slides down my face and falls to the ground. The mud-like substance moves across the forest floor like some sentient mud pie and disappears into an even larger pool of goo.

Sludge. *Level 8. Though not the smartest of creatures, sludges are hard to kill and even harder to get your hands on. They can only be destroyed by killing the core, which can move to any part of its body. Some are even known to hide poisonous stingers beneath their slimy exterior.*

"Can't a guy just walk in peace?" I ask the sludge, but there is no response, just a dull gurgle from inside.

Instead, a ghost-like pile of sludge rises from the pool and tosses another mud pie at me.

"Alright, you walking pile of diarrhea, let's go!" I take off after the sludge, but immediately notice I'm moving slower. My normal troll movements that I've grown accustomed to feel almost…human. I pull up the notifications from the background to see what is going on.

Alert! *You have been slowed. Movement and attack speed reduced by 50%.*

Well, that's annoying. Another mud pie comes whizzing by. I attempt to dodge it, but the debuff makes it impossible for me to move out of the way and it hits me in the chest, turning my green skin a murky brown.

Remembering the Tiger's Eye Pendant that Jira gave to me, I mentally activate its ability, removing the slow, and immediately move faster. The sludge tosses another mud pie, but this time, it sails over my shoulder as I shift to the side. I can't get hit again because the cooldown on the pendant is ten minutes.

I cover the distance between me and the sludge in a few quick steps and bring down my axe with a mighty swing. It cuts through the sludge but does no damage at all. Instead, the sludge seems to move around the blade, almost as if it's cutting through water.

"You have got to be kidding me. How am I supposed to kill something I can't hit?"

A long, scorpion-like tail rises from behind the sludge and strikes at me like a cobra. I jump to the side and it whirs through the air where I had just stood. Something hard and metallic protrudes from the end of the tail.

A stinger!

It strikes again, and I swipe at it with my axe, severing the tail. The stinger falls to the ground and crawls back to the host.

I have no idea how I am supposed to kill this thing when it can separate at will.

The damage I've taken has given me enough rage to use Intimidation. I let out a roar, expecting to confuse the sludge, but nothing happens. It rises as tall as me and six tentacles sprout out, assaulting me with mud balls. Unable to dodge them all, several of them hit me, slowing me and dropping my health down to seventy percent. Little by little, they are wearing me down. I might just have to say screw it and bail.

While I am still slowed, the sludge shrinks back down, retracting its multiple arms. Its stinger rises in the air and hovers like a snake about to strike.

Pain runs through my chest as the stinger penetrates my skin. Ten percent of my health vanishes instantly. My HP continues to drop as a throbbing pain traces from the wound and down my right arm.

Poison.

If only I hadn't wasted my pendant's ability, I could cleanse the poison. I grab one of the health potions from my bag and down it in one gulp. It battles with the poison as my health drops and rises, drops and rises, caught in a tide of life and death.

Another barrage of mud flies into me, dropping my health by a chunk. I take the other two health potions and my health begins to recover faster than the poison can drain me.

Moving at a snail's pace, I'm still unable to dodge the incoming stinger and pain flares through my left shoulder.

I'm about to die to a soggy turd alone in the forest. If I had invested points into Iron Will, then I could at least null the effects of the slow for long enough to run away. As it is, I'm pretty sure the sludge could chase me down if I tried to run.

Then I remember. *Berserker Rage*.

I activate the ability, and immediately the slow disappears and the poison vanishes from my system. My health ticks up and my muscles seem to pulse with power.

I hack at the sludge with violent enthusiasm. The edge

of my vision glows red, which I assume is a side effect of full rage. I hack and slash at the amorphous blob, separating it into delicious-looking nougats that flutter around the forest floor. The stinger rises again, but I cut it down before it can attack and punt it deep into the forest. I continue to chop like a lumberjack on cocaine, but somehow, I'm unable to locate the sludge's core. With no way to beat the creature, I take off running into the woods before my rage wears off.

Sometimes you just have to know when to bail. As much as I would have loved to spend all day cutting chocolate, I have a quest to complete.

I wasted all three health potions for no reward, but at least I'm still alive.

I make it a few miles before I hear a rustle in the bushes and a lone wolf steps out into my path. Finally, something I can actually kill, hopefully quickly, and be on my way.

Forest Wolf. *Level 7. Quick and powerful, a wolf is not to be trifled with.*

The beast snarls, revealing a set of sharp teeth intent on seeing just how tough my troll skin is.

"Let's dance," I goad the wolf, but as soon as the words leave my mouth, two more wolves emerge from the bush.

Just my luck.

I don't wait for the pack to surround me. I attack with a mighty slash that gashes the first wolf on the shoulder. He yelps in pain and the other two wolves bite at my ankles. My health dips and dark blue blood streaks down my feet and stains the forest floor.

Before I know what is happening, a fourth wolf

pounces me from behind and a sharp pain flares through my shoulder as it sinks its teeth in.

Without thinking, I grab the beast by its neck and throw it into a nearby tree. It collapses to the ground and sways back and forth as it tries to regain its footing.

At four against one, the odds are not in my favor. Not that they ever will be in this game. I've lost twenty percent of my health from the three attacks, but it's already regenerating.

I swing my axe back and forth in an arc in front of me, keeping the wolves at bay while I attempt to come up with a plan. I only have twenty rage at the moment, but that is enough to use Intimidation. I roar, and the wolves' eyes roll in opposite directions, confused.

With a sweeping strike, I manage to hit all three wolves in one blow, gaining me fifteen rage off one attack. I use Bite and Claw at once, sinking my teeth into the middle wolf's neck while simultaneously raking my claws across its chest. When I toss it aside, it doesn't get up.

The confusion wears off, and the other two wolves attack just as the dazed wolf that bit my shoulder regains its footing. My axe catches one wolf as he lunges and scores a critical hit to his head, but the other manages to bite me in the side. It lets go and retreats just as I reach for it.

My body stings all over from the attacks and I find it hard to focus.

Shaking my head, I push the pain to the back of my mind. If I die, I'll probably lose all the items that they gave me. What kind of hero would I be if that happened?

Taking a step back, I try to assess the situation. Just because I can take the damage they are dishing out, it doesn't mean I have to. The wolves come forward and begin circling around me. If I let them, they'll attack from my blind side and try to weaken me that way.

I take a stamina and strength potion, close my eyes, and listen. Their heavy breathing is the closest thing to me, so I try to pinpoint it. There's an intake of air behind me just before I feel a stabbing pain in my calf. I open my eyes and kick out, but the wolf has already returned to circling. Another wolf digs into my other leg as I turn away and it retreats just as quickly.

Hot blood trickles down my leg, no doubt increasing the fervor of the wolves. I push it away and close my eyes again, listening to their breathing. My heart pounds in response to the two potions.

The intake of breath gives away the attack and I turn, slashing my axe through the air like a pro golfer. It connects with the wolf's jaw, splitting it in two. I'm not quick enough to stop the counter-attack on my rear, but I'm down to two wolves and fifty percent HP.

I repeat the process until only the final wolf remains. We square off in front of each other, the final showdown.

I'll give it to the guy, he has some major balls staying around after watching three of his pack sliced to pieces.

I make the first move this time, attacking with an overhead swing. The wolf is surprisingly fast and darts out of the way. He lunges and takes a bite of my arm before I can regain my balance. His teeth sink into me as he shakes his head back and forth. It hurts like a bitch, but I use Claw against his snout and he sets me free.

The wolf licks his muzzle, tasting both my blood and his that has caked into its silver fur, and lets out a huff. He eyes me intently and begins circling once again.

"I've had about enough of your shit," I say.

I feint a swing of my axe and the wolf moves to the side, but I'm already prepared for his movement and spin to the other side, bringing the axe down in a beautiful arc that connects with his side, ripping the remaining life out of him.

Congratulations! You have reached level 7. +1 stat point to distribute. +1 Strength and Constitution racial bonus. +1 ability point to distribute.

I notice that when I look at my abilities now, there is a new tab for melee weapons. It must be because I have Peacemaker equipped.

Sweeping Slash. *Form a sweeping arc in front of you, dealing damage and knocking your opponent off balance. Cost: 5 rage.*

Cleave. *Your next attack causes bleed damage, dealing 1% of opponent's health per second for 5 seconds. Cost: 10 rage.*

Battle Cry. *You let out a ferocious roar, increasing Rage by 20. No Cost. Cooldown: 60 seconds.*

Thinking back on my fight with the wolves, I elect to put my new ability point into Sweeping Slash. Battle Cry is a nice way to get the upper hand early, but due to my natural tankiness, I can increase my rage simply by taking damage. Having an ability that knocks opponents back is a great defensive maneuver and may come in handy if I find myself surrounded again.

I'm feeling pretty good about myself after taking on four wolves and the lowest they got me to was half-health. By the time this quest is over, I should be leveled up nicely.

After looting pelts from the wolves, I pull up my map and find the location Chief Rizza marked for me.

Focusing on the overlay, I'm able to see the ley lines that run beneath the surface. She did say she wasn't exactly sure where the obstruction was, but at least was able to pinpoint the source of the ley line that leads into the forest. The cause of the obstruction could be anywhere between here and there. I just hope it's something visible so I don't walk past it.

By the looks of it, it will take me several days to get to my destination. Two human settlements stand in my way, and unless I want to divert my course and go around them, I will have to thread the needle and hope I don't get caught. Since I don't know the exact location, I can't really afford to take any detours.

I am Dorothy and the ley lines are my yellow brick road. Let's just hope the flying monkeys stay away.

CHAPTER THIRTEEN

13. Walking, Walking, and More Walking

The first settlement isn't anything special. It's a typical medieval town complete with spiked wooden palisade and several soldiers standing around the entrance. What lies inside is a mystery because I don't feel like dying, and with a negative thirteen hundred and ninety-nine reputation, I will be attacked on sight. Still, I watch them, wondering what could have been if I were a less hated race.

People come and go. There is a road system where farmers and other traders travel on horses and in wagons. A man wearing full plate armor and a plumed helmet sits in a wagon with some reptilian horned creature tied to the back of it. The creature doesn't appear to be moving.

Could that be another real player? He doesn't look as stupid as Glenn in his mismatched armor, but it's a damned knight riding in a wagon. I have to assume anything as ridiculous as this is the product of player ingenuity.

I try to focus on him to see his stats, but he's too far away.

Something cracks behind me, but when I turn to see the source of the noise, nothing is there. It's enough to remind me that I shouldn't be so close to human settlements. I grab my bag and my axe and set off away from the town. If I go at least a mile, I should be far enough away that no one will see me.

A beautiful sunny day waits for me outside of the tree line, but I'm nervous to leave the forest. It's the only area I've been a part of since logging in to *Isle of Mythos*. As silly as it seems, it feels like home. Out there, in the open, I'll have a massive target on my back. An even more massive target on my back. And in here, I won't have Taryn to watch my back.

I stall for a moment, slaughtering a few rabbits and filling my belly while I still have the cover of the trees. After eating the roasted boar at the celebration, the rabbits don't taste as delicious as before. They are still serviceable, and it's nice to not have to worry about learning a cooking skill.

When I step out into the open, I feel naked, and not just because the crisp morning air is brushing against my undercarriage. In spite of my tough skin and hulking physique, I feel as vulnerable as I did at school when I had to walk up on stage once to accept an award for placing in a gaming tournament. All eyes were on me, but I kept mine focused on the floor, so worried I might trip and make a fool of myself. I didn't realize until later that my fly had been open the entire time and pictures of my exposed boxers were doing the rounds on social media. I need to get my head in the game. There are more painful things than being called 'Ballsy McChadwick' out here.

I take a deep breath and set out towards my destination. A golden field stretches before me, dotted with wild animals running through it. If I had the time and desire, I could level up nicely out here. An assortment of deer and bison roam freely, but I don't want to spend any more time in the open than I have to. It's too close to the humans for my liking. I cross the dirt road that splits the field in a hurry a half-second after a wagon approaches on the horizon.

At full speed, I rush through the field until I can no longer see the road or the town.

The other settlement is still a few miles from my location so if I stay on my current route, I should be able to avoid it entirely. Once I make it through the field, there is another stretch of woods that leads to the base of the mountain where the ley line begins.

Magic. I can't wait to see what happens to the troll village once magic returns. So far, the only magic I've seen has been from Jira and Glenn. Glenn's was brutal, up-close, and personal, while Jira's was simply amazing to watch. I'll never really get to experience it, but at least I have Peacemaker and with a little luck, I might be able to find some magical stones.

The sun is starting to fade across the horizon, turning the blue sky to shades of lilac and tangerine. With my night vision, I will be able to travel well by night and plan to cut out a day's travel, making it to the obstruction by tomorrow evening.

Eventually, the sun falls off the horizon and my nightvision takes over. New animals and monsters appear all around me. I avoid them as best I can, but one time, a lone gnoll attacks me when I step too close to his den. The humanoid hyena's primitive wooden spear is no match for Peacemaker. I see the glowing eyes of several other gnolls in the darkness, but they leave me be after that.

Several hours into the night, a notification flashes across my vision.

Warning! *Your body needs rest. If you do not sleep within the next two hours, your stamina, strength, and health regeneration will be greatly reduced. Recommended sleep: 6 hours.*

Well, that blows. I thought I was going to be able to travel all night. I wonder if the sleep requirement is because of the full immersion. Maybe my mind still needs a rest in order to function properly.

I travel for another hour before finding a place to camp for the night. A river that runs down from the mountain rushes before me. Several trees line the banks, and rapids form around the rocky underbelly. There's not a bridge as far as I can see, so I elect to cross through the frigid water. The current is swift, but I find a location where I can still see the bottom and cross over. My massive frame weighs me down and even though the water pounds me, my feet remain secure.

Once on the other side, there is a thicket of bushes where I set up camp for the night. I tuck my belongings underneath the bush and not long after, Camouflage sets in.

Owls hoot in the distance and frogs croak amongst the reeds that adorn the river's edge. Somewhere far off, beasts howl into the night. With the nighttime melody, it doesn't take long for me to fall asleep.

I awake with a start as two bulging yellow eyes struggle in front of me while tiny hands vigorously try to remove the pendant from around my neck.

CHAPTER FOURTEEN

14. Tinker Time

The creature pulls at my pendant again, its bloodshot yellow eyes manic with desperation.

"Hey, let go!" I yell, startling the creature.

"Ahh!" it screams and flutters back for a second before swarming to my pendant again.

It tries another heaving pull, and I swat it to the side. The buggish creature falls to the ground with a splat. Now that it's out of my face, I'm able to see it more clearly. Long, spindly limbs and a forked tail. Dull reddish skin. Bat-like wings and a hooked nose.

Imp. *Level 8. Small, angsty creatures, imps often align themselves with beings on the more chaotic side of nature.*

The imp rises to its feet, a little woozy from the impact, and sways back and forth. It points a long finger at me.

"Give it." It stomps its foot against the ground.

"What do you mean, 'Give it'?" I ask. "It's mine. Wait—how do you speak troll?"

"Limery speaks many languages. Mother taughts him well. Now, gives us the magic." He extends his hand, waiting for me to hand him my pendant.

"I'm sorry, Limery, is it? But this was a gift. I need it for a quest I am on."

The small imp drops to his knees.

"Oh, please," he wheezes. "We needs it. We really needs it." He clasps his hands together, pleading. Tears stream down his demonic face.

I almost feel sorry for the guy.

"Hey now, no need to cry." I try to calm him. "This thing is almost as big as you are. Can't you find something more to your size?"

He stops crying long enough to answer. "We don't wants to wear it. We needs its magic."

I know I should just kill the bugger and be on my way, but there is something about his bulbous eyes and child-like mannerisms that stays my hand. I'm curious as to what he has to say.

"Why do you need its magic?"

Limery stands up, straight as an arrow, as if he is giving a very important speech.

"The magics is gone. Makes life hard. Limery tries to make life easier for Mommy, but needs more magics. Now, please, gives it to us." He extends his hand again.

It sounds like he might be affected by the same lack of magic that the trolls are. Maybe I can kill two birds with one stone. Still, I'm not exactly sure how the lack of magic is affecting Limery.

"I'm not giving you my pendant, *I* need it, but I may be able to help you. Can you tell me a little more about your magic? What it does, how you use it."

His eyes light up at my words. "Oh, yes, Limery can do this. We builds things. Most times, magic makes them work. We takes the magic and puts it in the machines. But now, no magics. So we takes the items and they gives us the magics." He stands there, arms held neatly behind his back, smiling his sharp-tooth demonic smile.

"So are you able to touch magic too? Like trolls?"

He shakes his head violently. "Oh noes. Magics is too strong for imps to touch, but we can calls it. When it's there." He jumps into the air and his wings spread, keeping him aloft at eye level. "Comes with us. We shows you."

"Limery, I can't. I have a—"

"It's okay. Not far at all. Follow Limery, he shows you the way."

What have I gotten myself into?

Limery takes off with gusto, and I follow him to a rock formation about a half-mile from the river. When I get there, I realize it is actually an underground cave. He lands at the entrance and motions for me to follow him. The cave is plenty big for the small imp, but I don't know if I will fit.

"Limery, I might be too big." The last thing I need is to get stuck in a cave where someone can kill me while I'm helpless. I'm not even one hundred percent sure this isn't a trap.

"It's okay. You fits. You fits." He grabs my leg and pulls until I start walking.

I have to duck my head, but I'm just able to fit inside.

The cave is dark, but a faint glow emanates from down the tunnel. We turn a corner to see a female imp stirring a pot over an open flame. She looks the same as Limery, except for a patch of hair that runs across her chest. Her wings are tucked in, and she doesn't look up as we enter.

The inside of the cave has a cozy vibe to it. There are cabinets carved into the cave walls, several tables and chairs, clearly homemade, but they look to be sturdy. Small furs and tapestries line the walls.

"Mommy!" shouts Limery and she turns to embrace her child. "I broughts a friend. He is going to fix the magics."

She looks up and eyes me warily. "Is that so?" I get the feeling this isn't the first time Limery has brought home an unwelcome guest.

"I hope so," I say.

She laughs shrilly. "And how does a troll plan to fix magic when he can't even use it?"

"I'm not sure yet, but I'm going to give it my best shot."

She rolls her eyes. "Son, why did you bring him here?"

"To show him the magics. To show him what we builds."

"You know we can't do that. We have very little magic to use as it is. If we waste it on a demonstration, then what will we do when we need it?"

"Please, Mommy. We will find more magics. We must shows him. We musts." Limery gives her his best pouty face.

She lets out an exasperated sigh. "Fine, follow me. Don't knock over my mole soup with your giant legs, Mister Troll."

"My name is Chod, if you'd rather call me that."

"I'd rather be left in peace. Things are hard enough without someone meddling in our business. Limery should have known better."

Limery's mother conjures a fireball in her hand and shoots it across the cave. It hits a torch, bringing the cavern to life. The end of the cave is filled with a multitude of machines, each one made out of an assortment of parts and materials that clearly do not go together.

"What is all this?"

"We builds it," says Limery. He runs over to the pile and pulls out a contraption.

There's a small colored box with several rods that extend upwards, which then connect to another set of rods and curve around like a hook. A funnel empties into the box at the bottom. Limery picks the whole thing up and carries it past me to the soup. He pulls the ladle from the soup and attaches it to the end of the extendable arm so that the machine holds the ladle.

He runs past me again to a chest in the far corner, opening it and pulling out a ring.

Item. Ring of Stealth. +2 sneak.

Limery tosses the ring into the funnel and a moment later, conjures a fireball and drops it into the funnel as well. There is a moment of sizzling, and then the arm that holds the ladle begins to spin.

"See? So easy." He gives me his toothy grin.

He just melted a magical ring to make a magical mixer.

"Wow! That's really cool. How does it work exactly?" I inspect the contraption as it moves of its own accord.

Limery's mother is the one who answers. "When a magical object is destroyed, its magical essence returns to the earth. We are able to harness that power to run our machines. This cave used to be a fountain of magical activity. Our machines could run simply off the magical current in the air. Unfortunately, due to the disappearance of magic in this area, we've had to resort to more primitive ways of doing things."

The ladle continues to stir, and chunks of meat and vegetables rise and fall in the pot.

"How long will that ring power the machine for? And what do you do if you want it to stop?"

She walks over to the mixer. "A ring of that size should last for a day or more. If we want to stop it, we simply remove the container." She reaches down and pulls the box from the bottom of the machine. The ladle quits spinning. "Some magic is lost while it sits, but we are lucky enough to have come across some precious stones which better insulate the magical barrier." She puts the box back under the machine and the ladle resumes stirring.

"This is all really fascinating. I have so many questions. I mean, why don't you just move to another magical site? And what do you do with the machines? Couldn't you sell them?"

"Limmy, where did you find this troll?" She looks at me with wonder. "I've never met one who asks so many questions."

Limery is in the back of the cave searching through various machines.

"To answer your questions, though, this is our home. We've been here for many years. Why would we leave? One day, the magic will return, but until that time, we will live as we must. We sell what we can, but due to our size, there are not an awful lot of buyers in the area. Our creations are viewed more as novelties than anything. In other parts of the world, we could sell to dwarves or halflings or gnomes, but the humans have little need of our inventions. They despise anything they didn't create themselves."

Limery comes back with a machine that has a basin filled with some liquid and three ringlets attached to rods that connect to a motor underneath. He pulls the container from beneath the ladle machine and inserts it in a similar receptacle underneath the new one. Immediately, the machine comes to life and the three ringlets dip into the liquid. They come out of the water and a tube that exits from the motor blows air against the ringlets. A spray of glowing bubbles flutter across the cave and Limery chases after them, popping them with his tiny claws and letting out little demonic giggles. I look over and see his mother has an adoring smile on her face.

"Limmy is the youngest, but he has more aptitude for tinkering than the others combined. It's a shame he can't put his talents to maximum use."

Footsteps approach from the mouth of the cave and I turn to see an imp entering, carrying a small sack stuffed with items. He's slightly bigger than Limery, with a patch of black hair between his ears that resembles a mohawk.

He drops his sack upon seeing me and fireballs materialize in both palms.

"What's going on here?" asks the one with the mohawk. "Mom?"

"It's okay, Leo. Put your fire away. He's friends with Limmy."

Leo does as his mother commands, but he looks at me with distrusting eyes as he walks past.

"Let me guess, you send Limmy out to find magical

items and he comes back with a troll. Just like him. Useless." Leo dumps the contents of his bag out on the ground.

"Don't talk about your brother like that, Leo," his mother scolds.

"Well, it's true."

I scan the items on the floor. There's an assortment of things, some magical, some not.

Item. *Buckler Shield. +1 Constitution.*
Item. *Pearls of Wisdom. +2 Wisdom.*

There are also several bracelets and a necklace, none of which seem to be magical, as well as a broken sword. I wonder where he found all this stuff. If it was anything like what I experienced, then there are several people feeling pretty angry right now.

"What do you do with the non-magical stuff?" I ask.

"We will melt it down and use it for materials." She turns to Leo. "Good job, son. Now go place these with the others."

Leo does as his mother commands.

"Can I ask you one more thing?" I ask.

"This is the last question I'm answering, so you better make it good." Her patience must be wearing thin at my game of twenty questions.

"How is it we are able to understand each other? Every other race I've come into contact with sounds like grunts or nonsense."

Limery continues popping bubbles as they float through the air. His mother stirs the soup before answering.

"For a long time, imps were the preferred means of message delivery. If you needed anything sent anywhere in a timely manner and wanted to make sure it was delivered, the Imp Messaging Service was the best there was. Due to this, imps needed a way to be able to communicate with many different species all at once, without the hassle of learning every language and the risk of having meanings lost in translation.

"The solution was communication stones." She touches a tiny pendant that hangs from her neck. "They have the ability to translate any language in real time, and accurately, but they are very expensive. They can't be stolen, only given away willfully. Any imp who enlisted in the IMS was given one for free in exchange for ten years of service. Then it turned out that it was all a ploy by the wizard who created them to form a contractually-obligated demon army. There was a huge war, and the continents severed ties with one another."

"How does one get one of these communication stones nowadays?"

"I thought I said no more questions." She smirks and goes back to her soup. "You said you have a plan to restore magic to our lands, right? Well, do that, and I may just have one for you."

"Mom, are you serious?" interjects Leo. "That stone belonged to dad. You can't give it away."

"Your father is not here, Leo. The stone is mine to do with as I wish."

"But you could sell it, you could trade it, you could—"

"Enough!" Her shrill voice cuts through the cave and heat rises off her small body.

Even though she is small, I have a feeling she has a lot of power inside her.

"That is my offer for you, Mister Troll. Take it or leave it."

Quest Alert. *You have been offered the quest 'Restore the Magical Well—Part 2.' Something has blocked the magical stream that feeds into the imp cave. Find a way to clear the obstruction and return magic to the imp cave.*

Reward: Communication Stone.

CHAPTER FIFTEEN

15. Dungeons and Dragons

With a clay pot filled with mole soup in hand, I leave Limery and his family in the imp cave. The promise of a communication stone has me excited and ready to be on my way. It was nice to be able to just speak and be heard, even if Limery did talk like he has spent hundreds of years eating fish inside of a mountain cave system.

I plug the stopper tight into the clay pot, ensuring my mole soup doesn't spill. Despite its name, the soup offers some pretty good buffs.

Item. *Mole Soup. +3 Constitution, +3 Charisma for one hour.*

I'm not sure where the Charisma comes from. I wouldn't be too keen on believing anyone who was offering me mole soup. I'm pretty sure there was fur still attached to a few pieces of meat floating inside.

Most of the day is spent walking. I'm far enough out from the two towns that I don't risk randomly running into someone unless they are out on a quest. Studying the map Chief Rizza gave me while I walk, I find the ley lines interesting, the way they seem to clump in certain areas and are very sparse in others. They almost seem to miss the human settlements entirely. I wonder if the humans even know they're there?

There is actually a very dense clump of magical veins not too far from where I am. I can spare a few minutes to go check it out and actually see what I am up against.

When I come to the spot on the map where the ley lines converge, nothing looks out of the ordinary. There is a large copse of trees and bushes, but nothing special or magical. Maybe once I unclog the line, things will change.

I step into the copse and look around. In the middle, there's a large rock formation surrounded by giant herbs and mushrooms. One of the rocks has some sort of smudge on it, so I go to take a closer look. Once I get closer, I realize there are engravings under a thick layer of dust and dirt. It's in some language I can't read, but it's writing nonetheless. I wipe away the smudge of dirt to try and better decipher the engraving. When I do, a notification flashes across my vision.

Faerie Dungeon. *Would you like to enter?*

"Hell yes," I say without thinking. There is no way in hell I'm leaving a dungeon unexplored. There could be all kinds of loot inside. I know the magic lines need to be restored, but I just found my first dungeon! I can't pass this opportunity up.

The rocks shake, but nothing else happens. No door or cave or anything opens. Then another prompt appears.

Faerie Dungeon is currently unavailable.

Dammit! I bet it has something to do with the magic lines that are affecting the rest of these parts. I mark this spot on my map. When I complete my quest, this will be the first place I stop.

As evening approaches, the long windswept fields finally come to an end and I'm face to face with the forest that forms around the base of the mountain. It's very different from the forest I came from. This one is more evergreen. Pine, spruce, and cedar trees spread out for as far as I can see, running up the mountains like thousands of troll hands crossed in prayer.

When I step into the forest, everything is muffled. The millions of pine needles offer a soundproof insulation. There is still the occasional birdcall or scuttle on the forest floor, but it's so much quieter than the troll's forest.

It's beginning to get dark again, and I know I need to rest soon. Judging by the map, there are maybe twenty miles or so between where I am and the beginning of the magical vein. Tomorrow, I should be able to make it by late afternoon at the latest.

I tuck my belongings underneath me and prepare to Camouflage when I hear a leathery flap of wings at the edge of the tree line.

You've got to be kidding me. A red blur moves through the tree branches.

"Limery, what the hell are you doing here?" The red imp with bulging yellow eyes plops on a tree branch in front of me.

"Mom saids Limmy can come. Limmy likes Chods, wants to helps him." He gives me his best smile, but his razor-sharp teeth are not the most welcoming.

Imp moms must be really lax caretakers. Not that my mom was any different. I got to do pretty much whatever I wanted as long as I stayed out of her hair and didn't get into too much trouble. I'm not going to turn him away, though. I have a feeling I'll need all the help I can get.

"How long have you been following me?" I ask.

"Just a bits." He leans back and lets the momentum take him as his knees curl around the branch until he is hanging upside down like a bat.

"Okay, you can come, but I'm about to camp for the night. Do you want to keep watch?"

"Oh yes! Limmy will watch all the things. Night night!"

I lean back against a tree, the aroma of pine a welcoming smell that almost seems to cleanse my lungs. As darkness creeps in, Limery's bat-like ears are the last thing I see before drifting off to sleep.

I'm awoken in the middle of the night by something nuzzling against my chest. I look down to find Limery cuddled against my arm, his wings wrapped around him like a blanket. I almost wake him, but then he starts snoring, cute little bubbly snores, and I can't help but let him stay.

When I finally wake a few hours later, Limery is no longer in my lap, but once again standing watch on the tree branch in front of me.

"How'd you sleep?" I ask.

He gives me a toothy grin. "Limmy slept good."

I share my mole soup with him and we start our day. When the buff hits me, I get the usual increase of heartiness that comes with Constitution, but there is something else. I feel more confident, like I could walk up to anyone and start a conversation. Is this what Charisma feels like?

It feels so good that I almost unload all of my remaining attribute points into Charisma just to chase that high. I stop myself before I complete the action, but damn, that feeling is something else.

I try to shake my head and focus on the task at hand. The obstruction. With my Charisma bonus, I know I won't have a problem fixing things. Hell, it'll be a piece of cake. When I get back to the troll village, I'll take my crown and before long, the whole island will be mine.

Over the next hour, I continue to contemplate how good of a ruler I will become. Limery jumps from branch to branch, flying in between. When the buffs finally wear off, it's like a moment of clarity.

Holy hell, Charisma is powerful stuff! Is that what it feels like to be a celebrity or a politician? I felt damn near invincible for a moment there. I make a note to be very careful with Charisma buffs in the future. There's no telling what they could make me do.

My foot suddenly sinks into the earth and I'm buried up to my knee. Grabbing hold of a nearby tree, I pull myself out. There's a faint glow beneath the surface where I fell through. Looking at my map, we're right on top of the ley line.

I bend down and look into the hole. It's a tunnel about three feet deep and two feet wide. A blue, jelly-like substance clings to the walls in places. Then I notice that there are dozens of holes spread throughout the nearby forest. My first thought is that maybe this is what caused the obstruction. My next thought is what kind of creature could do such a thing?

"What could make these holes?" I ask.

Limery jumps down from his tree branch and takes a

look at the hole. He reaches in, touching the blue goo, then screams in pain and shakes it off his finger.

"Limmy doesn't know." He sucks on his thumb, eyes watering in pain.

That's weird, it didn't burn me when my foot fell through. I take my finger and rub it against the same spot where Limery just touched. The gel is warm to the touch, but it doesn't burn. I remember Chief Rizza mentioning that trolls were one of the few races that can handle raw magic. Is this raw magic or something else entirely?

"Are you okay to keep going?" I ask Limery.

He nods, and we continue onward.

The farther we go, the bigger and more spread out the holes seem to be, like whatever made them has been growing. The same blue gel covers the inside of every new hole we see.

Limery has taken a seat on my shoulder, his tiny claws digging into me with each step. Whatever caused these holes has soured his normally playful disposition. I hold Peacemaker at the ready for whatever may come, carefully watching each step I take.

We come to a spot where the holes are so wide that full-grown trees have fallen through them, their tops sticking above the earth like bushes. Twenty-foot wide tunnels weave through the forest, the blue gel now appearing in globs as big as Limery.

Then I see it: the source of all the trolls' problems. The reason for the magical drought. There is a huge cavern where the earth has collapsed in on itself. Dozens of large glowing blue eggs, each one nearly as big as me, radiate magical energy. So much energy that the air is distorted around them.

The earth quakes and debris falls into many of the holes around us. Something slithers underground. It moves so fast through one of the tunnel openings that all I see is a trail of blue.

Limery clings even tighter to me when, suddenly, the ground erupts and a massive blue creature towers over us.

Wyrm (Mana-infused). *Unique Monster. Level 20. These legless, wingless dragons burrow deep underground, producing a natural toxic slime that allows them to glide through rough tunnels unimpeded. With magic-resistant scales, strong jaws, and powerful elemental magic, wyrms are some of the most powerful creatures in all of Mythos.*

The wyrm glows, and a neon blue, toxic gel runs down its body, dripping onto the ground. It hunches over us like a gargantuan cobra, ready to strike.

Limery takes off from my shoulder, flying into the canopy above and leaving me face to face with my doom.

The good news is that I found what is obstructing the ley line. The bad news is that it is about to kick my ass.

CHAPTER SIXTEEN

16. Big Bad Boss

Blue slime oozes from the wyrm's scaly body. Its massive dragon head strikes at me, and I jump to the side, barely dodging the attack as it burrows underground. Its hooked snout rips through the earth like a spade as it disappears beneath the surface.

"Limery, destroy the eggs. I'll handle the monster."

"Whatever yous says." The imp darts off through the canopy, a fireball blazing in each hand.

My head turns like a sprinkler, searching for sight of the dragon snake, but it's nowhere to be found. The ground rumbles beneath me and I'm knocked skyward as the wyrm breaks through the surface. I somersault through the air and land on my feet, covered in dirt and dust.

Thank god for my troll reflexes. Reaching into my bag, I down my last potions. My stamina and HP both receive a boost, and I do my best to set my resolve for what is about to happen. This wyrm is so far out of my league that my only chance of winning is to outsmart it. But how can I outsmart something I can't even see when it goes underground?

The wyrm rears back and lets out a fiery attack of blue flames that singe the trees and set the forest ablaze. A stream of fire hits me in the shoulder and it sears with pain. The wyrm dives for me again and this time, I swing Peacemaker with all of my might into the side of its dragon head. It leaves a gash but barely does any damage. The beast knocks me aside and burrows underground once more.

In the distance, Limery tosses fireball after fireball at the mountain of eggs. I can't tell if it is doing any damage, but he zooms through the air, his bulging eyes focused on his mission.

I'm knocked into the air again before I have time to react, but this time, I'm not so quick on my feet and tumble into a nearby pine, snapping it in half. My back throbs from the blow, but I get to my feet.

The wyrm towers over me, blue smoke rising from its nostrils as its head weaves back and forth. I roar, using Intimidation, but nothing happens. Whether it is because of its magic-resistant scales or because it's too far out of my level, the confusion doesn't work. Instead, I'm scorched by another flame barrage. This time, it doesn't just graze me, but full-on roasts me. Every pain receptor in my body is on fire, even with my phoenix feather negating ten percent of the damage. My health drops by half from the attack, and my skin turns a darker shade of green.

A massive tail smashes into my side faster than I can react, dropping my health by another quarter. With the way things are going, one more direct hit and I'm dead. I don't know if I can beat this monster, but I have an idea that might just keep me alive long enough to try. If I screw this up, I will most certainly be dead. I'll lose my items and will respawn somewhere in the middle of the troll forest.

The wyrm dives at me, and I jump to the side. Its scaly body brushes past me as it burrows underground.

I have about ten seconds to put my plan into action.

"Limery! Over here, now!" I yell at the top of my lungs. The small imp flies in my direction, still holding a fireball.

"What does you needs?" he asks.

"Hit me with a fireball. I don't have time for questions. Just do it now." I pull the phoenix feather from my hair and place it on the ground. I don't need to block any of the damage.

Concern radiates from his enormous eyes, but he does as I tell him. The fireball collides with my chest, dropping my health down to fifteen percent.

"One more," I say with gritted teeth.

The second fireball hits me, and I drop to five percent health.

Just as I expect, my health regeneration kicks into overdrive. When I am under ten percent health, my regen is doubled. Now, it's time to abuse the system.

I order Limery back to the eggs and activate Berserker Rage, turning my vision red at the edges. Quickly, I re-attach my phoenix feather while my health bar climbs rapidly. Normally, Berserker Rage increases my health regen by five times, but since my regen is already doubled due to being so low, it's regenerating at ten times the normal rate.

By the time the wyrm smashes into me from underneath, my health bar is full. The damage from the impact disappears almost as quickly as it happens.

Getting up, my rage meter is full and my blood pumps with righteous fury.

I have thirty seconds of near invincibility. Please don't let me screw this up.

I throw myself at the wyrm just as it releases a jet of flame. The flames graze me, but aside from the burning pain, it's almost like I was never attacked. I use Sweeping Slash. It doesn't knock the wyrm off balance, but it does do a sliver of damage. Then I use Claw with my free hand and cast Bite, sinking my teeth into its scaly flesh. A tail-smack knocks me down, but just as quickly, I am on my feet and attacking once again. I hack, slash, bite, and claw, all while taking a massive beating that could have killed me ten times over. Every inch of my body is burned and regenerated, but still, I fight. A final tail-whip knocks me through a tree, its burning branches igniting the pine needles that cover the forest floor when it collapses.

The wyrm burrows underground just as my Berserker Rage fades away. I'm able to catch a glimpse of its health as its tail sneaks below the surface.

Ninety percent.

It still has ninety percent health. I hit it with everything I had and barely did any damage.

Fire rages all around me. Without my increased regeneration, I'm as good as dead. Not knowing what else to do, I jump in the tunnel the wyrm left behind. At least I won't burn to death down there.

The sides of the tunnel walls are slick with the wyrm's toxic sludge and I have to focus to hold my footing. It's only a matter of time before it attacks, and I have about zero ideas for how to get rid of the rest of its health. My best bet might be to run away and regroup. Maybe I can think of a plan while I level up in the surrounding areas.

I don't know if the trolls have that kind of time, though. Glenn has already had three days to regroup. How long will it be before he manages to gather forces for another attack?

I have to find a way to end this now.

Isle of Mythos isn't like any other game, where everything runs on a script. It is based on action and reactions. Every action sets a new course of events for the game. If I want to beat this monster, I can. I just have to figure out how.

The ground rumbles nearby and I know the wyrm has just resurfaced. A shrieking roar tells me just how close it is. Everything that has happened in the battle crosses my mind as I try to piece it together in a way that might help me. The crackle of fire lets me know the wyrm has just attacked. In about five seconds, it is going to burrow.

I jump out of the tunnel and pinpoint the monster. It has just sprung forward, and I think I know the spot it is aiming for. I take position right in front of it.

Instead of clamping its mouth shut and using its pointed snout to burrow underground, the wyrm reacts to my presence and opens its jaw, expecting to take a bite out of me. I've got other plans.

"Eat me," I say, lunging at the monster and targeting its

throat. I don't aim for its exterior throat, the part on the scaly underbelly. No, I aim for its actual throat, the part behind its enormous and extremely sharp teeth. The part that spews fire.

I land on its sandpapery tongue as its mouth closes and claw my way down its throat. Everything is warm and dark and clenching all around me. I imagine this must be what it feels like to be born. Inch by inch, I claw myself deeper into the wyrm, biting and clawing and jabbing with my axe. Notifications of critical attacks fill my vision. The wyrm continues to thrash and heave, but with my claws stuck deep, I refuse to leave. I'm stuck in its throat like the sharp edges of a broken tortilla chip it just can't swallow.

Minutes pass as I attack the monster from the inside. Slowly, its fight begins to fade, until finally, it moves no more.

Notifications flood my vision, but I push them aside. Right now, I need to get out and find Limery. We need to destroy those eggs ASAP. I've seen enough horror movies to know what can go wrong if those things are allowed to hatch.

Unable to cut my way out, I have to climb out the same way I came in, but it's a whole lot harder going feet first down a slimy tube. Eventually, my feet hit against something hard and I know I'm in the creature's mouth.

With a heave, I lift its mouth open and flop my slime-covered body on the ground.

There's an explosion next to me and I look up to see Limery hurling fireballs at the dead wyrm. Tears stream down his face.

"You killeds our friend. You killeds Chods." He runs up

to the wyrm and claws and punches the dead monster. His desperate cries fill the air. He pounds his fist until he falls into a crying heap on the ground.

I had no idea he was so attached to me.

"Limery…" I say, but he doesn't look up.

"Limery, it's okay. I'm fine."

He looks up and recognition dawns on his face.

"Is okay?" He stands up. "Chods is okay!"

He leaps onto my body and gives me the biggest hug his small arms can muster. I hug him back. This might be the first time in my life someone has cried over me. Mom and Dad never have. Not even when they found out about my sentence. As I hug the small creature, I can't fight back the tears that creep into my own eyes. Perhaps for the first time in my life, I feel loved. And it's by a creature that doesn't really exist.

"It's okay," I whisper. "It's okay."

When we end our embrace, I clear my eyes and focus on the remainder of our quest. The eggs.

"Did you destroy the eggs?" I ask.

"We dids not. Eggs too strong, they only crack."

That's when I notice the cracks forming along the edges of several of the eggshells. They look almost like they're moving. Vibrating. A piece of shell cracks and breaks off, and I realized that it's because they are. A massive black snout pokes through the hole and a tongue licks at the air.

"Limery, we have to destroy those eggs now!"

I'm off and running before I even finish the sentence. I leap down into the cavernous nest just as the first wyrm hatches. It slithers by me and into one of the tunnels before I have a chance to kill it. Another one hatches, but this time, I'm able to lop its head off before it escapes. Limery tosses fireballs all around me, but it only increases the rate at which the eggs crack. The fire must be forcing them to hatch.

There's no way I can get them all. I need to attack the eggs themselves and crush them if I have too.

I use a Sweeping Slash and shatter the eggs closest to me. Bloody wyrm babies spill out and onto the ground. It's gruesome, but I have to do it. I prepare for another Sweeping Slash when the entire pile of eggs explodes, and I'm engulfed in a ray of bright blue energy.

For a moment, it's all I see. The energy washes over me. Through me. Nothing exists except for the purity that surrounds me. Then everything fades black.

CHAPTER SEVENTEEN

17. Summoner

Blue skies. That's all I see for such a long time.

The blue skies fade, and I feel two tiny hands push at my shoulder. My ears ring, and I try to remember what just happened. There was the wyrm, the eggs, an explosion. Then everything went blue. Did I pass out? If I died, I wouldn't be here right now.

I open my eyes, but there are no blue skies. Just charred branches and smoke. The fires no longer rage, but the damage has been done. Two pointy red ears cross my vision followed by bulging yellow eyes. Limery's mouth is moving, but the ringing in my ears blocks out everything he says.

I turn my head and the ringing fades a little.

"Chods, is you okay?" His words come in and out of focus. "Is you okay, Chods?"

The concern on his face forces me to smile.

"Yeah, I'm good." The truth is that I do feel good. It's like all my wounds from fighting the wyrm just disappeared. Aside from the ringing in my ears, everything feels fine.

"You dids it!" He jumps in the air. "You fixed the magics!"

I sit up and go to wipe my brow when I notice something strange. My skin is blue. Well, bluish-green. It's almost like there is an aqua-blue aura surrounding me. Not just my hand, but my entire body. Did the raw magic cause this?

"What the—What happened?" I stand up to get a better view of the canyon where the eggs were nesting. A stream of blue energy flows through the canyon. There's no trace of the eggs or the wyrms.

So that's what magic looks like. It's just flowing through the ground like an underwater river. The wyrm must have burrowed in it somehow, causing it to become mana-infused. Those eggs, though, I wonder what happened to all the babies. There is no way we destroyed them all.

"What happened?" I ask again.

"You smashes eggs, they goes boom." Limery mimics an explosion with his fingers.

"And what about me? How did I get up here? How long was I out?"

"Explosion knocks you up here. You sleeps for long time. Limmy wanted to help, but you was too hot. Magic burns Limmy's hands."

I guess I'm lucky to be alive. If I were any race other than troll, that blast probably would have killed me. I look at my hands, they almost glow. Could it be a buff of some sort?

I pull up my notifications to find out and am surprised to see there is a wall of text waiting for me.

You have defeated a unique monster. *Wyrm (Mana-infused).*

Item. Mana stone. 50% increased mana regeneration. Taken from the heart of a mana-infused monster.

Congratulations! You have reached level 8. +1 stat point to distribute. +1 Strength and Constitution racial bonus.

Congratulations! You have reached level 9. +1 stat point to distribute. +1 Strength and Constitution racial bonus. +1 ability point to distribute.

Congratulations! You have reached level 10. +1 stat point to distribute. +1 Strength and Constitution racial bonus.

Quest Alert. *You have completed the quest 'Restore the Magical Well.' Reward: Variable. Return to Chief Rizza to claim your reward.*

Quest Alert. *You have completed the quest 'Restore the Magical Well-Part 2.' Reward: Communication Stone. Return to the Imp Cave to claim your reward.*

Alert! *You have been infused with mana. New class option available.*

Regional Event Alert! *Mana-infused wyrms have descended upon Isle of Mythos. They will gravitate towards areas of magical affinity to lay eggs. Locate the wyrms and wipe them out before they infest the island. 20/20 remaining. Rewards: Each wyrm contains one mana stone. Failure: If wyrms are not eliminated, they will lay eggs and spread out from magical sources, devastating crops and towns. 20 days remaining.*

There's so much there that I don't know how to

process it all at once. I'm infused with mana. The raw magic that the trolls described, that must be the same thing as mana. Does that mean I can cast spells now? Will I be powerful like Jira? There are new class options available. I can't wait to see what's available to me now. Maybe I can be a badass troll wizard or a paladin. I'll also need to get back and claim my quest rewards as quickly as possible. Where do I even start?

Then there is the regional event. No doubt every player on the island received that notification. Twenty wyrms escaped and we have to eliminate them before they spawn across the island. I have no idea what the life cycle of a wyrm is, but if they manage to lay as many eggs as the one we just killed, this entire island could be taken over in no time if we fail. It worries me that others might not be able to kill them. I would try to warn them, but it's no use, even after I claim my communication stone. Everyone hates trolls so much that my only hope is to get a group together from the village and travel to the most magical areas on my map.

I'll just have to deal with that once I make it back to the village. Right now, I want to check out my new class options, so I pull up my character screen and take a look at my stats.

Chod, Level 10 Barbarian Forest Troll
  HP: 1960/1960
  Mana: 5000/5000
  Rage: 0/100
  XP: 64,153/85,000

. . .

Strength: 27 (+3)
Dexterity: 15
Constitution: 28
Intelligence: 7
Wisdom: 10
Charisma: 6

Five thousand mana? Wow. That must have been some seriously potent magic to do that when I had no mana at all to begin with. I have nine stat points as well as the one new ability point, but I'll wait to see what my class options are before I spend it.

Below my stats, a blinking box says, 'New Class Available.'

That doesn't make sense? Five thousand mana and only one new class option? Could it be because of my Wisdom and Intelligence stats? I focus on the box and the new class description pops up.

Class:

Summoner. *Magic users capable of summoning magical beings to fight on their behalf.*

Sub-Class:

Elemental. *Summon golems created from the elements.*
Brood. *Summon insects that evolve.*
Horror. *Summon monstrous creatures. Requires 20+ Strength and Constitution.*
Techno. *Summon robotic beings. Requires 20+ Intelligence.*

Undead. Summon undead creatures from nearby bones.
Champion. Summon one powerful creature at a time.

I only have one new class, but damn if it isn't awesome! There are so many intriguing possibilities for where this new class can take me. I can actually use magic and won't be forced to just slug it out. Techno is out of the question because I don't have the Intelligence requirement. I quickly disregard champion as well. With as much mana as I have, my power is going to come from summoning multiple monsters at once, not just one strong monster. Undead is too restricting based on the need for nearby bones. Plus, I'm already hated enough and could do without the stigma associated with necromancers. So, it comes down to elemental, brood and horror.

It's a big choice, and I'm not sure which one is right. I don't have a lot of ability power, so whatever I end up summoning is going to need to be able to crowd control my opponents while I still physically beat them down. With my low Intelligence and Wisdom, it won't matter if I can summon a hundred beings if they can't do any actual damage. I wish there was a way to see what abilities each sub-class has before I choose. There is something about the Horror class that calls to me. And the fact that there is a requirement of Strength and Constitution makes me wonder if the beings it summons feed off those stats as well.

To hell with it, my gut hasn't let me down yet. I select Horror and a new set of abilities pop up.

Summon Horror (Passive). Ability to summon a horror. Each horror grants a unique ability. For every horror active, gain 1% increased damage and health points. Horrors decay 10% every minute outside of combat.

Horror of Power. *Summon a horror with 20% of your Strength. Cost: 100 mana. Cooldown: 30 seconds. Bonus: Your next attack deals double damage.*

Horror of Vitality. *Summon a horror with 20% of your health points. Cost: 100 mana. Cooldown: 30 seconds. Bonus: Opponents near Horror of Vitality are slowed by 20%.*

Horror of Finesse. *Summon a horror with 20% of your attack speed. Cost: 100 mana. Cooldown: 30 seconds. Bonus: Your next attack heals you for damage dealt.*

I definitely made the right choice. All three of these abilities play off my strengths and two of them benefit from my racial bonuses. I can't wait to start summoning monsters, but first I need to decide which one to spend my ability point on. They all look so appealing that it is hard to decide. With five thousand mana, I could essentially summon fifty horrors if I were in a long, drawn-out battle. Especially considering my physical abilities rely on rage. I can pretty much summon my own army to take down the wyrms.

Even though I'm a big tanky troll, I was constantly running low on health in that last fight. If I were part of a team complete with healers and ranged attacks, I could probably take the power or vitality horror, but with it just being me and Limery right now, the Horror of Finesse makes the most sense. If it heals for damage dealt, then it is basically a one-hit potion.

After selecting the Horror of Finesse, I immediately cast it. A blue, gangly creature not much bigger than Limery materializes with a puff of gray smoke. It has long, pointy fingers, huge bat-like ears, and a dog snout. Basically a blue imp without wings.

Limery screams when he sees it and conjures two fireballs, hurling them with ferocity at my new pet.

"Whoa, whoa, whoa," I say. "It's okay, Limery, it's mine. It's not going to hurt us."

Limery holds another fireball in his hand, unsure of whether or not to trust me.

"Friends?" he asks, eyes full of suspicion.

"Friends." The two fireballs took out nearly half of the horror's health, making me wonder if it has the same weakness to fire that I do. It also makes me keenly aware of how fragile they will be in battle until I have the other two horrors unlocked. One horror is nice, but an army will be unstoppable.

Limery cancels his fireball and it disappears in a blur. He walks up to the horror and tries to talk to it.

"It's not much of a talker. It's here to fight and make sure we don't die," I say. That seems to be enough for Limery to leave the horror alone.

After the first minute passes, ten percent of the horror's health disappears. My chances of keeping a standing army are low because they deteriorate outside of combat. I'll worry about that when the time comes.

With my new class sorted, I elect to put all of my stat points into Dexterity to help benefit Horror of Finesse even more, bringing it up to twenty-four.

Looking at my stats, even though my mana pool is massive, my mana regeneration isn't very high, probably due to my low Wisdom. Luckily, I have just the fix. I pull out the mana stone left behind by the wyrm. It glows with the same vibrancy as raw magic, only crystallized.

Mana Stone. Would you like to equip mana stone to Peacemaker? 0/3 slots filled.

When I agree, the stone fits perfectly into the socket on the axe's side. I cast another Horror of Finesse and this time, my mana almost doubles its regeneration rate. I couldn't be happier with the results of beating the giant wyrm.

To my surprise, I look over and see Limery tossing a rock with the first horror I summoned. Though it doesn't speak, it seems to be enjoying the playtime with the imp. It makes me appreciate all the more how advanced this game is. Each horror acts of its own accord, not some preassigned robotic set of movements and commands.

"Are you ready to get going?" I ask Limery.

"Where's we going?" Limery stops the game of toss and the horror turns away, on guard duty once more.

I need to retrieve my quest rewards, but there is somewhere I want to go first. It seems like the perfect place for a mana-hungry wyrm to go.

The faerie dungeon.

CHAPTER EIGHTEEN

18. Dungeon Diving

We travel to the faerie dungeon without event. I use the time to practice casting Horror of Finesse. Every thirty seconds, I summon a horror. Since we are not in combat, they begin decaying after the first minute. It takes ten minutes for one horror to lose all HP and die, so I am able to summon twenty of them. The horrors of finesse have ten percent of my HP, giving them one hundred and ninety-six health upon casting. Due to the bonus increase in my own HP and Strength for having horrors summoned, I gain three hundred and ninety-two HP with all twenty horrors active. By the time they start dying off, the weakest of the bunch have twenty-four HP, hardly a threat to anyone.

For now.

I'm glad I put my stat points into Dexterity to bring it

up to par with my other stats and increase my overall attack speed, but I'm thinking it might be more beneficial in the long run to invest in Constitution. The longer they can last, the stronger I become, and in turn, the stronger they become. Once I have the other two horrors unlocked, I'll be able to summon a maximum of sixty horrors when I'm not in combat.

The days of trolls hiding away in the forest may be nearing their end.

Limery perches on the rock in the center of the copse where I first found the faerie dungeon. The mushrooms and herbs that surround the rock formation have changed slightly. The mushrooms all have an aura around them—it's faint, but I can definitely see it. A small blue furry creature with large round eyes sits atop one of the mushrooms, watching me intently. When I move forward with my small army of horrors, it scurries away.

I approach the carved runes and the same prompt hits me as before.

Faerie Dungeon. *Would you like to enter?*

This time, when I accept, the ground trembles beneath me. The rock Limery sits on rises higher into the air, causing him to jump off in surprise and revealing a cavernous archway that leads underground. Stone steps descend into darkness. Limery hovers in the air above my shoulder.

"We goes inside?"

"That's the plan."

I cast another horror and instruct them to lead the way into the dungeon. They respond to my thoughts just as quickly as my commands. It's dark underground, but my night vision allows me to see unimpeded. Limery must be able to as well, because he doesn't complain.

Rubble and dirt crunch underneath my feet with each step. It must have been a while since the last time someone was in here. Spiderwebs hang from the ceiling and small feet scurry away from our approach. A door closes somewhere beneath us with a thud. I continually cast Horror of Finesse, keeping my rotation at twenty. Whatever comes next, I want to be prepared.

Somewhere in the depths, the trickle of water echoes, but I can't pinpoint the source.

Light shines in from the foot of the stairwell. My horrors move into a large room where dozens of yellow wisps float through the air.

Wisp. *Level 10. Harmless unless touched, these ethereal creatures are light incarnate.*

The wisps range from level ten to fifteen. At the other end of the room is a door. Whatever scurried away must have gone through there. Limery could probably make it through without touching the wisps, but I'm way too big.

While I'm in the process of formulating a plan, one of my horrors bumps into a wisp. Electric bolts shoot out from the floating ball of energy, killing the horror in one shot. The oldest horrors are always at the front so that they can disarm traps or take lethal blows without risking the HP of the stronger ones.

The next thing I know, the rest of the wisps come swarming towards us.

"Oh noes!" Limery shouts and tosses a fireball, sending one of the wisps up in smoke.

The wisps swarm my horrors, electricity filling the air as bolts zap out like an electrical storm. The horrors attack, but their blows seem to be missing entirely and I've already lost a quarter of those with low HP.

I activate Sweeping Slash and swing for a nearby cluster of wisps, hitting them square on, but my blade passes straight through, doing zero damage. Several arcs of lightning strike the axe and travel down the handle, stunning me in place and taking out a chunk of my health.

Limery seems to be the only one having success as he fires fireball after fireball at the incorporeal damage dealers.

"We need to get to that door!" I shout.

With my horrors falling by the wayside, the wisps have turned in my direction now. Limery zooms through the air, too quick for their lightning strikes. Several bolts hit me even as I try to dodge and make my way across the room. With so many of them, all of the damage is beginning to add up. None of my physical attacks are working, not even Intimidation, and without anything to land a blow on, my healing from casting Horror of Finesse isn't working either.

Every third lightning strike stuns me in place. If I don't find a way out of here soon, I'll be swarmed and unable to move at all as I'm hit with bolt after bolt.

I'm stunned once more when a group of wisps pin me against the wall. Limery tosses a fireball at the cluster of wisps and it sets off a chain reaction, exploding four at once. There's still a minefield of wisps on the other end of the room that haven't moved. As it is, there's no way I'll make it without being hit unless I waste Berserker Rage in the first room. I wish I had a giant bubble of protection around me to just barrel through them.

That's it! I call what horrors I have left to me and

instruct them to climb on my body. I don one of them over my head like a helmet along with one on each shoulder, two on my back, and several more on my legs and arms. Their health begins to drop as the wisps converge on us.

I take off running like a bat out of hell, the crack of lightning raging all around me. The horrors' HP drop in droves as we cannonball across the room. I lose the imp-like monsters clinging to my arms first and take a shock to the shoulder. The one on my head goes and I dive through the open door just as two final strikes kill the horrors on my back.

The door closes behind me and the wisps disperse back into their original positions like we were never there.

"Holy shit." I let out a sigh.

Dungeon diving is not for the faint of heart. I probably should have put together a team before attempting something like this, but there's no turning back now.

I send one of my horrors down the hall, and a dozen poisoned darts shoot out from the walls, killing it.

Better him than me.

"Chods okay?" asks Limery.

"Yeah, I'm good. Thanks for your help back there. I didn't know those things only responded to magic attacks."

"Nasty little balls. Limmy doesn't like." He shakes his head in disgust.

Hopefully, the next level will treat us better. I wait for my health to regenerate as we sit in the corridor that leads to the next level. There is another wooden door at the end of the hall. Limery peeks through the slat in the door we just came through. The wisps managed to kill all but three of my horrors, pinpointing my weakness against anything that isn't flesh and blood. Maybe Jira will have answers for how to deal with monsters like that once I get back. All of this mana has to open more opportunities than just summoning.

As I heal, I continue to cast horrors, hoping this next batch fares better than the last. Ten minutes later, I have twenty ready to go. At the door, something scuttles on the other side. It's almost a clacking sound, like horse hooves on pavement. There is no slat to look through on this door, so once it opens, it's game on.

"Ready?" I ask Limery.

He nods.

With a quick heave, I open the door, and my horrors spill into the room. A chittering sound rings out and the clattering intensifies. Torches line the walls of this room, casting eerie shadows from large columns that stand throughout. I immediately spot the source of the noise. Large beetles, the size of a golden retriever, rush towards us, their shells a shimmering iridescent rainbow. Pincers hinge open and close with each step. Wingless faeries sit astride the large beetles while faeries with dragonfly wings zoom through the air firing arrows.

The fairies are bigger than Limery, but not by much. They have ivory skin, colorful hair, and daggers for teeth.

"Stay behind me and target them with your fireballs. Me and my horrors will push the attack."

The first row of horrors collide with the beetles and are immediately mowed down. The wingless faeries shoot bolts of magic from their hands while those airborne fire imbued arrows across the room. One hits me in the chest and I get a notification that I have been poisoned. I have my Tiger's Eye Pendant to clear the poison, but I want to save that until we clear the room. For now, I'll use my healing bonus to keep the poison at bay.

I cast Horror of Finesse and the icon telling me my next attack will heal flashes in the top left corner of my vision. I jump the line and bring my axe down with a powerful strike that tops off my health. Luckily for me, most of the faeries are attacking the horrors that rush to them like ants on a fallen ice cream cone and leave me be.

Behind me, Limery hurls his fireballs all the while yelling "take that" and "stupid faeries." His attacks are pretty accurate, incinerating the wings of many airborne fairies and forcing them to fight on foot.

I kick and claw as I continue to summon more horrors as time allows. One faerie comes running at me, hands glowing, and I stomp him into the stone floor with a crunch.

My horrors attack like rabid animals, moving from one beetle warrior to another. The pincers rip at their flesh, but they remain undeterred, sinking their claws and prying the shells apart with sheer numbers. I continue to raise more as soon as the cooldown allows, using each opportunity to fill my health with a basic attack, countering the poison that continuously damages me.

Though I lose more than half of my horrors, it doesn't take us long to overwhelm the faeries. With my Tiger's Eye Pendant, I clear the poison that runs through my veins.

The door out of the room opens and we enter another corridor.

So far, this dungeon hasn't been so hard. I don't know

if I'm overqualified with my new class or it's really just a beginner dungeon. Careful not to become skewered by darts or some other contraption, I send one of my horrors out first. It trips a tile and the floor collapses underneath it, sending it falling into darkness that not even my night vision can penetrate. I hear a splash and then can no longer feel the horror's presence.

I toss the rest of my horrors across the pit, and when they make it to the door unmolested, I follow.

We exit the corridor into a wide room with a large fountain at its center. Glowing blue water illuminates the room, eliminating the need for torches even if we didn't have night vision. The water reminds me of the nanites in the pod where my body is.

The room itself is similar to a Roman bathhouse with the way water drips down from the ceiling and spills out from an obelisk in the fountain's center. The fountain overflows into a large pool with channels that carry the water into drains. It explains the dripping I heard when entering the dungeon. I remember passing a stream not far from the dungeon's entrance, and I bet it runs underground and into the dungeon as well.

Aside from the fountain, the room is empty.

This has to be where we fight the boss.

As we wait for something to happen, I continue to raise horrors, making sure I am continually topped off. After several minutes of nothing happening, I approach the obelisk in the center of the room.

At the room's center, the stone floor quakes, sending out ripples through the pool where the obelisk rises. There's movement in the water and something moves beneath its depths. I take a defensive position with my axe, ready for whatever vile monster is about to emerge.

I'm surprised when a humanoid creature with beautiful eyes and hair rises to the surface.

Water Nymph. *Level 17. Guardians of the world's most beautiful places, nymphs are wild and spirited, embodying the elements of the locations they protect. They are naturally charismatic towards all manner of creatures.*

Her skin is light blue and only a few thin pieces of cloth cover her curvaceous body. Blue eyes stare out at me and she speaks, but I can't understand her.

"What is she saying?" I ask Limery, wishing I already had my communication stone. I keep my eyes on the nymph but turn my head towards Limery.

His yellow eyes bulge even larger than normal. "She says, 'Prepare to meets your doom.'"

There's a splash from behind us and I turn just in time to see two wyrms slither through the drainage pipes and into the room. They rise up like cobras, ready to strike, their scales glistening with the toxic slime that seeps from their skin.

Wyrm (Mana-infused). *Level 12. These mana-infused wyrms have been mesmerized by a water nymph, answering her beck and call.*

CHAPTER NINETEEN

19. Fire and Water

The twin wyrms sway back and forth, their hooked snouts hissing like snakes. They aren't as big as the wyrm I faced in the woods, but they are still massive. At least seven feet tall. Plenty long enough to wrap me up in a tight embrace, and not the warm and fuzzy kind.

The nymph continues to talk, even though I can't understand a word she says.

"Limery, I'm going to need you to translate everything she says until we make it out of here. Got it?"

"Yes! Limmy can do it! She says, 'You is not welcomes here. This dungeon is hers. Prepare to die.'"

"Alright, Limmy. I hope you're ready for a fight."

I hear the familiar crackle of fireballs igniting in his palms and know I can trust the imp to have my back.

Without waiting for my opponents to get the fight

started, I send my horrors on the offensive. They split and claw at the towering wyrms, dropping slivers of health with each raking scratch.

Blue flames erupt in a cone from the wyrms, setting the horrors on fire and destroying the front line. I cast another horror and a blast of water from the nymph knocks me off my feet, taking five percent of my health. There's a dull ache from the blow, but it's nice to put my actual tanking to use against something that isn't breathing fire at me.

I rise to my feet just as the wyrms slither across the stone floor, knocking the horrors aside. Evidently, the wyrms aren't strong enough to burrow through solid stone.

Not yet, at least.

Limery tosses fireballs at the wyrms, but they do very little damage against those magically-resistant scales.

"Focus on the nymph," I say, not knowing if he will fare any better against her.

I swing at one of the wyrms as it passes by to join its master, connecting with its side and healing myself just as a massive tail smashes into my ribs from the other side and knocks the breath out of me.

Horrors rush to my aid, blocking a wall of flame meant for me. Several of them die to the blast. I cast another and land a claw in the side of one wyrm as they retreat behind the nymph in the fountain.

Every fireball that Limery throws her way is negated by a water bubble that shoots out from the pool, intercepting the blast in a puff of steam.

We are truly fucked.

A wave of luminous water rises from the pool and

rushes across the stone floor. It collides with my horrors, scattering them around the room like bugs in a rainstorm. I stand my ground, unable to move against the rushing torrent as the toxic water slowly burns me. The toxic slime from the wyrms has contaminated the water and it damages both me and the horrors with every touch. When the water recedes into the drain, I call my horrors to me and lead a charge toward the fountain. Flames target me and I barely dodge to the side as puddles of water sizzle on the floor, causing a curtain of steam to rise into the air.

I'm hit in the face by a giant water bubble that surrounds my head, cutting off my air and obstructing my vision. I try to pop the bubble, but my axe and claws just cut through the water like jelly.

My lungs start to burn, and I don't know how much longer I can hold my breath, when the bubble dissipates and hot steamy air coats my lungs.

Limery zooms through the air as streams of water and fire chase him across the lair. The effect of both elements intertwining causes a huge layer of steam to rise. If this continues, we won't be able to see anything soon.

Maybe that's the key to winning this.

I cast another horror and instruct them to spread out. I have twelve still alive at the moment and since we are in battle, they no longer decay over time. If only I had a way to heal them, then I would be unstoppable.

They take their positions around the edge of the room. I don't want any of them to be hit in a cluster. A dozen orbs of water rise from the pool and hover in the air. My horrors have attack speed but no agility, so when the orbs come soaring across the room, only one manages to dodge the attack. Luckily, the water negates some of the fire damage by simply boiling their skin instead of burning them. It's not ideal, but the damage is a little less. Steam rises with each attack, until I can barely see the horrors on the other side.

We're still screwed, but I'm hoping an opening will appear at some point. As of right now, the wyrms still have ninety percent of their health and the nymph has all of hers. Limery and I are topped off, but my horrors won't last forever.

I'm far enough away from the nymph to dodge the next drowning glob she sends my way, but when she uses tidal wave again, the horrors are tossed aside like spiders in a shower. I lose two more horrors to the flames that follow before I am able to cast another.

The steam is thicker than ever, and I can only see the horrors closest to me. However, I can still sense the others as they retake their positions. If only there was a way to stop the inflow of water, then the wyrms might actually evaporate it all, leaving the nymph powerless.

Even if we could stop the inflow, their positioning makes the fountain inaccessible.

Limery flies too close to the nymph and a beam of water hits him in the chest, knocking him to the floor. I'm quick to his rescue, narrowly dodging a stream of flame, but the little guy is dazed.

I hide him in a corner and instruct one of my horrors to make sure he isn't carried away by a wave. It puts me a body down on the battlefield, but I can't lose Limery. He's become a friend, and he's part of the reason I'm even here right now. There's no way I'm letting anything happen to him.

If I don't figure out how to deal some actual damage, then my horrors will die and we'll have no shot at defeating this dungeon.

It's time to go all-in.

I take off towards the fountain, casting another horror along the way while calling all of the others towards it as well. We're almost there when a wave comes roaring, knocking us down and scattering my horrors once again. The water stings against my skin, but as quick as I can, I'm on my feet and rushing the fountain once more. I can see another wave forming, so I use Berserker Rage. This time, the wave has no effect on me other than slight damage and I carry on, hopping the ledge of the pool and diving into the abyss. I feel an intense heat near my feet, telling me that the wyrms are trying to roast me in the water, while the toxic water burns my eyes.

Hacking at anything near me, my axe connects with flesh and then a tail collides with my side, knocking me against the pool wall. My vision goes dark at the edges, but I do my best to gain a sense of direction. The pool is deep, and I wonder how the wyrms are floating on its surface. It must have something to do with the nymph's water magic. My head breaches the surface and I gasp for air before swimming below again. The water grows hotter as another set of flames boil the area where I just was.

With all the focus on me, my horrors have managed to climb into the pool and now join me in its steadily heating waters. I send them after the nymph, content to keep her distracted, even if it means sacrificing my horrors. The hot toxic water drains my HP, but the increased healing from Berserker Rage is keeping it steady. For now.

Another flame attack and the water grows hotter still.

I can sense the horrors dropping like flies. I come up for air and the steam is so thick, it's almost like breathing in water. Flames bear down on me again and it feels like the water is melting off my skin. Berserker Rage wears off and my HP starts dropping rapidly. Bubbles rise all around me. The water is actually boiling from all the heat. Cooking me alive.

This is it. All or nothing.

I activate Sweeping Slash right before my last horror expires, doing my best to focus on anything but the burning pain that engulfs my body. The blow connects with the nymph, and the knockback sends her out of the fountain.

Notifications flash across my vision, but I push them from my mind. Right now, all that matters is her.

She lays on the ground unmoving as I crawl out of the fountain and fall over the edge with a splat. I'm tired and in pain, every pain receptor on my body screams at me, but my rage meter is full.

She says something, but I use Intimidation before she can finish, sending her into confusion for two seconds. Using Claw and Bite, I take out her remaining health before collapsing on the ground beside her.

For the longest time, I just lay there. The fact that I haven't been roasted alive means the wyrms are dead.

"We dids it!" I hear Limery's voice somewhere above me.

The steam is starting to fade, but it still takes up the majority of the room.

"We did, didn't we?" I sit up and take in the chaos around me.

There's not a single horror left. My skin is covered in

boils, even though my increased regeneration is doing its best to heal me. Rising to my feet, I walk over to the fountain, where the two wyrms float lifelessly on the surface.

Limery perches on the ledge of the fountain and mumbles something about "filthy wyrms."

I never really believed the story people told me about frogs. That if you slowly heat up a pot with a frog inside, it'll boil to death before it realizes what's happening. In the chaos of the battle, the nymph had no idea her new pets were actually boiling her alive. Not until it was too late. They even managed to kill themselves while they were at it. If not for Berserker Rage, I'd no doubt be joining them.

Then I notice the obelisk in the middle of the fountain. There's a crack running along the edge of it. Not a crack like it was broken, but an opening with something glowing beneath it.

"Hey, Limery. See if you can open that?" I say, pointing at the obelisk.

He flies over and presses his tiny fingers in the crack and slowly pulls up. It flips open like a clamshell and a bright yellow glow emanates from within.

Item. *Elemental Stone. Boosts the power of elemental attacks by 20%.*

Item. *Water Potion x2. Allows user to breathe underwater for 10 minutes.*

Item. *Aquatic Boots. Allows user to walk on water.*

Not a bad haul. Along with what's in the chest, the two wyrms drop Lesser Mana Stones, which increase mana regeneration by ten percent.

I don't really have much use for the elemental stone, since I have no elemental attacks. I bet Jira would make good use of it if I took it back with me, but he wasn't here to help me win it. Instead, I give it to Limery.

"For me?" His eyes glisten with tears as I hand him the stone.

"I couldn't have done it without you."

"Oh, Chods." He wraps me in his tiny arms as his tears run down my shoulder.

"Give me a second to look over my notifications."

Limery releases me and immediately starts testing out his new item. He casts a fireball and it seems to burn brighter than before.

I pull up my notifications.

You have defeated Faerie Dungeon. Claim dungeon prize.

Congratulations! You have reached level 11. +1 stat point to distribute. +1 Strength and Constitution racial bonus. +1 ability point to distribute.

Congratulations! You have reached level 12. +1 stat point to distribute. +1 Strength and Constitution racial bonus.

Regional Event Alert! Two mana-infused wyrms have been slain. 18/20 remaining. 19 days remaining.

"Come on, Limery. Time to get the hell out of here."

Once we exit the dungeon, the rock formation falls back into place, making the entrance no longer accessible. I swipe my hands across the runes.

Faerie Dungeon. Would you like to enter?

I focus on yes, just to see what happens, but I'm not surprised at the response.

Faerie Dungeon is not currently available. 7 days until respawn.

CHAPTER TWENTY

20. Rule the World

At level twelve, I'm one of the strongest trolls from the village now. If that doesn't get Gord to respect me, then I don't know what will. I'm actually looking forward to rubbing my new summoner class in his smug face. Gah, he was such a dick. But that will have to wait, our first stop is the imp cave to collect my communication stone.

I also need to assign my new ability point. There are still a few abilities I haven't unlocked in my barbarian class as well as the melee weapon abilities I unlocked after acquiring my axe, but with the way I plan to level from here on out, upgrading my horrors makes the most sense. I want to be unkillable, a true brute capable of taking pain and dishing it out.

Summon Horror (Passive). *Ability to summon a horror. Each horror grants a unique ability. For every horror active,* *gain 1% increased damage and health points. Horrors decay 10% every minute outside of combat.*

Horror of Power. *Summon a horror with 20% of your Strength. Cost: 100 mana. Cooldown: 30 seconds. Bonus: Your next attack deals double damage.*

Horror of Vitality. *Summon a horror with 20% of your health points. Cost: 100 mana. Cooldown: 30 seconds. Bonus: Opponents near Horror of Vitality are slowed by 20%.*

It's a tough call. More power or more life? The slow that Horror of Vitality offers is a game-changer, though. I'll finally have my own crowd control abilities. And the twenty percent HP that these new horrors will have is essentially double what my current horrors have. I do the math in my head. At level twelve, I have two thousand and four hundred HP. If I gain one percent health for each horror and I'm able to summon forty now that I have two classes, that's a nine-hundred and sixty HP bonus. Holy shit! At full power, my horrors of Vitality will have almost seven hundred health.

I add my attribute point to Horror of Vitality and summon my first new horror since leaving the dungeon.

There's a puff of smoke and then a rotund, furry monster with orange and blue stripes appears. Its head is orange and the stripes run horizontally across the rest of its body. It has two black ram's horns that protrude from its head and curl around its fuzzy orange ears. It has the same round and bulbous eyes as the other horrors, but its body-type is completely different. Sharp tusks stick out from its jaws not that much different than my own.

It reminds me of a stuffed animal, if a stuffed animal could eat your face off.

A bison roams through the golden field not too far

ahead, the perfect victim for a test run. I motion for Limery to stand back and instruct my horror to do the same as I approach as quietly as possible. Crouching through the tall grass, I move like a lion on the prowl until I am only a few feet from the grazing animal.

I attack it from the rear, drawing a critical strike and when it turns to charge, I summon a Horror of Vitality. It pops into existence and the bison slows noticeably, allowing me to sidestep its charge like a matador. It doesn't take me long to kill the bison without taking a single point of damage.

The next day, we arrive at the mouth of the imp cave and something feels different. The rattle of machinery echoes out of the cave's mouth.

"Mommy!" Limery yells as we enter the cave. "We dids it! We kills the wyrms and the baby wyrms and then we goes to the dungeon and Chods gives me magics stones!" He's speaking a mile a minute as he recounts our adventure and finishes by pulling out the elemental stone and showing it to his mother.

She laughs at her son, embracing him against her furry chest. "It seems I may have underestimated you, Mister Troll. I'll be honest, I didn't think you had it in you." Her eyes run up and down my body, taking in my new look. "Blue looks good on you, by the way."

I don't pay much attention to the comment as my eyes wander around the cave. It's almost nothing like the primitive cave I left a few days ago. All of the machinery that was piled in the back of the room is whirring with life. There are contraptions weaving blankets, sweeping the floor, turning a rotisserie over an open flame. A giant pot of stew is continuously stirred, and there are several others that I can't even begin to grasp their purpose. One is shaped like a giant mixer and pops little blue cubes out of the bottom. There's even a line of glass tubes that cast light from the ceiling. They have magical electricity!

"Magic does all of this?" I ask.

"When it's around. The machines pull it from the very air. It's hard to make them much bigger than this and have them work effectively, but considering this isn't a fountain of magical activity, it works pretty well. We also have a battery maker. It takes the magic from the air and stores it in common stones that last up to a day."

This has me even more excited to see what is happening at the troll village. The magical veins that run underneath it are massive compared to here.

"If I remember correctly, I promised you a reward if you brought magic back to our cave. Let me go and grab it right quick."

She disappears in the back of the cave, and Limery pulls strips of meat off the rotisserie. His mother pops his hand when she returns and hands me a small circular stone with a hole in its middle.

"Most people wear them around their necks, since they only work when they are on your person. May it help you in the days ahead."

I pull a strip of leather from my bag and run it through the communication stone. There's nothing special about the stone, nothing to signify that it may be one of the most useful tools in this entire game. Communication will be the key to me leading the trolls out of the forest and into better times.

"I hope you will stay for dinner before heading out." She flashes me razor-sharp smile. "We're having roasted deer. I also have more mole soup you can take with you on your journey. You are more than welcome to rest here for the night if you desire."

Thoughts of the last time I had mole soup cross my mind. The last thing I need is another Charisma high.

"Dinner sounds lovely."

I'm anxious to get moving, but after receiving the communication stone, I feel I owe it to Limery's mother to stay for dinner. Besides, twilight is approaching and I'll need to rest for the evening anyway.

We fix our dinner and take it outside to eat, just as the sun begins to set over the horizon, casting the sky with streaks of watercolor.

There is a delicious smoky and spicy flavor to the deer meat. It reminds me of Indian food. For a second, my mind drifts back to the real world, to the many nights I called in takeout from the Indian restaurant on Sixth Street because neither Mom nor Dad were going to be home in time for dinner. I wonder if they even know I'm here? If they even care? Do they know I feel real pain when I'm hurt here or that there are violent criminals who want nothing more than to kill me on sight just because of my in-game race?

Suddenly, I'm not so hungry anymore.

"Where's Leo at?" I ask, trying to take my mind somewhere else. I hadn't seen Limery's brother since we came back.

"He's off on his own. Since magic returned, we no longer need the constant influx of magical items, so he's taking a well-deserved break. He received news of the regional event and is going to form a party to try and defeat one of the wyrms." She laughs. "If he knew Limmy had managed to help defeat three already, I'd never hear the end of it."

In the distance, I watch Limery as he zooms through the air, blasting glowing bugs out of the sky with tiny fireballs.

"He's a good kid. Smart, talented, heck of an aim."

"You best take care of him," she says, her face suddenly serious.

"What do you mean?" I thought Limery would be staying here once we returned.

"He's taken a liking to you. I can see it in his eyes, Chod. He'll follow you to the ends of the world."

That's the first time she has called me by my name since I've known her. It must be something intimately cultural about referring to someone by their name for the imps. I still don't know hers.

"Then I will do my best to protect him."

We sit in silence after that. The sun sets and the only light comes from the stars above and the occasional fireball in the distance. My entire life, I've been an outsider. My fans who watched me stream were only there for the entertainment. Maybe part of the reason I've been a loner is because I always push people away, afraid of getting hurt. I've never really let anyone other than Taryn get to close to me, never really had anyone who wanted to.

I wonder what Taryn is up to right now. What I would do to be able to tell him about my adventures so far. He'd love this place.

I don't know what the future holds, what will happen when my time in *Isle of Mythos* is over. All I know is that right now, this two foot tall, energetic, insane, loving, demonic spawn wants to be a part of whatever adventure I'm on now, and I'll be damned if I let him down.

I officially have a party. And before this is over, we're going to rule the world.

"Can I ask you something?"

"You are a curious troll. What is it this time?"

"You mentioned that all the continents used to be accessible to one another before the great war with the wizard. What happened?"

"Come inside and I'll tell you about it." She cleans up the leftovers from dinner and I follow her inside. The gentle whir of magically-powered machines hum and purr. There's a machine against the wall where Limery's mother places our plates. It lifts the plates, scrubs them, then dips them in water to rinse them off.

She pulls a bottle of amber liquid off a shelf and grabs two clay cups, motioning for me to take a seat against the cave wall. Due to our size differences, none of their furniture is large enough for me, but she does offer me a leather hide to sit on.

She pours the bottle, nearly filling the cup, and I pray it doesn't have a Charisma buff.

Item. *Imp Mead. -3 Intelligence for 1 hour. Useless, but it feels so good.*

We tap our glasses together and the sweet flavor of honey coats my throat. Then an uncontrollable smile comes, and everything seems to be just a little bit funnier than usual.

"It's terrible for you, but damn if it doesn't take the edge off." She laughs, but then her tone grows more serious. "The world used to be such a wonderful place. People traveled to different continents, all the various races traded together, and the world was a better place for it. There was less hate back then. After the war, the wizard that started it all retreated to his homeland and sealed off the magical transport portals. Now, the only way to travel to other continents is by ship. And there are things that lurk in the oceans that have the power to devour them whole."

"Do you think the portals will ever reopen?"

"I have no doubt it will happen. No spell lasts forever, no matter how powerful. My worry is what the wizard has been up to during all this time. Most of the imps were able to escape through the portals before they closed, but some races were not so lucky." She gives me a half-smile.

"Which races?" My chest feels tight as I ask the question.

"There was a large number of giants and goblins, no doubt the wizard made promises to coerce them to his cause. They don't often engage in large-scale warfare. The real threat were the dark elves, though. It was said that some could raise the dead to fight on their behalf."

That's not what I was expecting. I thought maybe I had found the reason the trolls were hated so much. Will I ever find out the true reason?

"It's nothing to worry about now," she laughs. "For now, your focus should be the wyrms or else there won't be an island left."

CHAPTER TWENTY-ONE

21. Welcome Home

When we set off the next morning, it is a tearful goodbye. As much as she encourages his adventure, I can tell his mom will miss him dearly. I mean, who wouldn't miss a clown like Limery. He's like the little brother and the pet I never had all rolled into one.

His mother even gives me a hug around the knee.

"I am glad to have met you, Chod. You are more curious than the average troll. Take care of my boy."

"I will."

"Lillith, you may call me Lillith. Now, get going before I regret telling you my name." She releases her embrace, and Limery and I set off towards the forest.

It's a beautiful day and excitement fills the air. Two days from now, I'll be back at the troll village claiming my reward. I still don't know what I will ask for. Chief Rizza offered me literally anything I wanted. Tormara seemed to think I would want the village, but truthfully, I have no interest in ruling a small village. I want adventure. The thrill of fighting the wyrm, of exploring the dungeon, that's what I'm truly after. Not council meetings and planning how to stay hidden from the outside world.

I want to make trolls respected so that we don't have to stay hidden. If I can't make them respect us, then I will at least make them fear us. Enough power and people like Glenn will think twice about attacking the village.

When we come across the river, I pull out the Aquatic Boots I won at the faerie dungeon. They're made out of green leather with pearls sewn into the upper half. They must have some enchantment that sizes them to the wearer, because they manage to fit my giant troll feet, claws and all.

I step into the rushing river and it's like I'm walking on sand. The water gives a small amount, but then it's firm. Rapids form around my feet with each step until I am safely on the other side. Limery flies beside my shoulder.

Pretty cool.

Limery and I chat the day away as we travel. He tells me about some of his favorite games he likes to play with his brother. One of them is similar to tag, but they throw fireballs at one another.

"We meets you family soon, Chods?" he asks.

"I— I don't have a family here." I don't know why I say it, but I start talking to him about my life outside of the game. "I have a mom and a dad where I'm from, but we're not really close. I'm their only child, and we're not close. How sad is that? I honestly can't remember the last time

Mom gave me a hug or Dad took an interest in any of my school activities. You're lucky, Limery. Your mother loves you."

"You mother loves you, Chods. You good son." His tiny hand pats me on the shoulder.

"I don't know about that. Maybe it's not them. Maybe it's me. Maybe I'm not the son they wanted." I never had an interest in business, especially when it was always more important than I was. How many tournaments did I have to win for them to notice me? Not enough, apparently.

"Don't says that, Chods. Don'ts. If they don't likes you, then you comes and stays with me."

I don't know what I did to deserve his love, but I'm glad to have it. If only I had a Limery in the real world.

"It's not all bad. I have a friend named Taryn and he's about the closest thing I have to a brother." He's been there for me more times than I can count. He's not much of a talker, but whenever I just needed some company, anything to break up the loneliness, we'd sit and play games for hours in silence. There's a lot to be said for that. "We're going to go see my people, though. They're like me, but they aren't my family. You'll like them."

I hadn't really thought about whether or not the trolls would be welcoming to Limery. They live in a closed society, so they may not be accepting of outsiders, even if they're non-human. He's a big part of the reason they even have magic at all.

We're making our way across the golden field when a notification pops into my vision.

Regional Event Alert! *Jason Montoya and Lester Hobbes* *have slain a mana-infused wyrm. 17/20 remaining. 17 days remaining.*

Maybe I underestimated the other players. Three days in and they've slain their first wyrm.

Out of the corner of my eye, I notice a black splotch moving across the golden fields in the distance. Straight in our direction.

I contemplate running for a moment, but then my mind clears and I realize I don't have to. I have natural abilities to conceal me. If I simply quit moving, Camouflage will take effect.

"Limery, come here. We need to hide, nestle against my arms."

I take a seat and Limery climbs against my chest. I cover his body with my arms until he can't be seen, his skin is warm against my own.

The black splotches continue to grow in size until I can clearly tell they are two humans on horseback. The clop of horse hooves is all I hear as they trot towards us.

A dark-skinned man in boiled black leather armor wears a black cape that flows in the wind. He rides next to a man in a ruby red robe holding a scepter made of a dark wood that's fitted with a piece of obsidian on the end. Several runes are engraved down its side. A gray beard falls to his chest and blows in the wind. The man in black wears a sword to one side of his hip, but I can see several daggers strapped along his leg. He must be some kind of rogue.

They pull the reins of their horses and come to a halt a few dozen yards away from me. They both wear the same emblem, a white skull with a sword and staff crossed together in the background.

"This is where I saw it," says the rogue.

"I don't care what you say. Doesn't look like there is anything here," says the wizard.

They both scan the area and I focus on them, displaying their stats in my vision.

Randy Billson
 Level 17
 Rogue
 Human

Don Othello
 Level 16
 Mage
 Human

"Fuck off, Don. I know what I saw. There was something big and blue moving over here right next to that giant rock." He points to me as he says it. "I have advanced eyesight. It was a monster, I tell you. A big, ugly monster. Could have been one of those wyrms."

"Well, like I said, whatever it was, or wasn't, it ain't here now. Regardless, we need to be getting back to town. Word is that Glenn attacked the damn trolls again." Don rolls his eyes.

"Fucking Glenn. I don't know what his fascination is with those things. There are much better options for leveling up that don't rip your face to shreds. Trolls are so stupid that the best loot you're gonna get is a stone club.

Like we could even lift the thing to use it. He's lost all of his items, what, three, four times now? No, I'll stick to dungeons and finding actual loot. Glenn can have his trolls." Randy laughs.

"Still, the mayor wants us back at town by sundown in case the trolls try to exact revenge."

Randy pulls a dagger from his leg and spins the blade around his fingers with precision. "I'd like to see them try. Besides, if they were going to attack, they would have done it by now."

With a quick pull of their reins, both men are off towards the other town.

That was a close call. I didn't take into account that other players might have enhanced senses as well. I'm lucky it wasn't a ranger or someone capable of tracking my footprints. I wait for another ten minutes before removing my camouflage and setting off again.

One day with my communication stone and it's already paying dividends. I can't stop thinking about what Randy said as I walk. Apparently, not everyone is out to destroy the trolls. Yes, they hate us, but they're more content exploring dungeons.

Still, if Glenn is continually out to get us, then he needs to be stopped. Soon.

We do our best to stay away from the two human settlements that stand between us and the forest as we camp for the night. I refrain from casting horrors just in case we need to hide. If what Don said is true, and the mayor of one of those towns is recalling his people, then we need to stay as far away from them as possible.

The next day, we make it past the towns without trouble. I'm so excited to get back to the village that I don't even spy on the humans this time. There's plenty of opportunities to level up, but the priority is to make it back in one piece without drawing any extra attention.

When we cross into the forest, it feels like I'm back home. The vines, birdcalls, and the musty smell of the forest floor calm my spirit for the first time since I stepped out into the larger world.

I cast a Horror of Finesse and Vitality, thankful to be under the safety of the canopy and away from prying eyes. As soon as the cooldown is up, I cast another, until I'm trampling through the forest with my own personal army of forty horrors. They're loud as they walk, gnashing their teeth and grunting as we move along. Limery zooms in and out of them, occasionally landing on one of the Horror of Vitality's heads and holding on to their horns.

With such a large force, I draw the aggro of several woodland creatures as we walk and my army tears through them like it's nothing. I know I've only scratched the surface of my power and that if I keep leveling, there could be even more summoner abilities for me to unlock. I'd like to see Glenn try and attack us now.

As we make our way to the village, nothing really seems all that different with the ley lines returned. There are a few exotic animals roaming the forest, and I'm pretty sure I spot a centaur at one point, but by and large things are the same.

I'm surprised when I come upon the boundary of the village that there are no trolls on guard. When I left, I saw several in Camouflage around the village's edges.

Behind my army of minions, we cross the line into troll lands.

A barbaric grunt stops me in my tracks, and it's like a veil is removed from my eyes. The empty forest I was looking at disappears and I see the translucent shapes of several trolls on guard. The troll closest to us abandons Camouflage and charges into my horrors with a club, obliterating several of them and tossing others aside.

Fire crackles next to me as Limery readies his fireballs for battle.

"Wait!" I yell as several more trolls come from the nearby area. "Wait! It's me, Chod! I'm back."

The troll is about to take another swing at my horrors when I hear a deep voice bellowing to my right.

"Trogden, halt!" I'd know that voice anywhere. Gord steps into view from behind a massive oak, his metal nose ring reflecting the fire in Limery's hand.

He looks me up and down with disgust, then over my minions, and finally to Limmy.

"Blue skin. You finally decide to reveal your true colors? You are welcome, but outsiders are not permitted on troll grounds."

I know I shouldn't take his bait, but he really pisses me off with his smug attitude.

"Are you fucking kidding me? I look this way because of you. I risked my life for this village and actually succeeded, and now you're telling me I can't bring my partner on troll grounds."

"Partner," he scoffs. "More like vermin." The other trolls chuckle at his joke. "Rules are rules, even for you."

"I'm not going anywhere without him."

"Then stay and rot." He turns to leave.

"I'm not as weak as I was when I left." When I check his stats, I see we are now the same level.

"Is that a challenge?" he roars.

I call my horrors by my side and they hiss and snarl in a violent mob. I still have over thirty left and hear the crackle of Limery's fireballs behind me. The other trolls take a defensive position and I see more approaching. This isn't exactly what I imagined my return to look like, but if I have to fight my way in, then so be it.

I twirl Peacemaker in my hand. "If you want to dance, then let's dance."

Gord's lip curls above his broken tusk and he jumps through the air, club raised to attack.

A fireball hits him in the chest and then all hell breaks loose.

"You no hurts Chods!" screams Limery.

Three trolls rush me, but I send out my horde, stopping their push with the horror's AoE slow and overwhelming them with sheer numbers. The trolls fight against the horrors, slinging them off with ease, but with every horror they remove, another takes its place as I continue to cast every chance I can.

A loud screeching caw cuts through the chaos and Jira appears on the battlefield.

"That is enough!" he yells. His dreads seem to rise from his body, an unearthly heat emanating from him.

I call off my horrors and the trolls cease to fight.

"Now, what is the meaning of this?" he asks.

"This fool is attempting to bring outsiders on tribal lands," spits Gord.

Jira recognizes me for the first time. "Chod, is this true?"

"We completed the quest together and I want him

there when I choose my reward. As for the others—." I motion to the horrors. "—they are mine."

Jira gives me a curious look. "What do you mean they are yours?"

I cast a Horror of Vitality in front of him. With a puff of smoke, the rotund orange creature appears at his feet. As strong and as powerful as the other trolls are, they still gasp at the showing.

"I see. As village shaman, I grant access to the imp. Everyone, back to your posts."

Gord cuts his eyes at me as he walks away, but I take pride in the scorch marks that stain his chest.

The walk to the village center is long and quiet. There's no parade of thanks or even any real acknowledgment for what I've done. Is it because I have blue skin or is there more at play than I know? Now that I'm not being attacked, I notice that everything since crossing into the troll lands is different from when I left. Evening has come upon the forest, but there are glowing flower bulbs, like light posts, lighting our way. They light up before us and when we are out of range, they shroud the forest in darkness once more. Is that the power of troll magic?

"Jira, what happened back there? I couldn't see anything and then suddenly trolls were everywhere."

"There is a reason that trolls have survived in the forest for so long. Using the power of the magical well, we are able to conceal our location among the trees. Think of it as a barrier of sorts, reflecting the world outside our lands back to those who pass by. Those who aren't trolls will even have a desire to travel in other directions. Unless they cross the boundary, they will never know we are here. Even sound stays within our grounds."

"How is that even possible?"

"All in good time. I apologize for Gord. He's not quick to trust an outsider, and many of the other trolls look up to him. We are grateful for the journey you made, and I look forward to hearing all about it. As well as why you are now blue."

Whispers and pointed fingers greet me as we walk into the village. All of my horrors have expired, but Limery sits on my shoulder. The village has changed too. I can't quite explain it, but it feels more alive, like there is power running through the very trees. In the short time I was gone, the village seems to have healed itself. There are no traces of the fire to be found.

Jira leads me to the council area. The chairs carved from nature itself have blossomed and flowers adorn them, framing the council members in lilies and roses. Shocked faces gaze upon me and Limery as we kneel before the council. Even Tormara's scowl has disappeared for the moment.

Chief Rizza tells me to stand, and I feel Limery poking at my side. The chief and I stare at each other for a moment but the imp continues to poke me until I acknowledge him.

"What is it?" I ask.

He points at the foot of Chief Rizza's throne. I'm not sure what he is showing me until something slithers and two bright blue eyes stare back at me.

CHAPTER TWENTY-TWO

22. Magic and Mayhem

"Welcome back, Chod," says Chief Rizza.

I should respond but the only thing I can think of is, "Why in the hell is there a wyrm wrapped around the foot of your throne?" The wyrm raises its head, licks the air, and lays down once again.

"As you can see, your efforts were successful and the trolls are once again hidden away from the prying eyes of men." She smiles, her small tusks framing her face. "I believe the undying one will trouble us no longer."

My hand grips a little tighter on the axe handle as I force myself to look away from the creature. They had to have received the same notification that I did about the wyrms. They must know that unless they are killed, they will infest the island. These aren't ordinary wyrms that burrow in a small area, these are mana-infused, and they will grow into the size of a barn if left unchecked.

"We are all interested in what led to the obstruction. If you don't mind, please recount the events of your adventure."

For the next half-hour, I have their full attention. Chief Rizza, Tormara, Guilda, and two others hang on to my every word. One of the council seats is empty, but I don't recall who sat there. Jira stands behind me, but I know he is following every word as well.

I tell them about the wyrm, the eggs, my new abilities, the regional event, the dungeon, and my communication stone. When I am finished, it is Guilda who speaks first. Her gray braid marks her as the oldest of the bunch.

"It has been many years since we last had two magical trolls in the village. I believe this is a warning of grave things to come."

"Hardly," scoffs Tormara. "It was a freak accident, not some divine intervention. Now that magic is restored to the forest, I think it is time to focus on rebuilding what we lost, on building up our tribe."

"There are no accidents, Tormara. Everything prepares us for what is to come next. That is the way it has always been."

"Heroes are not influenced by the wills of the gods, Guilda. You know that as well as anyone. They are pure chaos and I would have them on their way before any more damage is done."

Limmy stands quiet beside me, the quietest I have ever seen him. Even at such a young age, he knows more about troll customs than I do.

Chief Rizza raises her hand, and the debate ceases.

"Before you left, I promised to reward you with anything within my power if you completed the quest. You have succeeded. Now it is time to claim your reward."

The wyrm adjusts itself beneath the throne. *How in the hell am I supposed to kill it without making the chief irate?*

"Chod?" she asks again.

"You know you have to kill the wyrm, right?"

"I have to do no such thing. It will one day be a great and powerful protector of our village." She reaches out her hand and the wyrm uncoils, rising to rub its head against her palm.

"It's what blocked the ley lines. It's the reason there is a regional event. The thing is infused with mana and attracted to magical energy. That's probably why it came to the forest. If you allow it to live, then it will breed and sooner or later, this will all happen again." *They can't really be so obtuse to think that keeping a violent monster as a pet is a good idea, can they?* "Jira, back me up here."

I turn to face the shaman, thinking he may at least be thinking rationally.

"I'm sorry, Chod, but I stand with the chief. For too long, we have been hated and oppressed, forced to hide away from the men that would do us harm for nothing more than the color of our skin and the tusks on our faces. Let the humans destroy the rest, but this one, it is ours, and it may one day be the difference in our survival or extinction."

"And what if it cuts off your magic again? What if it rises up and kills you?"

"How is it you know so little of troll ways?" asks Tormara. "Were you raised on an island?"

"Enough, Tormara. There is no need to worry about the wyrm." Chief Rizza stands and the wyrm rises next to her, equaling her height. "We are bound and the wyrm will do as I command. Now, Chod, tell me what you would have of me."

I don't know. I could ask her to kill the wyrm. Would she honor that? It seems like such a waste if there was actually a way for me to convince her on my own. Would she really hand over the village to me if I said that's what I wanted? I really have no desire to rule, but I've done too much to just stand by and watch them destroy themselves. And what did she mean about me not knowing troll ways? What am I missing here?

"Can I have more time?" It's the only rational solution to make sure I get this right.

"Very well. You may have one day. If you do not request your reward within the next twenty-four hours, then it is forfeit. Jira, show him to his quarters for the night."

I don't get it. She was so welcoming last time I was here. It was like I was the savior of the village that they had all been waiting for, but now it feels like I'm the outsider Gord claimed on day one. Is the magic having this effect on them or had they lost so much hope that an outsider was all they had to believe in?

Jira leads Limery and me away from the council area and back to the village. The glowing flower bulbs make the village feel alive as we walk.

"You will be staying here tonight." He stops in front of a small hut.

"What am I missing about the wyrm? Why is no one else worried about it destroying the village?"

He raises an eyebrow at me, but then motions into the hut. "Step inside."

The inside of the hut is warm and welcoming. Vines adorned with tiny glowing berries run along the ceiling like Christmas lights. Branches form a bed layered with living leaves that looks incredibly comfortable. There is a small table against an open window that has shutters that open and close, all made out of living foliage. A small bush grows from the wall, ripe with berries. Limery picks one off and tosses it in his mouth, mumbling something about how good it is. This all has to be crafted with magic somehow. If not, it would take years to bend each individual piece into the correct shape. And to do that for every hut, the manpower it would take would leave time for nothing else. I for certain want to learn how it is done, but first I want to understand what the chief meant.

We take a seat, and Jira pulls the shutters closed.

"She's right, you know," says Jira, his red eyes boring into my own.

"Who?"

"Tormara. You know so very little about our culture, yet it is undeniable that you are one of us. Well, it was." He looks down at my arms and hands, my blue skin so different from his own. "You know the seaside trolls are the only ones with blue skin, but they don't glow quite like you do. They're much smaller, too. If you were raised a troll, or rather, raised by female trolls, you would know of their inborn ability to bind with creatures that most other societies view as monsters. Once they bond, they bond for life, until one or the other dies. A mental connection forms between them, one that remains no matter how far they are separated."

"Then why don't all of the women bond?" I ask.

"It is not always an easy task. The creature must first be subdued. Once that happens, a bonding of blood must take place. All of this while not dying to the creature. Chief Rizza is lucky to have found a newborn."

Newborn…yeah, seven feet tall and loves to snuggle. I can see why it's not worth the risk for most.

"And the men, it's not possible?"

"No, most were blessed with great strength only and the ability to go into a powerful rage. It's the women who have the high intellect. I'd be lying if I said I trust the temperament of most males to control a bond."

I agree with that. The last thing we need is Gord running around with a fully-grown wyrm at his beck and call.

"If women have higher intellect, does that mean that if they went through the same process that I did, that they would have stronger powers?"

"Perhaps, but they do not have the constitution that you have. That much raw magic would surely rip them apart."

There's always a catch. The ones who could use this power best are not strong enough to survive getting it.

"You know we cannot complete the regional quest while the wyrm still lives, right?"

"Indeed, but that does not mean you can't save the island. Chief Rizza's wyrm will not breed, it is one of the consequences of the bond. If not for this, the trolls would never have been forced into hiding to begin with."

"How do I save the island then?"

He stands and smiles. "I will leave that for you to figure out."

As he walks to the door, I call out one last time. "Jira, one last thing. Will you show me how trolls control the magic?"

"Tomorrow." He half-smiles before leaving.

I think about Jira's words long after he leaves. Limery curls up at the foot of the bed and goes to sleep. Soft snores fill the hut as I'm left to ponder my future.

How can I save the island without completing the quest? The other players are already out hunting the wyrms, what will they do if they reach the last one and find out that it is here?

I already know the answer to that. By allowing the wyrm to live, the trolls are dooming themselves.

No, ourselves. I am one of them. It doesn't matter if my skin is green or blue, I went on the quest because I believed in these people. They might not be perfect. Hell, they suffer from many of the same flaws that humans do —pride, arrogance, anger—but that doesn't make them monsters.

Or maybe I'm looking at it all wrong. Who gets to decide that being a monster is a bad thing?

I know what I want for my reward.

I'm awakened the next morning to the clatter of wooden clubs. The troll children run through the village, beating each other as they duck, roll, and otherwise tumble around learning the ways of battle.

Limery flies out into the chaos, juggling fireballs above their heads. The children laugh at his antics until the instructor comes over.

"Excuse me, Chod," she says. Even though she is female, she is seasoned from battle. Scars run down her dark green arms, making her look like a tiger in places, and one stretches across the entirety of her face. Her hair is pulled into two ox-horn buns on the side of her head. I'm sure I'm about to be reprimanded for Limery's behavior.

"Yes?"

"My name is Ismora. I train the children during the day, but I have also fought many battles for our village. I have heard that you are a great warrior yourself, that you raise demons from thin air. I just wanted to say thank you for bringing magic back to our village. For protecting the little ones."

"Uh, you're welcome."

"Thank you to your little one as well. I can tell he has the heart of a warrior."

Limery continues tossing his fireballs as the children watch, then he catches one in each hand and slams them into the third, making an even bigger fireball that vanishes into the air. The children laugh with delight.

"I see you are providing entertainment now," Chief Rizza says from over my shoulder.

I turn to see her with the wyrm following close beside her. She's smiling, at least. The wyrm licks at the air and watches me with its icy blue eyes.

"I have decided on my reward," I say.

Ismora nods to the chief and leaves to rejoin her students.

"Let it wait for now. There is something I want to show you first. There is no doubt you have taken in some of the changes to the village since your return, but I want to show you why it was so important to clear the obstruction. What it really means to our people."

Limery joins me and we follow her to the village center, where several of the other council members, along with Jira, stand around what looks like a well. To one side, pigs roast over an open flame in one hut and a woman tans leather in another. When we arrive, Jira removes the lid that covers the well and a dull blue glow can be seen coming from inside.

"This is the fountain of our village. It is one of very few wells on the entire island that tap into the ley lines directly. They were formed long ago, long before the trolls were hated. When we all simply roamed the lands. A new well has not been created in many years. Most of the humans do not understand their true power, because they are not able to touch or control raw magic. It has the power to rip through their very flesh. There are those, the imps being one of them, who have managed to pull a fraction of the magic's power from the air around magical areas and harness it, but even they cannot do this."

A chain goes down into the well. Jira turns a crank and it slowly pulls up, the glow growing brighter as it does. When the crank will turn no more, a bucket filled with bright blue energy, the same energy that passed through the ground when I fought the wyrm, sways back and forth.

Chief Rizza reaches into the bucket and cups some of the energy in her hands. It jiggles like slime but doesn't spill. She walks over to a tree and gently forces the energy into its bark. When it's gone, she presses her hands to the tree and closes her eyes.

The tree shakes momentarily, its roots rumbling the

earth and its leaves swishing far above. As quickly as it started, the tree moves no more.

"What happened?" I ask.

"Tell your friend to throw a fireball at the tree. The biggest one he can make."

"Is okay, Chods?" Limery's eyes radiate concern.

"Give it your best shot," I say.

Limery flies from my shoulder to the ground about twenty yards from the tree. He looks back at me as he takes his position, and I nod for him to go ahead. He gives a small bow to the chief, then turns towards the tree.

A small fireball erupts in his hand. He pushes both hands together and the fireball grows between them, doubling and then tripling in size. He raises his hands over his head and the fireball grows even larger, until it is bigger than he is. The air around the fire is distorted to the point that I don't know how Limery is even controlling it.

With a flick of his wrist, the fireball erupts from his hands and soars toward the tree. It sends nearby leaves up in smoke before colliding with the tree in an explosion of fire and smoke.

The smoke dissipates and I expect the tree to be charred, thinking that the magic might help it heal faster, but the tree isn't damaged at all. The grass and leaves beneath the fireball's path are singed, but the tree itself is undamaged.

"How?"

"Magic." She smiles.

That fireball probably could have dropped me for half my health, maybe even more, and yet the tree looks like nothing happened.

"We have the power to infuse mana into living objects. If the object accepts our will, then it may continue to pull magic from the ground itself until no more magic remains. We can't infuse weapons or non-living items; only certain mages may do that. Animals are tough because they very rarely accept our will and can only use the magic we infuse in them, unable to replenish it from the earth, but plants, they love anything that will make them stronger."

"How do you do it, though?"

"Come, let me show you."

She leads me to the well and dips her hands in the bucket of swirling energy.

"Hold your hands out," she orders.

I cup my hands and she pours the energy into mine. It's hot, but it doesn't burn. Hot like a bath that's not quite ready. The kind you can put your feet in for two or three seconds but then it starts to hurt. Except this doesn't hurt. It's like being constantly on the edge of hurting, definitely not a pleasant feeling.

"Now, pick a tree."

Looking around, I try to find a tree that suits me. I settle on a small but sturdy maple, not much bigger than I am.

"Now, try to focus your mind and pour the magic into the tree."

I do as she says, and the tree absorbs the magic like a sponge.

"Good, now place your hands on the tree, close your eyes and feel the tree within your hands. When you do, impart your will upon the tree. It will let you know if what you wish is possible."

When I close my eyes, I feel something reach out to me. Another presence, but entirely inhuman. It's like I can feel the tree's energy in the blackness. There's nothing there, but at the same time, something very special. I try to do what Chief Rizza says, focusing my intention on the tree before me. I go crazy at first, willing it to uproot itself and walk, but I'm met with a forcefield of resistance in the darkness.

Something simpler, then. A shield perhaps. I focus on the tree using its branches and leaves as a shield, protecting it from anything that might harm it. This time, there is no resistance and the tree accepts my offer.

Congratulations! You have unlocked the skill 'Magical Infusion.' You are now a level 1 Infuser (Novice). Increase your skill and learn advanced techniques for working magical infusion by finding an advanced infuser (Apprentice or above). Crafting Ranks: Novice, Apprentice, Journeyman, Expert, Artisan, Master, Grandmaster.

I open my eyes and look to the chief for confirmation.

"Well?" she says.

"Well, what?"

"See if it worked."

I feel stupid doing it, but I pick up a rock and toss it at the tree. I don't use my axe just in case it doesn't work and I kill the tree. Just as the rock is about to hit the tree, several of the tree's branches move with blazing speed and block the projectile. It's almost like the branch has an invisible forcefield around it, because the branches aren't even damaged.

"Wow. This is amazing."

"It truly is. And we have you to thank for it. Now, tell me, Chod. What is your reward?"

As I lay in bed last night, I kept thinking about Jira's words and about the trolls. Even though I've helped them the best I could, I haven't really embraced their culture, embraced my new culture. I've treated this game like every other, content to fight and level, assuming that humans are the main race and that nothing could be done to counter that.

It doesn't have to be that way. I've been given an opportunity to make the trolls relevant, to make them powerful.

"I want two things. One, I want to become a citizen of the village, with a seat on the council to have my voice heard in all council decisions."

Tormara and the other women shake their heads and whisper among themselves.

"And secondly?"

"I want to take a party of women to hunt down the remaining wyrms."

"What makes you think that I would allow that?" She crosses her arms, but behind her, I can see Jira's eyes light up.

"Because I want them to bond together so that if the humans attack again, we can wipe them from the map."

CHAPTER TWENTY-THREE

23. Beggars Can't be Choosers

Tormara stares at me from across the council area. Her red hair blazes vibrantly against the white flowers that bloom from the headrest of her chair. I don't know if she is angry or intrigued by my request to form a party in an attempt to bond the remaining wyrms to the women of the troll village.

"The humans have already killed one mana-infused wyrm. Limery and I slew two others. Taking away the one Chief Rizza has already bonded with, that leaves sixteen. We don't know where they went, all we know is that they are attracted to magical areas. We'll be racing against time to find them before the humans as it is, so I think we should get a group together as soon as possible."

"How many trolls do you require on your adventure?" asks Chief Rizza. Her wyrm lies coiled beneath her feet.

"It is not often we send our people outside of the forest, but the cause is worthy of the risk. I have no false hope that we will bond with all of the wyrms, but even one can turn the tides of battle when fully grown."

If it were up to me, we'd take sixteen women in the hope of bonding every wyrm, but I know the chief will not allow it. We still have our reputation to consider. If we are met out in the open by humans, they will attack us on sight. The village can't afford to risk that many lives, no matter how good the reward may be.

"I think at least five should come with me. That will give us the trollpower to tackle any challenge that comes our way and if we succeed in bonding all five, then we will come back and journey out again. I want Jira to come as well."

The council sits in silence, letting my words sink in.

"It's too much," says Guilda. "The village cannot afford to be without Jira. To lose one magic user is enough, but both will leave us in grave risk even with our protections."

"I agree with Guilda," says Kina, one of the other councilwomen. She has bluish-black hair and is the only one who doesn't have it braided or in a bun of some sort.

"I'm sorry, Chod, but Jira must remain here. I'm sure you understand," says Chief Rizza.

I nod. I do understand. Taking Jira was a long shot, but I had to at least ask. Limery and I will be the only magic users in our party.

"I cannot offer you five women either. Many of these magical sources are located within dungeons. You will have to defeat each dungeon just to be able to see if the wyrms are inside. With luck, they may be, but us trolls are not known for our brilliant luck. Every troll I send with you risks death. If they die, they will not come back like you heroes do. For us, death is the end of this world and the beginning of another. Therefore, I will offer you three. If you succeed in bonding all three, then we will send more upon your return."

A party of five to clear a dungeon. Pretty standard. I was hoping for more, but we will have to make it work.

"Do I get to choose who comes?"

"Since anyone who joins you risks death, I will not force them to go against their will. We will have a village gathering where you will ask for volunteers and may take your pick from them."

The council doesn't take long to gather up the villagers. We meet in the village square and for once, I'm able to see the entirety of forest troll society. I now see why they are so worried about leaving the forest. Even with all the male trolls and children present, there can't be much more than a hundred trolls here.

Are the other troll sub-species this depleted as well? If so, why not gather together? There is safety in numbers.

Chief Rizza steps up onto a small pulpit constructed out of living trees. I know for a fact it wasn't there last time that I was here. It's definitely mana-infused. There's still so much I don't know about that aspect of my power, like how to remove the buff or if it's even possible. Could I press my hands against the podium and return it to its natural shape? There's so much I don't know about trolls and about this game in general.

She lifts her hand, and everyone falls silent. "As you know, Chod is now a member of our village. He has also been granted a seat on our council."

There are many nods of affirmation, but the grumbles

among some of the trolls are not lost on me. There are those who think I have risen too quickly within the tribe.

"The recent event with the mana-infused wyrms has granted us an opportunity if we are bold enough to take on the challenge. These wyrms, while already strong and powerful, are ripe for bonding if we manage to locate them and subdue them to our will. You all know the power of a full-grown wyrm. Imagine if we had several to protect our village.

"Chod and his companion have volunteered to lead a party out into the world to search for these wyrms so that we may bond them to our cause. I have authorized three females to go. It will be dangerous and there is the very real possibility you may not return, but it is a cause that I find worthy. Now, who among you will join Chod on this quest?"

Silence.

Not a single person volunteers. Whether it is because of how dangerous it is for a troll to leave the forest or because it's me who is leading the expedition, I don't know, but I had at least hoped for three volunteers.

The silence hangs in the air for far too long until Limery pokes me in the back.

"What?" I ask.

He points to the pulpit. "Talks to them. Makes them believe in Chods."

Whispers begin to snake through the crowd. If I can't convince three of them to follow me, then what the hell am I doing here? I might as well be out there alone, being the loner I always have been. If only I had some mole soup right about now. I've never had a problem tearing people down with words, but now, I need to lift them up.

Chief Rizza moves to the side, allowing me to take center stage on the pulpit. Hundreds of eyes, some angry and others ambivalent look back at me. Most of them are probably content to stay in the village and live their lives. With the ley line restored, what do they have to lose by staying?

I've never been one for public speaking, avoiding it at all cost. Streaming was different—no matter how big the audience, it was always just me. Every person watching was nothing more than a number on a screen. I take a deep breath, searching deep inside for something to help me convince these living and breathing pieces of data that I'm worth following into possible death.

"I know you don't know me that well. To many of you, I'm just an outsider who has come into your village and stirred up trouble. To others, I'm nothing more than a tool to help accomplish your objectives, someone who can be sent on foolhardy missions because death doesn't come for me as it does for you. The truth, though, is that I am one of you. I may not have been born here and my skin might not be as green as it once was, but I've been on the outside looking in for my entire life. All I ever wanted was for someone to notice me. I've hidden away for most of my life, just like you. Now, we have that chance to change that. We have the opportunity to make sure the entire island remembers the trolls. If we capture these wyrms and bond them to our cause, we can forge a path for greatness and annihilate anyone who stands in our way. I say the days of hiding away and hoping no one stumbles upon the village are over. We aren't just another monster to be beaten. We are trolls, and we are mighty!"

Congratulations! You have unlocked the skill 'Public Speak-

ing.' You are now a level 1 Orator (Novice). Increase your skill and learn advanced techniques for public speaking by finding an advanced orator (Apprentice or above). Ranks: Novice, Apprentice, Journeyman, Expert, Artisan, Master, Grandmaster.

By the time I finish my speech, I'm ready to tear down the whole fucking forest and siege our way across the island, taking town after town until it's the Isle of Trolls. My blood is pumping, and I'm ready to rumble, but when I look out over the crowd, I see I didn't have the same effect on them. No one is cheering. There's no pounding of chests or thumping fists in the air, only silence.

Long bouts of silence.

If no one volunteers, the mission is off.

There's movement in the crowd and Ismora, the scarred female who trains the children, steps to the front.

"I'll go. I've been aching for a good fight."

Tormara joins by her side, her red braid falling down one shoulder. I've already witnessed the damage she can inflict on a battlefield.

"What the hell, the kid has spunk. I'm in." She actually flashes me a smile for once. "Screw this up, and I'll kill you myself."

For a long moment, no one else volunteers, until Tormara shouts at the crowd.

"Come on! I thought you were braver than this. I remember stories of when the trolls were feared above all others on the island. When we adventured and roamed and battled man and beast alike. Chod is offering us our lives back. A chance to be the warrior tribe that our ancestors were. Will no one answer the call?"

Whispers turn to mumbles until eventually the entire

crowd is talking. Women step forward, and the men cheer them on. The ground begins to quake as feet stomp, chests pound, and a roaring chant fills the air.

Damn, Tormara is good.

I practically have my pick of anyone in the village to take with me, but since Ismora and Tormara volunteered when no one else would, they are my first choice.

"Who else should we take?" I ask.

My two new companions look out over the crowd. Ismora whispers something in Tormara's ear and she nods.

"Yashi."

I have no idea who that is.

"Yashi," I yell above the chaos and the roar dulls.

The crowd parts along the middle and I search for Yashi. It's not until she reaches the front that I am able to fully see her. She's small for a troll, even by female standards, and can't be taller than five feet. Her body is composed of nothing but lean muscle, like a young gymnast. Her black hair is split into two braids that flow over each shoulder and two tusks frame an almost innocent-looking face.

"She's not the biggest, but she is sneaky and fast," says Tormara. "We may need her skills."

"Very well. Welcome to the team, Yashi."

She nods and takes her place beside the others.

Chief Rizza steps up beside me and once again the crowd quiets. The respect they have for her is astounding. It makes me wonder how she was able to come into such a position of power.

"There you have it. The future of our tribe rests in the fate of these five individuals. I pray that—"

"Wait!" a booming voice cuts through Chief Rizza's speech. "Wait!" A giant green body pushes people aside as he makes his way to the front, his giant metal nose ring bobbing with each step.

"I want to go," demands Gord, his broken yellow tusk accentuating his snarl. "The others can keep watch without me."

The chief doesn't speak for a moment. "I'm sorry, Gord, but that is not my decision to make."

He stares into my eyes, but he doesn't speak. I've never noticed that his eyes were so green, like a moss-covered tree.

Gord's an asshole, there is no denying that, but he loves this village like no one else, save the chief. Letting him join us could either be a great advantage or a total mistake.

Fuck it, at least it'll be interesting.

"Let him come."

CHAPTER TWENTY-FOUR

24. Empty the Chest

My merry band of trolls and I meet inside of Jira's hut along with the chief to gather our supplies before setting off in search of adventure. Chief Rizza's wyrm waits outside, a blue-eyed sentry. The smell of incense inside is once again overwhelming. Limery sits quietly on my shoulder and Gord broods silently in the corner while Tomara, Ismora, and Yashi talk in excited voices about what's to come. They've been to the edge of the forest and looked out into the world, but none of them have ever set foot outside of the forest since they were born.

Time is of the essence, so we need to grab our supplies and get a move on as soon as possible.

"As far as weapons go, we need to play to our strengths, but we also need to build a decent team composition," I say.

"Meaning what exactly?" asks Ismora. She's a great fighter, but I don't feel that the trolls have ever been one for tactics.

"Meaning all of you shouldn't be swinging clubs. We need some ranged attack. Variation means that one obstacle doesn't shut us all down. Since Gord and I have the most Constitution, we'll be the frontline."

Gord snorts at my suggestion. He doesn't like the idea of me telling him what to do, but it was part of the agreement allowing him to go, so he better get used to it. This is my party and what I say goes.

"Daggers are my specialty, but I'm also decent with throwing knives." Tormara takes a stone dagger from her belt and spins it around her finger.

"I can use a bow." Yashi pulls at one of her black braids and runs her sharp fingernail through the tip. "We have taken several from the humans over the years. They're too small for most trolls, but they're just my size."

"Perfect. What about you, Ismora? What weapons can you use?" Being the one who teaches the trolls to fight, I'm interested in what she brings to the table.

"As you can see…" She displays her scarred arms. "I'm not one to shy away from battle. I am skilled with most melee weapons, but my greatest strength is hand-to-hand combat."

I think we can make this work. "What about other skills?"

"I am quite adept at gathering and potion-making." Yashi still twiddles her braid. "My mother taught me when I was young."

"And I'm a high-level mana-infuser, though I am not

sure how useful it will be once we leave the forest," says Tormara.

Neither Gord nor Ismora respond, so it looks like that is what we are working with for the moment.

Jira opens the chest from where he pulled Peacemaker before my journey to the wyrm.

"Chod, your time with Peacemaker has come to an end. It served you well on your quest, but there is another who is worthy now. Remove your magic stone please."

I take out the mana stone and hand the axe to Jira. I knew I wouldn't have it forever, but I was really getting used to having it by my side. I guess it is back to swinging a club until I find something better.

The double-edged battle axe glitters in his hand. Through all the muck and battles, not once did it ever lose its luster. Perhaps one day, I will find some dwarven-made weapons once again.

"Gord." Chief Rizza takes the axe from Jira. "You have been a watchful guardian of the forest for many years. Your loyalty has never been questioned, and therefore, I believe there is no one better to carry our most revered relic of days past. I present you with Peacemaker. May it serve you well."

There's a glitter in Gord's eyes that I have never seen before. He clears his throat and stands taller than before. "Thank you." His voice thunders.

"But that is not all." She moves closer to the chest. "There are a handful of weapons that have been passed down through our people for many years. We have not dared to bring them into the open, for fear of them being lost in battle when so few still remain. However, I feel now is the time to empty our troves and bet everything on ourselves. Jira, if you will."

He reaches into the polished trunk and pulls out a wondrous shield. The trunk must be enchanted, because there is no way that shield should have fit inside. It's made of black steel with a ram's head engraved in the front.

Item. Shield of the Ram. +5 Constitution. Capable of blocking one attack and reflecting damage back to attacker. Cooldown: 60 seconds. *Forged in high altitudes by the Mountain Dwarves, this shield is lightweight, yet unyielding.*

Gord takes the shield and straps it to his arm. It protects the majority of his body and looks like it would weigh several hundred pounds.

Next, Jira pulls out a folded leather pouch and places it on the ground. Untying the leather belt that secures it, he unfolds it, displaying five glittery silver daggers.

Item. Daggers of Light. +3 Dexterity. +3 Strength. Double damage against dark-aligned monsters. Bonus: Cleanse. Removes all debuffs. Cooldown: 5 minutes.

He lifts a dagger and places it in Tormara's hand. She spins it around her finger, feeling its weight before nodding in approval. Those daggers will be much more durable than the stone ones she currently uses.

Over the next few minutes, we are gifted with an array of weapons, clothing, and jewelry meant to make our journey easier.

Yashi receives Arrows of Truth, increasing her Dexterity and accuracy with the bow, as well as a Blighted Quiver, which infects each arrow with poison.

Ismora is gifted with Boots of Swiftness and Warrior Gauntlets, increasing both her movement speed and strength.

Several small rings go to Limery, boosting his Intellect and Wisdom and no doubt making him even more deadly.

Everything we are gifted goes to my companions. They are the ones who risk true death, so I'll do my best to keep them alive by taking as little as possible.

It hits me hard when I realize how easy all of this would be if we had the opportunity to walk into town and buy weapons or armor from a smith. Instead, everything the trolls have was either taken in battle or passed down from ages ago. No one would ever pick to play a troll after finding that out, no matter how great the physical benefits. The difficulty in competing against other players who have access to everything from the start, I wouldn't be surprised if they came into this world with a small amount of gold already in their pockets.

"We have one final gift," says Chief Rizza. "Chod, you have proven yourself an asset to the village in the short time you have been here. For so long, Jira has been the only magic wielder in our village. I was not sure if we would ever find someone worthy of this next item. Now, it is yours."

Jira pulls a rust-colored staff from the chest and then closes the lid with a thud. The staff looks like a gnarled branch, but it gleams like polished stone. Three sockets run down its side, the same as Peacemaker.

Item. Petrified Staff. An enchanted staff capable of taking on the properties of up to 3 attached stones. +3 Intelligence. +3 Wisdom. Bonus: *While holding Petrified Staff, the user can cast ranged physical attacks once every 10 seconds.*

I take the staff and it feels natural in my hand. The gnarled head will be strong enough for blunt attacks and the ability to cast a ranged attack every ten seconds means

I can stand back while raising horrors and still do damage.

These new items have me feeling better about our chances already. That is until a notification flashes before my eyes.

Regional Event Alert! *Percy McDonnell has slain a mana-infused wyrm. 16/20 remaining. 15 days remaining.*

CHAPTER TWENTY-FIVE

25. Knowledge is Power

After receiving the notification of another slain wyrm, it feels like we're racing against the clock. Fifteen wyrms remain in the wild, and there are at least twenty-four other players after them, not to mention NPCs. The entire reason these criminals are in here is to play the hero, to vanquish monsters and claim loot using their violent tendencies for good. We just happen to be the ones they consider monsters.

Our work is definitely cut out for us, but we have something they don't.

The map of ley lines.

I superimpose the magical map the chief gave me over the map of towns and landmarks and it paints a pretty good picture of where we need to look.

There are a total of thirteen human settlements across

the island as well as two castles, one on the southern tip and one on the northern tip. A mountain pass separates the island in the middle. Curiously enough, the ley lines bypass every single settlement on the map, aside from the northern castle. It's like the humans have no idea that there is a hotbed of magical activity underneath the surface.

This is good for us because it means we can stay away from humans as much as possible while we try to complete our goal.

The dungeons are hidden from the main map, but based on the way the magical veins converge in certain areas, I think we have a good shot at finding them. The faerie dungeon was right on top of a cluster of ley lines. Limery's cave was over a small vein. He is the only one who might be of any help in locating the dungeons since he alone has knowledge of the world outside the forest.

It's time to follow the map and see what comes of it.

We go south this time around. The original location of the eggs was northwest in the forest, and I don't think it's likely the wyrms went north into the mountain because of where we found the first two. Chief Rizza's managed to find the forest rather quickly as well. There are more magical spots closer together in the south, so it should be easier to hit those first if we go south. If we manage to bind three wyrms, then we can save time by regrouping at the village on our way north.

It takes a little longer for us to reach the southernmost part of the forest and by the time we do, it is already dusk.

"Let us go ahead and camp under the safety of the forest tonight and we can leave first thing in the morning," I say.

No one complains, not even Gord. They must all be incredibly anxious, whether or not they want to admit it. They might be seven feet tall and full of rippled muscle and destruction, but right now, they're kids about to go to their first day of kindergarten.

I'm lost in thought when Yashi approaches.

"Would you like to accompany me to gather herbs? There are certain varieties that only bloom at night and they may aid me in potions for our journey. I would be glad to teach you." There's a twinkle in the small troll's eye when she says it.

"Yeah, that sounds good." I'd like to add more skills to my repertoire anyways and herb-gathering could be particularly useful.

I tell the others we'll be gone for a bit and follow Yashi to the edge of the forest. The sun dips below the horizon and the edge of the forest takes on a silver hue, bathed in moonlight. The hoot of owls is calming and somewhere deep within the forest, howls sing across the night.

Yashi bends down next to a large oak and runs her green fingers along its mossy bark. The moss shimmers under the moonlight.

"Snowy moss," she says, using her claw-like nail to cut the moss from the bark. Even in the moonlight, I can see how it gets its name. The moss has snow-white tips. "It's used in perception potions. They will allow us to boost our Wisdom and see things we might normally miss. Now, you try."

I extend my finger and run my claw underneath the moss. It peels it away from the bark like a sticker on a glass bottle.

Congratulations! You have unlocked the skill 'Herbalism.' You are now a level 1 Herbalist (Novice). Increase your skill and learn advanced techniques for herbalism by finding an advanced herbalist (Apprentice or above). Ranks: Novice, Apprentice, Journeyman, Expert, Artisan, Master, Grandmaster.

Suddenly, I'm able to spot snowy moss all along the forest's edge. A faint green outline appears around it, almost like a notification. Yashi notices my reaction.

"The more herbs you learn, your ability to locate them will improve. Now, gather as much as you can so we may return to the others."

We spend the next twenty minutes cutting moss from the trees until we have a sizable amount and return to our camp, where Gord is roasting some sort of meat over an open flame.

"Do you think it is safe to have a fire blazing at night?" I ask.

"No humans for miles." He turns his back on me, returning to his roast.

"He's right." Tormara leans against a tree, sharpening her new daggers. "We should be safe."

I don't argue, but instead join Yashi as she pulls several clay pots from her bag and places them on the ground next to a mortar and pestle. Some of the pots are filled with a red liquid that looks like blood.

"Your snowy moss, please."

I take it from my satchel and hand it to her. She rips a piece off and places it in the mortar, using the pestle to grind it to a fine pulp. Once the moss is ground up, she pours in some of the red liquid and continues until it forms a dark pink paste. Then she adds more, this time stirring until it becomes a milky-pink liquid and I can finally analyze it.

***Item. Perception Potion.** +2 Wisdom. This potion heightens awareness of details and that which might normally go unnoticed. Duration: 2 hours.*

Yashi empties the contents into an empty pot and passes the mortar and pestle to me.

"Now, you."

The moss rips easily in my hands as I take a small amount and place it in the mortar. I follow Yashi's steps exactly until it is time to add the liquid.

"What is this?" I ask, carefully pouring it into the bowl.

"Jackal's blood."

That's when I remember the jackal that spotted me on my first day in the game. It had known I was there even though I used Camouflage. It makes me wonder what other potions are possible in this world. What could we make using the toxic slime from the wyrms?

After mixing in the blood, I'm greeted with notifications.

You have created Perception Potion. Item. +2 Wisdom. This potion heightens awareness of details and that which might normally go unnoticed. Duration: 2 hours.

Congratulations! You have unlocked the skill 'Potion-Making.' You are now a level 1 Apothecary (Novice). Increase your skill and learn advanced techniques for potion-making by finding an advanced Apothecary (Apprentice or above). Ranks: Novice, Apprentice, Journeyman, Expert, Artisan, Master, Grandmaster.

Sweet, if I keep hanging out with Yashi, there's no telling how much I'll learn by the end of this trip.

Once we mix the entirety of our snowy moss, we all

join around the fire to eat. The meat is juicy and fatty as we devour it with gusto. Limery's sharp teeth rip through the meat like an imp possessed.

After dinner, we all lay down for the night. Limery curls up against my arms, using my Camouflage to conceal him from whatever may pass by in the night.

I'm awakened by Limery's tiny hands shaking me and two pointy red ears bouncing in and out of my vision, an event I've grown accustomed to.

"Get up, Chods. It's times to goes." He's like a needy younger brother waking up his sibling for Saturday morning cartoons. His bulbous yellow eyes radiate excitement.

Everyone else is already packed by the time I wipe the sleep from my eyes, even though the sun is just now breaking the horizon. They must be anxious to get off to an early start. I am, too. Once we find our first dungeon, I'm sure everyone will relax a little, but for now, the anticipation is like another member of our party.

"Morning," I say.

Tormara cleans underneath her claws with her new daggers as she leans against an oak. Gord faces the rising sun with his massive shield strapped across his back. The eyes of the engraved ram's head seem to stare at me ominously.

Yashi and Ismora talk quietly together, but when they notice I am up, Yashi runs over to me.

"We're excited to get started." She looks up at me. "I've been thinking, in order to save our perception potions, we should only take them when we are close to where we suspect a dungeon to be. That way we don't waste it out in the open."

"That's a good idea." If snowy moss is uncommon outside of the forest, then it might be a while before we find any more.

Ismora walks up beside her. "I would like to scout ahead if possible. My Boots of Swiftness will allow me to travel faster, and I can spot any trouble that may threaten our passage."

They all have the same map that the chief gave me, so there's no worry of her not knowing where we are going. It would be so much easier if we had party chat and she could just tell us what was ahead. Instead, we'll have to do it the old-fashioned way.

"Go ahead. If you see any danger, return to us at once." Ismora is a seasoned warrior and I trust her judgment.

Ismora is almost to the forest's edge when Limery calls out to her.

"Waits!"

She stops and turns to the imp with a curious expression. He flies over to where she is and scrounges through his small pack, pulling out a small sphere made of clay. A short piece of string hangs from it.

"Limery, is that a bomb?" I ask.

"Noes. If they's is trouble, lights this and we finds you." He hands the item to Ismora and she looks it over.

Item. Signal Flare. *10 seconds after activating, a beam of light will explode into the sky.*

"Sorry, little one, but we do not carry fire like you." She attempts to hand the flare back to Limery, but he has his fingers to his chin, deep in thought.

"It's okay. Don't needs fire. Just pulls the string and

throws it." He flashes a toothy grin and flutters through the air to Ismora's shoulder. "I goes with you. It's okays, right, Chods?"

"Okay, buddy, you lead the way."

Ismora and Limery take off ahead of us, the troll in a dead sprint and the imp flying close behind her. The boots give her noticeable movement speed, but I wonder if my natural boosts to Strength and Dexterity put me at much of a disadvantage. Either way, we will conserve our stamina for our first dungeon.

"Do you really think you'll be able to control the wyrms when they are fully grown?" I ask Tormara as we walk.

It's something that has concerned me since we left. The wyrm seemed well-behaved in the village, but what happens when it's digging tunnels big enough for us to walk through?

Gord rolls his eyes, but he says nothing.

"You don't understand, do you?" She spins a dagger around her finger, its glittery metal sparkling in the sun. "When we bond with a creature, our wishes and desires merge. The bonded creature becomes part of the tribe and would never do anything to hurt us."

Never say never. "I guess that after seeing the mother wyrm in the forest, I have a hard time believing that. I mean, it was so big and powerful that I don't see how anyone could control it."

"One day, you will see."

As we journey south, we pass through wooded areas populated sparsely with trees and bushes. Yashi identifies several new plants for me, such as demon tea leaf, brown creeper, witch's mint, and bloodfennel, and before long, my herbalism skill is at level two. At level five, I will graduate from novice to apprentice.

Midday comes and goes until we aren't more than a few miles from a large batch of congested magical veins. Ismora and Limery return, informing us that the terrain is about to change, and we all down our perception potions. Immediately, I notice a difference, particularly with my herbalism skill. The outline of the plants I can identify glow from further away, even some that are hidden between other plants where only a fraction of it is visible.

The area where the veins converge is full of rolling hills and scattered boulders. Gnarly trees reach out with branches that grasp like fingers at the sky.

We spread out and scan the area, searching for anything out of the ordinary. I cast my horrors, instructing them to move out and scour the area. Before long, our group looks like a search party combing the woods in a horror movie. My HP and Strength are boosted by the forty horrors that roam the hills like ants.

"Over here," Gord's deep voice rumbles.

I find him standing next to a stone entrance carved into one of the hills. The door is closed, and two gnarled trees extend from the top of the hill, their branches blocking the entrance.

Underground Dungeon. *Would you like to enter?*

I accept and wait for the branches to move out of the way.

Underground Dungeon is not currently available. Occupied.

CHAPTER TWENTY-SIX

26. Tales of Old

"Occupied? Someone is inside?" asks Tormara.

Gord tries to smash the gnarled branches that block the entrance to the dungeon with his axe, but they don't give. The magic that powers the dungeon must be protecting them.

"Looks that way." I hadn't expected to encounter other players so soon. Thinking on it now, they have been here for an entire month before me, why wouldn't they have spread out to explore the island? With so many human settlements, it was stupid of me to think they were all in the two nearest the forest.

"What do we do?" asks Ismora. Her warrior gauntlets clink together when she touches them.

"Well, either we stay and wait, hoping they fail the

dungeon and it opens up for us, or we try to get a head start to the next magical area."

Two of my horrors die off in a puff of smoke and I cast two more to take their place. The blue impish horror and the fat furry orange one join their siblings on a nearby hill.

Regional Event Alert! *Jude Duggan and Michael Didato have slain a mana-infused wyrm. 15/20 remaining. 14 days remaining.*

"You have got to be kidding me," I mumble under my breath, knowing everyone else just received the same notification. Whoever is in that dungeon just killed a wyrm. "Everyone, take positions behind the hills. We don't have time for anything else."

We scatter to both sides of the narrow valley that leads into the dungeon. Yashi and Limery join me on one side, and Gord, Ismora, and Tormara take the other. For a long moment, all that can be heard are the soft grumbles of my horrors as they huddle together.

There's a twist of a knob and the door to the dungeon opens. A group of four exits. They are laughing and cajoling one another even though they are covered in blood and gore. The branches rise, allowing the group to pass, then cross together once more.

Two of the men are the players who killed the dragon. Their stats display in my vision.

Jude Duggan
  Level 14
  Fighter
  Human

Michael Didato
  Level 14
  Paladin
  Human

Jude is broad shouldered with an unkempt beard and shaggy brown hair. He wears a brown boiled leather vest while carrying a small round shield and a shortsword. Several knives hang from his belt and a couple of glittering rings adorn his fingers, but there doesn't appear to be anything remarkable about him. Michael, on the other hand, is clad in massive blue and silver armor with a billowing cape that flows to the ground. The armor swallows him whole and might actually fit me if I put it on. He carries a broadsword at least four feet long. His shield is nearly as big as Gord's and is emblazoned with a white raven on a blue background. He screams heavenly power as his golden hair blows in the breeze, and somehow, he is the only one not drenched in blood. He must have the holy dry clean service on speed dial. The other two are level ten foot soldiers wearing the same blue and silver as the paladin, small white ravens adorning their chest pieces. One carries a spear and shield and the other wields a crossbow.

"Sorry about your friend," says Michael the Paladin. He places his hand on the spearman's shoulder. "He fought valiantly and will be reveled in the next life."

"Price of doing business," says Jude the Fighter.

The two soldiers nod.

"Glad to be of service," one says.

"The king will be glad to know Timothy died for the cause," says the other.

Gord's head rises from behind the hill across from us and I suddenly remember they don't understand what these men are saying. Limery and I are the only two with the communication stones.

A wild fury burns in Gord's eyes when we make eye contact, but I shake my head. We're not that far out-leveled by these guys, but we don't need to rush into a fight if we don't have to. Let's just stay put for the moment.

"Where to now?" asks Jude.

"Do you think we should head back to the castle and try to round up a few more men for the next one? I hear that the Paltras Ruins are tougher than this dungeon. We might need the extra manpower. It would be smart to deposit these items as well."

Several more of my horrors have vanished while we hide, but I don't want to risk giving away our location, so I don't cast anymore.

"Paltras Ruins? Is that the old castle by the sea? The one they say is haunted?" asks Jude.

"Good luck finding men to follow you there," says one of the soldiers. "That place is cursed. They say the dead still roam the halls of the castle."

"Ha." Jude smacks the soldier on the back, knocking him forward. "The dead don't bother us. Michael here is a paladin, for fuck's sake. What do we have to worry about?"

"Paladin or not, not many men will risk their lives for

Paltras. Not after what happened," the other soldier chimes in.

"What happened?" asks Michael.

They all stop and listen to the soldier while he recounts his story.

"Trolls. It was many ages ago, back when there were four kingdoms on the island. The humans divided the south between Paltras and Vanaria, up north, the dwarves presided over Seascape, and the trolls ruled over all the forest, mountain, and desert between the humans and dwarves."

"The entire thing? I thought there were barely any trolls left?" asked Jude, suddenly serious.

"Now, yes, but back then, trolls were the most populous race on the island. They had access to magic the others did not. While only some of the humans and dwarves possessed the power to use magic, the trolls were able to control it directly, as long as they had access to its source."

"So what happened?" Michael moves in closer.

"What always happens. The trolls got greedy. They wanted more and they attacked Paltras. It's said that they rode in on the backs of giant wyrms and dragons, burning the city alive and tearing down its walls. The male trolls went into violent rages, their skins so hot that swords melted when they touched them. It was a massacre."

"That's insane. How were they defeated?"

"Once word of Paltras's fall reached the other two kingdoms, they formed an alliance out of fear that what was happening to Paltras would happen to them. No kingdom alone could stand against the trolls, but perhaps together, they would have a chance. Before the trolls knew what was happening, the women and children that had been left behind in the forest were slain and put on display around its edges as a message. When the troll army returned home, many of the trolls went mad upon seeing them. It's said that the troll king surrendered his army that day, his desire to fight completely gone. They had nothing left to fight for with their offspring dead. You see, they care more about family than most of us in their own twisted way. Take away what they fight for and they crumble like dirt. With no clear direction, the troll kingdom fell apart into what it is today."

"Haha," Jude bellows. "Ghost stories…that's all it is. I'm not gonna say no to fortune and fame because of a few old wives' tales. Not when I've got my man Michael here. When we get back, tell your friends that they have nothing to worry about, okay?"

The two soldiers respond with nervous laughter before following the men away from the small valley between our two hills.

When they are far enough away, I stand and motion for the others.

They gather around me, but I can't stop thinking about the story the soldier told. I finally find out why the trolls are so hated, and it's for a reason that's intrinsically human. Greed. In my time with the trolls, I never would have thought them a greedy race, but yet they wanted to expand their empire just like everyone else. They paid the price for it. A price the trolls are still paying to this day.

"What did they say?" Gord thunders as he looks in the direction the men left in. I can tell he is aching for a fight.

"They were talking about the battle at Paltras," I say. "Is it true?"

Tormara responds, her red braid whipping through the air like a snake. "That they murdered our children and women in cold blood while our ancestors fought to save the princess who had been kidnapped? Yes, it is true," she snaps.

"Wait, what? They said that the troll kingdom was expanding, that they tried to take over the castle out of greed."

All four trolls roar at the same time, snarls on their faces. The roar of frustration is so intense that I can't make any sense of what they are saying.

"One at a time!" I cut them off, and they stare at me in silence. "Will one of you please tell me what happened?"

"I will." Tormara takes a deep breath, letting some of the anger subside. "In ancient times, the troll kingdom was the strongest on the island. Our queen governed and our king led our warriors in battle and adventure. We had the respect of the dwarves in the north and the humans in the south. As we grew more powerful, resentment began to build among the humans. The dwarves were not worried, content to build and mine in their mountainous fortress, but the minds of men are weak and grow troubled when they are not in control. On many envoys, they asked how we were able to control magic simply by touching it, for they had tried and many had died. When we told them that it was simply our way, they refused to believe, certain that we were hiding a powerful secret from them.

"One day, they sent spies into the troll kingdom and stole away the king and queen's daughter, believing that the princess had answers that could be coaxed out of her. And if not her, then certainly the royal family would tell all they knew to get their daughter back. When the queen found out, she ordered the king to gather all of our forces and march on Paltras. He was ordered to tear their kingdom to the ground if the princess was not returned. When the king arrived at their gates, Paltras refused to return the princess. Their human king had gone mad and no rational argument could be made to convince him to let her go. He said that if we would not give him our secrets, then he would kill the princess.

"Our king tried to talk to him, but there was no reasoning to be had. When we had no secrets to give, the princess was burned alive." Fires burn in the eyes the other trolls, angry for a crime none of them were alive to witness. "In a fit of rage, our king attacked the castle, killing everyone inside. When he returned to the forest, the bodies of children and women lined its edges, his queen among them. Many trolls killed themselves in that moment, certain that our race was doomed and unwilling to live a life without their loved ones. On that day, the troll kingdom crumbled. With the majority of our women dead, our population grew smaller and smaller each year, until we split off into the tribes you know today. We were once a mighty and proud kingdom, but now we hide in the shadows."

A solemn anger radiates from the four trolls before me, and even Limery seems on edge by the story. The truth is that I am, too. I know it's a game, but the situations, the history, it's all so reminiscent of real life. And when I look at my party standing before me, the hurt and the hatred feel real, too.

The trolls have had one shitty hand right after another. Even when they were the most powerful kingdom on the island, a lack of understanding caused them to be hated and feared for no other reason than the fact that they were different.

Tormara was right. The minds of men are weak.

The creators at Mythos Games think it's okay to put prisoners in a game and use their violent tendencies against a misunderstood people because it will make them seem righteous and good.

Let's see how they feel about it when we fight back.

CHAPTER TWENTY-SEVEN

27. Heaven and Hell

My heart pounds in my ears as we run through the hills. With each lumbering step, the power that flows through my body makes itself known. Trolls are something special, and I'll be damned if I'm just going to sit back and watch while their society slowly erodes and their people, no, my people, fade away. For once, Gord and I are on the same page. We hunger for reckoning. Our plan is to ambush the group that just left the dungeon, take their items, and make it to Paltras Ruins before they have time to replace their armor and supplies. They'll also lose a level upon dying, setting them even further behind. After that, I'll talk with the council and we'll make a plan for what comes next.

If they want to make us the villains, then it's high time we acted the role.

Ismora runs ahead of us, her Boots of Swiftness proving useful as she scouts for the group. She comes to a stop and raises a fist, letting us know she found them.

"Does everyone know their roles?" I ask when we all gather. Less than a hundred yards away, the group walks, oblivious to our impending attack.

They nod in affirmation and then we break into our positions. The terrain is jagged and rocky, rolling hills splotched with bushes, and small trees offer just enough concealment for us to attempt an ambush. Gord, Tormara, Ismora, and I, along with my army of horrors, descend upon the group from behind while Yashi and Limery flank them from the sides. Their objective is to cause as much chaos as possible so that we can attack them without being noticed.

As we approach, our footsteps sound like a herd of buffalo. If Yashi and Limery don't draw their attention soon, then there is no way they won't hear us coming.

The flick of a bowstring lets me know the battle is on. Yashi's poisoned arrow soars through the air, penetrating the neck of the footsoldier carrying the spear. He staggers back and forth for a moment before pulling the arrow from his neck. Blood sprays from the wound in an arc. She scored a critical hit! That'll be one less opponent to worry about. Each spurt of blood grows weaker and I'm certain the soldier is about to die, until a stream of holy light shines upon him and the wound closes.

Yashi fires off another arrow, but this time, the men are prepared. The paladin rushes forward, blocking the arrow with his shield. He yells something and then a white aura surrounds all four men.

A fireball soars across the battlefield, striking the

fighter in the back. He falls forward, losing a sizable chunk of health, the back of his boiled leather armor scorched black. The two foot soldiers make to escape, but a fiery wall erupts in front of them as Limery zooms overhead. He taunts them, calling the men 'filthy humanses and dirty scoundrelses,' all the while peppering them with fireballs the size of softballs. A crossbow clanks and a bolt narrowly misses his giant head, forcing him to retreat further into the air.

In that moment, the fighter rises to his feet and sees us coming. The look he gives us is one of pure hatred. As he raises his sword to attack, a wicked grin creeps across his face. This is a man who loves to fight.

"Gather up," he shouts to the two soldiers and they prepare for our onslaught. "Cedric, take out the bitch up on the hill. The rest of you, follow me. Michael, cast an aura of protection overhead to ward off the fireballs for now."

The paladin raises his sword and a silverish barrier, almost like glass, appears overhead, repelling Limery's fireballs as if they were nothing.

We charge at the three men, the soldier with the crossbow having fallen back to target Yashi.

"Gord, take the lead. I'll be right behind you. Ismora and Tormara, if you see an opening, then make them bleed."

Gord runs straight ahead, using his shield as a battering ram. He collides with the paladin, knocking him aside and into the spearman. The fighter jumps to the side and does a barrel roll, springing back to his feet. He raises his sword to attack Gord's blind side, but I use Petrified Staff's bonus ability to fire a stream of physical energy that hits him square in the chest, knocking him off balance and causing him to miss.

A wave of ten horrors scurries on the group, slowing them and attacking with their razor-sharp claws and teeth. The paladin raises his sword in the air and a beam of holy light tears through the horrors, sending them up in a puff of smoke.

The foot soldier hacks and slashes against the horrors, giving as good as he gets, but his health depletes with each hit he takes until the paladin washes him with holy light, replenishing lost health. Out of the edge of my eye, the soldier with the crossbow makes his way towards the hill where Yashi continuously fires on the larger party.

Gord and the fighter square off in the rear as my staff cracks against the paladin's shield.

"Trolls! The blight of the earth!" he shouts as his imbued strike slashes through an entire row of horrors. Half of them die, but I immediately cast two more in their place.

Tormara and Ismora pick at the foot soldier who desperately tries to free himself from the horrors surrounding him. The movement speed debuff of Horror of Vitality thwarts his efforts, and the two trolls make short work of the man.

That leaves us five on two while Yashi and the crossbowman play their game of cat and mouse in the distance.

"Ismora, go help Yashi. Tormara, assist Gord. Leave this asshole to me."

The paladin looks up in surprise at the fact he can understand me, momentarily forgetting about the horrors that surround him. It's like he just now looked at my stats for the first time.

"You're a hero? But how?"

"Just lucky, I guess." I shoot him in the chest with a ranged attack from my staff. I cast another horror and use Claw, but he blocks my attack with his shield. My claws grate against the shield, shrieking through the battle.

"No matter, you will die just the same."

Limery continues his attacks from above and eventually, a crack forms in the heavenly barrier overhead as the fighter and paladin move back to back.

With at least twenty horrors still alive, my HP and damage are pretty high. I attempt to move in to use Bite, but a blast of light knocks me back, taking out a chunk of health. I cast Horror of Finesse and my next attack heals me even though the paladin blocks it. He's tough, a great defensive tactician, but our sheer numbers will overwhelm them in the end.

A powerful swing of his sword connects with my ribs and pain flares through my side. I look down to see a massive gash where blood spills down my side.

I retreat as my regeneration takes effect, letting my horrors have the frontline. I need to get back in the fight to use heal, but all I can think about right now is the stinging pain in my side.

A deep yell from beyond the paladin draws my attention and for the first time, I realize the true difference between a hero and NPCs.

Blood streams down Gord's body. His shield drags against the ground. Something is wrong with his arm, keeping him from lifting it. Tormara looks no better, a gash runs along her face and her clothing is drenched red around her midsection. They both look on the verge of exhaustion.

In a blur, the fighter moves from Gord to Tormara, his blade moving quicker than I can see it. The only evidence he attacked at all is the fresh wounds on both of my party members. He pulls a dagger from his waist and throws it at Gord, lodging it in his ribs.

Gord keels over in pain before removing the dagger and tossing it to the ground. He takes another step towards the fighter when a new pain takes over.

"Poison…" He stumbles and almost falls to the ground.

The fighter twists the pommel of his sword in his hand for show. Tormara attacks with a dagger of her own, but the fighter sidesteps it with amazing speed, leaving a shadow in his place. The shadow explodes and the dagger clatters to the ground. A fireball comes hurling towards his head, but he raises his shield at the last moment, absorbing the attack. The shield glows red, but he takes no damage.

He takes a lunging step and a wave of energy erupts from his sword, knocking both Gord and Tormara to the ground. If I don't do something soon, they will both die. A death neither one can come back from.

I leave the paladin to my horrors for now, even though his holy attacks seem to be having a greater effect on them.

At full speed, I slam into the fighter from behind, using Bite and sinking my teeth into his neck for a critical attack. I follow up with Claw and rake his side. There's a grunt of pain just before something stabs into my stomach. I roll to the side and spot a dagger held in a reverse grip in the fighter's hand. He stumbles to his feet, facing me.

"So you're the big bad champion of the trolls? Chod, is

it? We were all wondering who it was that managed to start a regional event. Looks like the higher-ups have a few tricks up their sleeves." He lets out a cold laugh. "I bet Glenn would love to have a crack at you. Too bad I'll be the one popping the cherry."

Tormara slings another dagger and once again, the fighter moves in a blur, leaving a shadowy trail in his wake.

"I've about had enough of you," he says. With a flick of his wrist, another dagger strikes Tormara just above the heart. She grimaces in pain and grasps at her wound, her health nearly depleted.

I feel my bonus HP dropping as the paladin continues his holy war against my horrors. If I don't do something now, I'll lose any advantage I might have.

"Limery, cut him off," I yell, and a wall of flame erupts between the fighter and the trolls.

I use Berserker Rage and my vision reddens at the edge as power and chaos take control of my body. Quickly, I summon two more horrors and feel my HP grow even more. Without wasting any time, I charge the fighter. I feint a swing of my staff, but instead, fire a bolt of physical damage, taking him off guard. He counters with a quick slash of his sword, but my increased health regeneration barely drops from the attack.

"After I kill you, tell your friends that the trolls are done hiding. You can either make room for us in the world, or we will make it ourselves."

He wipes away a drop of blood from his lip and spits blood to the ground.

"You have no idea what you're doing." He smirks. "You have no idea what we're capable of."

I summon a Horror of Vitality right next to him, slowing his movement speed. Limery's fireball engulfs him from behind.

The paladin raises his sword to perhaps cast a heal, but his spell is interrupted by an arrow finding the soft spot in his armor. He falls forward as my horrors dogpile on his body.

I use the moment to cast Intimidation, and the fighter's eyes glaze over for a moment. My staff connects with the side of his head, dropping his health to twenty percent, and I follow up with Bite and Claw. Limery casts a giant fireball that swallows the man whole like a hungry sun. By the time the fireball dissipates, all that remains is the man's armor and weapons.

With the fighter down, I focus my attention back on the paladin. Only glimpses of his armor can be seen beneath the pile of blue and orange miscreants. Gord tries to join me, but I can see the anguish in his face and motion for him to sit. Yashi, Ismora, and I will finish this.

Above the grumbling, gnashing teeth, and claws that grate against the paladin's armor, I hear the sound of singing. It reminds me of the choirs I heard on the few times my family attended church, usually on a holiday. A gentle, warm hum pervades through the chaos and death.

And then, an explosion of light. My health depletes in an instant as every last horror vanishes in the light, taking my entire bonus HP and Strength along with it.

The paladin takes to his feet, still at half-health. He must have just blown his ultimate ability. It reminds me of every cheesy action movie where the hero rises from the ashes. Cue corny dialogue.

"Is that all you've got?" he roars, his blond hair blowing in a breeze only he seems to be standing in.

"Hardly."

Limery lands on my shoulder, and Yashi and Ismora approach from the paladin's rear. Tormara stumbles over, clutching her chest and grimacing.

I quickly cast one of each horror and my health and Strength rise a small amount.

"Why don't we show this asshole what hell feels like?" I say, and in that moment, I know I'm finally one of them.

Everyone, even Tormara, manages to smile.

"Yous funny, Chods," says Limery, a fireball crackling in his palm.

An aura of white light surrounds the paladin and his HP slowly replenishes.

"Now!" I take off into battle as fireballs, arrows, and daggers find their mark. They do little damage against the paladin's stout defenses, but his defenses won't last forever. I'm several yards away from the paladin when I use my staff to pole vault over his body, leaving him swiping at air as I land behind him. Ismora arrives beside me just as I land. She punches him with one of her gauntlets, leaving a dent in his armor at the same time as I kick him like I'm breaking down a door.

His legs curl under as his body flies forward. Yashi's poisoned arrows stack their damage and deplete his health faster than he can regenerate. A holy beam descends from the sky, burning my skin, killing my horrors, and dropping my health by ten percent.

The paladin rises to his feet, his sword and shield bathed in divine enchantments. He tosses his shield aside and runs at me, sword held over his shoulder with both hands.

A massive force smashes into him from the side. Steam rises off Gord's emerald skin, his wounds healing before my eyes. Berserker Rage. Gord hacks at the paladin with otherworldly force, and I'm taken aback by the beauty in the destruction. The paladin raises his hand as if to say something, but with one final chop, Gord separates head from shoulders.

Notifications fill my vision, but I push them away. Ismora and Gord are already gathering weapons and armor and placing them in a pile. The paladin's body has already vanished, but the two foot soldiers remain. They drag the bodies over, and I notice the one with the crossbow has an arrow lodged in his eye.

"You all fought bravely. It was a good fight, but our teamwork could use a little work. It's nothing that fighting side by side won't fix. Yashi, next time you get singled off like that, I want you to retreat to the group. You're more useful fighting alongside us than pulling away a single opponent." She nods. "Gord, what took you so long to go into a rage?"

He tosses the fighter's shield on top of the pile. "For us, we do not choose when the rage happens. It is in our blood," he thunders, but for once, his answer isn't contemptuous.

Once we strip the men of their armor, we have a pretty sizable pile of loot. I pass the rings from the fighter off to Ismora and Tormara. They are an assortment of Strength and Dexterity buffs. I offer Gord the paladin's armor, but he refuses, saying that his skin is the only armor he needs. It's a bit foolish, but movement speed is key for his battle style. Ismora takes the crossbow, and Tormara adds a few more daggers to her collection.

When we have what we want, we wrap the rest of the items up in the looted clothing, forming makeshift bags. If we happen to come across a boar, then maybe I can fashion another leather satchel to help carry the extra items. The paladin's shield is too massive of a burden, so we leave it behind, even though I'm sure it would fetch a good amount if we ever had the opportunity to sell it.

With everything sorted, I pull open my notifications.

Congratulations! You have reached level 13. +1 stat point to distribute. +1 Strength and Constitution racial bonus. +1 ability point to distribute.

Warning! *You have killed a human NPC. If word of this reaches a human settlement, your reputation among humans will be decreased by 100. Stop your enemies from reaching town before it is too late. Current reputation with humans: -1399. (-1000 Racial Penalty)*

Warning! *You have killed a human NPC. If word of this reaches a human settlement, your reputation among humans will be decreased by 100. Stop your enemies from reaching town before it is too late. Current reputation with humans: -1399. (-1000 Racial Penalty)*

Warning! *You have killed another player. Your reputation among humans has been decreased by 100. Current reputation with humans: -1499. (-1000 Racial Penalty)*

Warning! *You have killed another player. Your reputation among humans has been decreased by 100. Current reputation with humans: -1599. (-1000 Racial Penalty)*

Alert! *You have failed to stop your enemies from reaching town. Your reputation has decreased by 200. Current reputation with humans: -1799. (-1000 Racial Penalty)*

Not that I expected anything less. As soon as the players respawned, our reputation was bound to take a hit. It might as well be negative one million at this point. But the good news is that I have another ability point and I can finally unlock my final summoner ability.

Horror of Power. *Summon a horror with 20% of your Strength. Cost: 100 mana. Cooldown: 30 seconds. Bonus: Your next attack deals double damage.*

I summon my new horror and it appears in a puff of smoke. It looks completely different than the other two. While Horror of Finesse is lean and quick, and Horror of Vitality is fuzzy and tanky, Horror of Power is solid muscle. It walks on all fours, wide-stanced like a pit bull with a massive head, sharp teeth, angry red eyes, and tusks that shoot out of its jaw like a warthog. Its fur is golden with a black mane around its head. A barbed tail with four spikes swishes through the air like a mace.

It paces like a lion on the prowl, ready to battle whatever comes its way.

Everyone stares at the horror in admiration. I'm pretty sure I see a fleeting smile cross Gord's face. Our army just got a hell of a lot stronger. As I look around, I notice everyone else leveled up from the battle as well.

I still have three stat points to use from the last few times I leveled up. I elect to put them in Intelligence in the off chance that it helps me with my casting and am surprised when I receive another notification.

New Class Ability (Summoner). Each ability requires one ability point.

Sacrifice. *Sacrifice X amount of horrors to receive a temporary buff. Horror of Power: +1 Strength. Horror of Vitality: +1 Constitution. Horror of Finesse: +1 Dexterity*

Kamikaze. *Sacrifice a horror to deal a burst of damage.*

Holy shit! I don't know why I just assumed that there were only three abilities for being a summoner. It's a magical class, so of course, there are perks to increasing my Intelligence. Probably some for increasing Wisdom too. I can't wait for another ability point so that I can unlock one of these new abilities. All the more reason for us to get a move on.

"Is everyone ready? We are officially in a race to Paltras Ruins."

CHAPTER TWENTY-EIGHT

28. No One Said There Would Be So Much Walking

Congratulations! You are now a level 2 Leatherworker (Novice).

I finish the last stitch using the technique Gord taught me and neatly place the clothing and weapons we looted inside, along with the mana stone the wyrm dropped. Maybe Jira will be able to use it once we return. Mine is much more powerful so there is no need to equip it to my staff.

We have made great progress throughout the day, managing to go the entire day without seeing any humans, so now we can finally settle down for the evening and enjoy the great boar that Ismora shot with her new crossbow. It's twice the size of a normal boar, plenty big enough to feed all six of us.

Gord roasts several giant slabs of meat over a spit that

Limery built, his natural aptitude for building machines benefiting us all. Yashi is off picking herbs for potions. After the battle today, it's more important than ever that we manufacture our own health potions.

"How are you feeling?" I ask Tormara, who is leaning against a tree and sharpening her daggers.

She moves aside her red braid and rubs at a sage-colored scar just above her chest, the only remnant of the brutal wound she suffered earlier.

"I'll be fine. A little sore. My pride was hurt more than anything."

I know that's not true. The fighter would have killed them both if not for my intervention. She and I both know it. The fact that heroes have these special abilities makes such a big difference in battle. The NPCs with magical abilities are the only ones in the same ballpark. It's like taking a knife to a gun-fight for most of them. Sheer numbers can do a lot, but one on one, there's no comparing. Which is all the more reason we need to make it to Paltras Ruins before Jude and Michael have a chance to regroup. If we manage to bond with these wyrms, they will even the playing field for our side more than anything. Well, those and my horrors.

The whole thing seems a little unfair, how I and the other heroes come into this world and level up in days what it takes these people years to do. We unlock abilities most of them can only dream of. I can't imagine what it would be like to witness something like that in the real world.

Real world, ha.

Aside from the mythical creatures and magic, this honestly doesn't feel that different.

By the time Yashi returns, the rest of us have already finished our portions of the boar. The gamey texture of wild meat is something I've grown accustomed to. She carries an armful of thorny brambles and sets them down in front of me.

"Tonight, you are going to learn one of our most ancient potions. It's hell tracking down this particular ingredient, because it grows high in trees and is not often visible from the ground. But with the perception potion we made yesterday combined with my high herbalism skill, I was able to find some. While we are natural healers compared to most, I'd rather not leave our fortune to chance if we find ourselves in a grave battle once again."

"What is this?" I pick up the plant to inspect it.

It resembles a brier, with a long, thick stem covered in thorns. Pink berries the size of grapes blossom from its fuzzy leaves. Each stem is about a foot long.

"It's Horned Thimbleberry. Both the stem and berries have properties that aid in healing. We are going to mix it with the bloodfennel and powdered crow's feet for an even more potent product. When we add the final ingredient, we'll have a rapid healing potion that might just save your life one day."

Or yours, more likely.

Her knowledge of herbalism is astounding. "Yashi, what did you do back in the village? With all the excitement, I never thought to ask." I already know about the others. Ismora trains the children in combat, Tormara holds a seat on the council, and Gord is a guardian, but Yashi is a mystery.

She gives me a smile. "You couldn't guess? I make potions. Not that we have a particular need for them, but every now and then, someone has need of my skills. In the old days, it was said that our potions were widely regarded among both men and dwarves, but times have changed. I know potions to help with sleep, to heighten senses, even to conceal one's scent from animals. It's best to have someone knowledgeable in the art of potion-making and not need them than to be lacking when the time comes. Now, grab your mortar and pestle and get to work."

I do as she says, taking the horned thimbleberry and mashing it until it forms a paste before adding in the bloodfennel, a bright red stalk, and doing the same. Once they are mashed, Yashi pours a little of the powdered crow's feet into the mix. Out of the corner of my eye, I spot Limery and Gord having a conversation. Did today's battle actually soften his hard exterior?

"What's the final ingredient?" I ask.

Tormara pulls one of her daggers from her belt and tosses it towards me, the blade landing in the earth.

"Blood," says Yashi.

"Wait, what?" Nobody said anything about blood magic.

"Blood activates the bloodfennel, which combined with the horned thimbleberry and crow's feet will form the health potion."

"Does every race use blood in their health potions?" I know it's always been red for health potions and blue for mana, but have gamers secretly been drinking blood all these years?

"No, there are other ways, but we are lucky that our blood has such power. It cuts out a lot of ingredients, and the horned thimbleberry is the only one difficult to find. Now, if you are done being squeamish, I'd like to finish these up before the sun rises."

To be so small, Yashi has a lot of sass. She takes the knife and pricks my finger, squeezing several drops of blood into the mortar. The paste steams and bubbles for a moment before turning into a semitransparent liquid.

You have created Health Potion. Restores 10% health over the course of 20 seconds.

That's not bad at all. Then a thought dawns on me.

"Whoa, wait a minute. Whose blood was in the potions I took with me to fight the wyrm?" I ask, but Yashi just rolls her eyes at me.

I level up my potion-making skill as we fill up several clay jars with the potion.

"Why do you keep pricking my fingers?" I ask. "There's five of us. Couldn't someone else help out?" Even with my tough skin and regeneration, the force it takes to draw blood stings just like a real doctor would.

"Because you're the student," she laughs, revealing her small tusks.

When I wake the next morning, a notification crosses my vision.

Regional Event Alert! *Kevin Harris has slain a mana-infused wyrm. 14/20 remaining. 13 days remaining.*

Someone had a late night. Not counting the chief's wyrm, that means thirteen wyrms still remain out in the wild. I'm feeling less confident about finding three wyrms by the day and it's becoming even more important that we reach Paltras Ruins before anyone else. There are plenty of options for leveling up in the countryside, but I aim to reach the ruins by nightfall.

Tormara falls in line beside me as we walk. Far ahead, Ismora is but a small dot on the landscape as she scouts for anything out of the ordinary. Gord pulls up the rear, and Limery flies high overhead.

"What is it that you hope to accomplish with all of this?" she asks.

"What do you mean?" I thought my intentions have been pretty clear.

"Once we have the wyrms, once we are back in the village. What then? What happens to our people?" Her face radiates concern. I've only ever seen Tormara as strong and powerful, spitting fire and challenging others with an iron tongue, but deep down, she cares for her people above all, just like Gord. These trolls are just as complex as any real person.

"Honestly, I don't know. I've only been here a short while, but you all have accepted me as one of your own. Some of you took longer than others. I feel a great connection with this community, and I don't like the way you're constantly shit on by the other races. If everyone wants to stay in the forest and hide out, then that's fine, I won't push the issue. But I'm sure you feel the same as I do, that there is something in our blood that begs for greatness. The greatness the trolls once had."

She gives me a half-smile. "Many will die to attain greatness and our numbers are already low. You know there will be retribution for our attack on the undying ones, right?"

"Yes, but if we get a wyrm before it is killed, then I believe it will be worth it. Once we have them, we can lay low until they are grown."

"They will come looking for us," she counters.

"Will the magic from the forest not keep us hidden?" I ask.

"From most, but you have already seen the power of potions. Those who know where to look can always find us."

"Then we will just have to make sure we are ready."

We carry on in silence for a while. Yashi identifies several new plants as we walk and eventually, my herbalism skill increases again, allowing me to spot the plants I have identified from further away.

At one point, I hear a loud caw and look up to see a falcon diving for Limery. A shimmer appears around his pointy little fingers and there is a sizzle before the bird falls with a thunk to the ground. Gord picks it up and bites off the head.

"What?" he asks as the bones crunch in his mouth.

By late evening, Ismora comes to a stop, and we catch up to her on the top of a high hill. From atop the hill, the coastline is visible and near its edge, Paltras Ruins.

The castle is indeed in ruins, the exterior walls are crumbling in places and vines and other plants have overtaken the castle. Moss covers the stone walls, and trees grow above them in places, evidence no one has been there in years. Several large black birds perch along the parapet. The castle hugs the coastline, only walled on three sides, the keep sitting far back against the rocky cliffside that serves as its own form of defense.

It is still several miles from where we are, but with a little luck, we will make it by nightfall.

"Let's speed it up, team. We can rest once we make it."

By the time darkness falls and the moon casts its silver glow over the ocean, we are within a mile of the castle. The salty air of the coast fills our lungs. Limery perches on my shoulder, and there is a look I haven't seen before in his bulbous yellow eyes.

"This place no goods, Chods. Limmy no likes it one bit."

My eyes fall on the castle and I know what he means. There is something unsettling about the abandoned structure. Deep within its walls, I swear there is a green glow coming from the keep.

"I agree with the little one," Gord thunders. "Something is very wrong with this place."

I'm reminded of our encounter yesterday. The human soldiers were adamant about this place being haunted. Looking at the map, this location is a hotbed for magical activity. Maybe it's more than the average dungeon.

Sounds of the night come alive as we approach. Crickets chirp, owls hoot, and something a little more haunting seems to linger in the chilly air. The hairs on my neck rise the closer we get until finally, we arrive at the entrance to the castle. The portcullis that once kept out intruders lies rusted and broken.

When we step beneath the gateway, we are greeted with a notification.

Paltras Ruins. *Would you like to enter?*

I accept and we walk through the gateway. Limery's claws dig a little deeper into my skin.

There's a loud clank, and I turn to see the portcullis moving of its own accord. It rises from the ground and flies into the gateway, hinging itself in place and blocking our exit.

CHAPTER TWENTY-NINE

29. Paltras Ruins

The portcullis secures itself in the outer gateway, blocking our escape. Our only way out is to go forward. Before us stands a second wall with another gatehouse that bars our way to the courtyard. Everyone holds their weapons at the ready, and Limery clings ever tighter to my shoulder. High above, clouds frame the moon, lighting the sky with eerie shadows.

"Somethings is here, Chods," Limery whispers.

I peer around the decaying castle. Everything is empty and desolate, except for the faint green light that glows from behind the furthest windows of the keep.

"That's where we need to go." I point to the keep.

We step into the gatehouse, where murder holes remain from long ago, though they are now mossed over. I'm sure that this castle was magnificent once, full of life and bustling activity, but now it is nothing more than a skeleton. And more than that, a graveyard. Along the battlements, several of the stone walls are still scorched from the battle long ago. I can only imagine the force it must have taken to wipe this place off the map.

The other trolls seem somewhat in awe as they take the castle in. Sure, they have had battles, but they've never experienced anything like this. To be able to tear down one of the greatest human structures on the island on a whim is not the same as winning a battle in the forest. I'm sure it just reminds them of how far the trolls have fallen.

"Let's find the wyrm and then leave," says Tormara.

Suddenly, there's a flash of silver behind the murder holes and I swear for a moment an arrow is pointed in our direction. As quick as it appears, it is gone.

"Did anyone else see that?" I look deeper into the murder hole, but nothing is there.

"See what?" Ismora faces me, always the first one on alert.

They all look around, but whatever I saw has disappeared. Goosebumps erupt along my arms, and the hair on the back of my neck reaches for the stars. This place is really giving me the creeps.

"Nothing, let's just get through here." Before this turns into a horror movie and we all die.

A cloud passes in front of the moon, and I'm struck with a shooting pain in my shoulder. Yells of anguish ring out around me, and I turn to see a shimmering ethereal arrow protruding from my right shoulder. An angry silver face shouts at me from behind a slat in the wall.

Ghost. *Level 12. The haunting remains of those unable to pass into the next world.*

Limery slings a fireball at the ghost but before it connects, the silver man vanishes once more. I reach to pull out the arrow, but it is no longer there either, only the bloody wound where it had entered.

"They were right. This place is haunted." Blood continues to stream down my arm.

Gord, Tormara, and Ismora all have blood streaming from various spectral injuries.

That's when I notice the courtyard is bathed in the light of the moon once more. It doesn't take a genius to see the connection.

"It's the moonlight. Whenever it disappears, that's when the ghosts come out. Let's get out of this gatehouse before they return and we're sitting ducks."

"Sitting what?" asks Ismora, not understanding the reference.

"Nothing. Before we're dead."

As soon as we are out of the gatehouse, I find the moon. It's a cloudy night and they shuffle across the sky, able to blot out the moon at any point. There's no way to know if there are ghosts everywhere or just outside the castle until we make our way inside.

"Get moving before the clouds come out. We need to make it to the keep."

Before we are even halfway across the courtyard, an army of silver foot soldiers erupts before us. One rushes at me, sword raised, and I use my staff to block its attack, but the blade passes through my weapon and cuts into my skin. I cast a Horror of Finesse and attempt to use heal, but my attack goes straight through his translucent body. The horror wanders around, unable to attack until the ghosts bludgeon it to death.

The strained cries of my teammates surround me as archers fire a volley of spectral arrows down upon us, dropping our health in droves.

"We can't attack. We can't defend," yells Gord. "What the hell are we supposed to do?"

"Take thats!" screams Limery, tossing a fireball at a nearby soldier. When the fireball hits him, the ghost goes up in a puff of smoke. He follows up with another fireball just as I'm hit in the chest with an arrow. I reach to pull the arrow out, but my hands pass through it and then suddenly, it vanishes.

Everyone breathes heavily as they try to patch their wounds as best they can. I continue to cast my horrors. Even if they can't attack, the bonus health might just save my life.

"Yashi, the potions. Pass them out." Her small frame has left her unscathed so far. "Magical attacks are all that work against the ghosts. Limery, we're going to make a run for the keep. If the ghosts appear again, I want you to cast a wall of fire on both sides of our group. It's the only way to keep the ghosts off of us. Can you do that?"

He nods and flies in the air. "Limmy is ons it!"

The rest of the group downs health potions and we take off running towards the keep. The clouds blot out the moon, and once again the courtyard becomes a battlefield. I can't even count how many soldiers surround us before flaming walls rise on both sides of me. The heat is uncomfortable, but it beats the alternative. Arrows sizzle into nothingness as they enter Limery's wall of flame and several ghosts vanish trying to rush through it. Yashi and Ismora race ahead of me, and the entrance to the castle keep comes into view.

The door is closed when we arrive, but with our strength combined, Gord and I are able to force the rusted hinges.

The door shuts with a thud and we all take a moment to gather ourselves.

"That…was intense," says Ismora. Her normally neat ox-horn buns are messy, with strands falling over her pointed ears. Our entire team looks like they just went through hell.

Then I notice a hulking black figure cloaked in darkness on the other side of the room. Several more figures spread out along the first floor of the keep, none of them moving. I rise to my feet, ready to fight, but the cloaked figures stand pat.

Wraith. *Level 13. Although unable to attack while being looked upon, wraiths are deadly to those who pass by unaware. They shroud their victims in darkness, draining the life from them.*

The creature wears a black hood of tattered fabric, obscuring the face that lies underneath in total darkness that even my night vision can't see through. For most races, the inside of the castle would prove foreboding, the lack of light allowing the wraiths to swoop down upon their enemies before they were ever spotted.

We're not that unfortunate.

"We need to get to the glowing door," I say, pointing across the hallway. "Keep your eyes out for wraiths and make sure we are always focused on them. If you turn your back, they will move forward and attack, but if we stay aware, we should be able to pass through without incident. There is rubble all along the floor, so be careful where you step."

A set of staircases on each side of the entrance spiral up to what I imagine are the living quarters and a long, wide hallway extends forward to a set of massive doors where green light emits from underneath. I'm certain it is the throne room and that is where we need to be.

I take the lead, keeping my eyes focused on the wraiths before us. They hover in the air ominously, but aside from the swish of their cloaks, they don't move. Footsteps tell me my party is behind me, but I can't look to confirm.

"Is someone watching the rear?" I ask.

"I am," Gord replies.

"Limery, if any of the wraiths start moving, I want you to let us know."

"Limmy can do it."

We pass by a wraith that towers above us, hovering a dozen feet off the ground. Its tattered clothing sways ominously as we pass, and its cold raspy breath chills me to the bone.

We're a few yards from the door when a firm body plows into my back, knocking me to the floor.

"Oh no, I slipped!" says Tormara as we scramble back to our feet.

I turn my head and a wraith comes to an abrupt halt a foot from my face. Its arms are spread wide, opening the cloak and displaying the infernal darkness that resides within. The emptiness inside threatens to swallow me whole if I will only give in. It's mesmerizing, almost welcoming.

Peace surrounds me as I let the pull take over.

"Chod!" Ismora's hand grasps me on the shoulder, bringing me back to the world. "We're at the door."

I'm lost for a moment as I reacclimate.

"Okay, keep your eyes on the wraith, and when I give the order, we all rush inside."

The handle of the door is ice cold with a small streak of green light escaping through the keyhole. Whatever is on the other side, I pray there is a wyrm with it. My fingers wrap around the cold bronze handle and I pull. The door opens with ease, and we are all bathed in green light.

CHAPTER THIRTY

30. Ghost Stories

We hurry into the room, and the door slams behind us. Immediately, I feel my HP begin to drain. We're all bathed in a neon glow from the other side of the room, and I look up to see a decrepit man sitting on a rusted throne. His body radiates spectral energy, every part of him an opaque neon green. A crown sits lopsided on his head, displaying a wide gash that cuts from ear to nose. The other side of his face is covered in burn marks. An old robe lays curled around his feet.

To his side, three knights, all the same greenish hue, stand watch with their swords displayed in front of them, point down while their hands rest on the hilts. They're not quite ghosts, but also not quite living, caught somewhere in the middle.

King Bartholemy. Specter. *Level 16. A specter is a ghost gone mad. Their very presence depletes the life of anyone around them.*

What Tormara said appears to be true. The king did go mad. He is level sixteen, and the three knights are each level fourteen. He leans one arm against the side of his throne, oblivious or uncaring to our presence.

My HP drops to ninety percent and I notice that everyone else's is doing the same.

"Yashi, we need the health potions. Just being in this room is draining our life!"

"What do we do?" asks Tormara, eyes wide.

"We fight!" Gord thrusts his axe forward, "Instead of standing around and dying."

The king lifts his head, his pupil-less eyes finally noticing us.

"You will all die soon enough." He leans back against the throne. "They always die."

The robe around his feet moves and I realize that it is not a robe at all. Two blue eyes stare at me before falling back to the floor. This wyrm looks nothing like the others. It's deflated and shriveled, like it had the life sucked out of it.

Because it has.

The specter's ability must be constantly draining the wyrms HP while the mana source is enough to keep it barely alive at the king's feet.

"The wyrm," I say. "It's the priority. How do we bond it to one of you?"

Limery's claws dig into my shoulder just before he falls from it. I'm quick enough to catch him before he hits the ground, but his HP is nearly gone.

"Quick, health potions, now!" I shout, and Yashi places one in my hand. I pour it in the tiny imp's mouth and his bulbous eyes open, though he still looks a little dazed. All of the female trolls' health bars are dropping dramatically faster than mine and Gord's. It must be a flat decay and not a percentage. "Keep the potions for you all. Gord and I have higher regen."

I just hope we figure out what to do before we all die. I pass Limery to Yashi and she continues to nurture him back to health.

"There's no point in fighting it." The king stares forward blankly. "You will all die eventually."

He stands up from the throne, leaving the wyrm wrapped around its base, and steps forward. His knights lift their swords and follow him. There is something sinister about the way they walk, like they are puppets on a string.

"If we can keep them distracted, can you bond with the wyrm? He's already at low health."

Tormara and Ismora nod before rushing off to the wyrm.

"Alright, Gord, are you ready to fuck some shit up?"

He gives me a wicked snarl and lets out a roar so powerful it echoes off the walls.

The king unsheathes his own sword, the blade the same spectral green as his body, as we race across the throne room. My horrors follow me, nearly twenty in total, but they seem lost on what to attack. Our health is already over a quarter gone when we reach our opponents.

I fire one of my ranged attacks and it shoots straight through the specter king.

Gord charges two knights with his shield like a battering ram, but he passes through their armored bodies just the same. They turn to slash through him, drawing blood and taking a chunk of Gord's health.

The king slashes at me and I jump to the side, barely avoiding the attack. There's no way for us to fight them as my horrors run back and forth, unable to attack yet dying to the attacks of the king and knights.

"I's better now, Chods." Limery hovers next to me, his leathery wings flapping like sails, holding a fireball in one hand and a potion in the other. He tosses the fireball at the king and it explodes against his disfigured face, dropping his health for the first time. How in the hell are we supposed to defeat them without magic?

"You're the only one who can hurt them," I say. "Gord and I will distract them, but you need to deal the damage."

He takes a sip of his potion and slings another fireball.

I check my own health and realize it has dropped below fifty percent. "Gord, I'm going to need you to get real angry real soon or you are going to die."

The ladies need the health potions, and I'm certain we will run out before all of this is over. For Gord and myself, our only hope is to use Berserker Rage and counteract the decay so that we can bond the wyrm and leave.

I dodge a swing from the knight who isn't chasing Gord. His greatsword moves with ease and he follows up with another swing as if the weapon weighs nothing. Which, apparently, it doesn't. The blade connects with my chest, ripping flesh and spilling blood.

"You no hurts Chods!" screams Limery as he tosses another fireball that bursts against the knight.

Gord's health is down to thirty percent, but at least Tormara, Ismora, and Yashi have managed to get to the wyrm. They lean over it, Ismora and Yashi holding it down, belly-up, while Tormara cuts it open with her dagger.

Limery's attacks are not doing nearly enough damage, and Gord and I continue to lose health at a rapid rate. I cast horrors to try and counteract the effect, but they die quicker than I would like. With every bit of health we lose, the specters grow more powerful, replenishing their lost health with our own.

As our health continues to deplete, I don't see any way we make it out of this. Even if we bond with the wyrm, we're still locked in here.

Gord's health drops below ten percent. By the throne, the wyrm thrashes as it fights against its bonds even in its decrepit state.

Gord is going to die if he takes much more damage, so I do the only thing I can think of: I sacrifice myself. Running in front of Gord, I take the brunt of the attacks that were meant for him until my own health drops below ten percent. Using the same trick that saved my life with the first wyrm I encountered, I trigger Berserker Rage and use my rapid regeneration in conjunction with my bonus healing. My health spikes like it took a shot of adrenaline to the chest. Beside us, Limery continues his assault, but it's evident he can't do much against these creatures.

There's a violent roar behind me and I turn to see Gord's health increasing just like mine, steam radiating from his green skin.

Thank God.

The king's health has already replenished. The damage Limery deals is simply not enough and the horrors that I cast to raise my own health feed the specters just the same as we do. It feels like we are caught in a riptide, being pulled out to sea, and no matter what we do, we are destined to be pulled under.

A stream of flame sprays across the throne room and I turn to Limery to see what the hell just happened. He's just as shocked as I am.

Tormara steps down from the throne, the wyrm at her side. It's no longer shriveled and weak, but rises up proud and strong like a cobra, several feet taller than Tormara. It tilts it head back and a shrieking roar cuts through the room. The specters bend over as if in pain. The shriek actually deals a small amount of damage.

While they are distracted, the wyrm lets out another spout of flame, dropping their health even further.

Limery doesn't waste any time getting in on the action, peppering the specters in a blast of miniature fireballs. The specters seem panicked for once and slash out at anything and everything around them. I let my horrors fall and cast no more. It means I have less health, but I'll no longer be replenishing the HP of our enemies.

"Limery, box them in with a flame wall," I shout.

Two walls of fire form to one side of the specters, forming an 'L' shape and preventing them from escaping the wyrm. Another blast of fire pushes the specters back into the fiery corner and their health drops even further as they are assaulted on both sides.

Right now, I'm feeling about as useful as nipples on a breastplate as I bark orders, unable to actually fight.

"Okayy, Limery, it's time for the big guns."

The wyrm shrieks, momentarily immobilizing the specters while Limery lifts his hands over his head and a swirling ball of flame grows ever larger.

The specters recover from the shriek and the last thing I hear is the king's colorful curses as the megafireball swallows him whole. There is a clank as his crown falls to the floor, no longer a spectral image. Another fire blast from the wyrm finishes off the knights, and the green glow fades from the room. I push the notifications to the side to check on my party members.

Everyone's health begins to tick up with the specters gone. Tormara, Yashi, and Ismora's health bars are below twenty percent.

"Do we have any potions left?" I ask.

"That was the last of them, I'm afraid," says Yashi. "And not a minute too soon."

Tormara runs her fingers down the back of the wyrm, the toxic sludge it creates just beginning to seep through its scales.

"That was some good timing. How did you manage to get its health up enough for battle?" The last I saw of the wyrm, it was still shriveled up as they tried to bond with it.

"That's where the rest of the potions went." Tormara strokes the snout of her new pet. "I didn't see any other way, so I made a tough decision. Either heal the wyrm and maybe die or save ourselves for a bit longer and definitely die."

She made the right choice. Even at such a young age, the wyrm has already proved invaluable. I approach it with caution and when I extend my hand, it nuzzles its hardened snout against me.

"I wish there had been more than one, but I will count this as a serious win. I say we camp here tonight. No one can get inside the castle while we are still here and then we can set out for our next stop early tomorrow."

Limery steps up beside me and pushes the king's crown towards me. It's silver and sleek, encrusted with sapphires.

Item. *Kingly Crown. +10 Charisma.*

I still remember the bonus Charisma I received from eating mole soup. It only gave three Charisma for one hour and I felt like I was losing myself. I don't think I can handle ten Charisma even if I wanted to. It's just not me, even if it does make me a smooth-talking son of a gun. Maybe one day I'll have use for it, so I place it in my satchel.

Everyone takes their spot on the stone floor. It is well past midnight and we will need our rest for tomorrow. As I settle in with Limery tucked against my chest, I use the opportunity to sort through the notifications from before.

Congratulations! You have reached level 14. +1 stat point to distribute. +1 Strength and Constitution racial bonus.

I'm a little bummed I only got one level since I was really looking forward to unlocking that next ability, but considering we didn't actually defeat any wraiths and only a few ghosts, the fact that I leveled up at all is a blessing. Maybe I can farm on the way to our next magical area.

Something else bothers me, though. It's kind of strange that I only got the level up notification. When we defeated the faerie dungeon, there was a chest filled with loot and a notification that I had defeated the dungeon. Is there more to these ruins than just defeating the king?

Either way, we got what we came for. The endgame was never loot. Wyrms are more valuable than anything we could possibly find in these ruins. The fate of the entire troll race rests on the scaly backs of these two bonded creatures.

CHAPTER THIRTY-ONE

31. Liches be Crazy

Sunlight spills through the high windows of the throne room, urging me to wake. Daylight is a welcome sight since it means we won't have to worry about the ghosts in the courtyard. But that doesn't mean there won't be new challenges on our way out. Limery stirs as I sit up, his bulbous eyes groggy with sleep.

I cast my horrors as the others wake and gather their belongings. Tormara's wyrm curls in a ball by her side while she sleeps, a watchful guardian.

We are all out of potions, so whatever happens next, we need to be careful until we have a chance to replenish them.

Our goal is to get out of the castle without any problems. We have what we came for and I'd like to get as far away from this place as possible, regardless of what loot may be hidden on its grounds.

"Is everyone ready?" They all nod in affirmation. "Same routine as before, eyes on the wraiths at all times. I'll keep my horrors out front in case there are any surprises. Tormara, I want that wyrm by your side at all times, Chief Rizza would kill me if something happened to it before we made it back. Gord, pick up the rear."

The door opens with a groan and we are greeted by a troop of wraiths drifting aimlessly. Their dark presence watches over us, but we keep them in our vision, freezing them in place. This time, we make it to the door without incident and exit into a warm, breezy day by the coast.

My horrors are organized in line formations. Two rows of horrors of vitality lead the way, with their curling ram horns and furry orange and blue bodies ready to tank anything that comes near. Next, there are two rows of the horrors of power. They are the most vicious-looking of the bunch, pure muscle and elegance rolled into one. Muscles ripple beneath their golden fur as they prowl the hall, barbed tail swishing back and forth. They wear the black mane that surrounds their heads like a crown. Finally, the horrors of finesse bring up the rear, their gangly bodies swaying side to side as they walk. They may look goofy, but their claws are deadly.

The presence of the wraiths keep the horrors from decaying and by the time we exit the hall, I have over seventy horrors at my disposal. Due to their added buffs, I feel stronger and more powerful than I ever have. As we make our way down the steps from the keep and away from the aggro of the wraiths, the decay resumes, but I quickly cast another horror for each one lost.

We're walking across the courtyard when something rumbles in the tower along the wall near the cliff.

All eyes turn to the tower as its scorched walls shake, stone and dirt falling from the tower's base, then winding upwards as if whatever is causing the ruckus is moving up its spiral staircase.

There's a moment of silence and then a crack forms in the top-most section of the tower. A battle rages on the other side.

It doesn't make any sense. No one else is supposed to be able to enter the dungeon while we are in here.

The tower wall explodes and pieces of stone and dust rain down as a wyrm and half a dozen bodies tumble to the ground. The wyrm lands hard and slithers away. The bodies rise in pursuit as if nothing happened, though I'm one hundred percent positive one of their necks broke from the fall and hangs sideways.

That's when I see someone standing in the exposed section of the tower. Dark hair drapes down over a black robe, the shadows concealing the face beneath. Grey, deathly hands hold a scepter, its end glowing an eerie green.

Duchess Ravana. *Lich. Level 16. Once a powerful necromancer and sister to the king, it is rumored that her dealings with the dark arts led to the king's eventual madness. Unwilling to leave the mortal world, Duchess Ravana made sure she would never have to.*

The wyrm burrows underground and the trailing undead follow with outstretched hands and rotting flesh.

Duchess Ravana leaps from the tower, a fall that would seriously injure most, and lands silently, her feet hovering several inches off the ground. The robe she wears reveals her decayed chest, speckled with death, and pasty skin that has not known life in a very long time.

For the moment, she seems more focused on the wyrm than the rest of us.

"It must be our lucky day," I tell the group. "We get a chance to clear the dungeon and get the wyrm. If we hold off the lich, do you think you can bond the wyrm?"

"Leave it to us," says Tormara. She, Yashi and Ismora fall back to where the ground rumbles.

My army of horrors approaches the lich. She stops moving.

"Do not stand in the way of what is mine," she bellows, her voice shrill and cutting.

"Sorry, lady, but that wyrm is ours."

"Then prepare to meet your doom!" She lifts her scepter into the air and with a flourish, the ground beneath her rips apart. Hands reach out, grasping and covered in dirt. They pull themselves from the ground until heads break through the surface and dozens of fallen warriors with exposed bones and ribcages rise, ready for battle. The warriors carry rusted weapons, while some use the bones of their fallen comrades.

Gord and I make brief eye contact.

"At least it's something we can hit," I say.

The sunlight catches his nose-ring and a smirk crosses his face. "At least there is that," he rumbles.

There's another explosion of earth behind us as the wyrm breaks through the surface. The three female trolls chase after it, along with Tormara's new pet. I trust that they can handle the wyrm on their own. They have proven themselves.

The undead horde marches toward us, but I'm not

worried. I have an army of my own.

Keeping them in formation, my horrors march toward the undead madness.

They collide in the open courtyard, the wave of horrors of vitality slowing the movement of the undead. The demonic lions that are my horrors of power launch themselves off the backs of the horrors of vitality, catapulting themselves into the fray. Their powerful barbed tails swing back and forth, cracking bone and knocking the dead to the ground.

They've nearly demolished the undead when a new crop springs up to the left and then another to the right. Suddenly, my summons are surrounded on three sides.

"I think it's time we help out," I say to Gord and Limery.

Limery takes flight and fireballs dart through the air. They hit the skeletal warriors, but do little more than burn off the clothing, way less effective than the attacks on the ghosts.

Gord charges the horde nearest him, plowing through them with ease. The clatter of bones rings out as he slashes Peacemaker in powerful arcs. Horrors of finesse fall in behind him, watching his blind side as he wreaks havoc.

All the while, I continue to raise more horrors between attacks. I blast roaming dead with my ranged physical attacks and smash the skulls of any who stray too far from the chaos.

No matter how many we defeat, there seems to be a fresh batch of undead for the duchess to beckon to her call. How many died here so long ago?

My horrors swarm the dead, overwhelming them with

power and numbers, while the duchess continues to raise more. She stops for a moment and raises her scepter overhead.

A buzz spreads over the battlefield and a darkness surrounds the undead. It moves about their feet, turning the earth as black as night and slowly rising into the air. I feel the life of my horrors start to dampen. Whatever she has cast, it is draining the health of everything around the undead, including myself.

The duchess laughs. It's cold and deadly.

"Death always wins. It's the one thing you can never kill, only postpone. You will all make great additions to my army. And when I take the wyrms, I will bring death upon any who oppose me. I will—"

A fireball to the face cuts off her evil speech and her robe goes up in flames.

She swats at the flames and I dive into the moshpit of horrors and undead, allowing my inner beast to take control. Bite, Claw, Summon Horror, Summon Horror, Bite, Claw, ranged attack, Summon Horror. Rinse and repeat. Gord does his own thing off to the side and the growls of rage he emits let me know he's okay. In a strange way, they spur me on.

My health drains from her area of effect spell, but before it gets worrisome, I use Berserker Rage and tear through the undead like a troll possessed. I never worry about dying, not like last night. No, this is actually fun. This is the reason people will do anything to play this game once it launches.

My horrors of finesse have armed themselves with the bones of their fallen enemies and have now added blunt force trauma to their attacks. The duchess raises her hordes, but we destroy them all the same.

When the last of her undead falls, she simply stands there, mana depleted and useless. Gord does the honor of separating her head from shoulders, and several notifications fill my vision.

On the far end of the courtyard, our companions gather around two wyrms coiled together. We run over to find that Tormara's wyrm has overpowered the wild wyrm and holds it in a death grip. Arrows and daggers stick out of the wild wyrm's legless body while Yashi leans over it, dagger in hand.

She presses the blade between a slit in the scales and peels it back. A trickle of blood runs down the wyrm's side. Yashi then cuts her own finger and presses it into the wound. There is a sizzle, and the wyrm writhes as if in pain, then the wound heals and the wyrm quits fighting. Tormara's wyrm loosens its grip, and the newly bonded wyrm coils around Yashi's feet, its wounds healing miraculously fast. Its tongue licks at the air and Yashi gently pets it on the back of its head.

She flashes me a smile. "We did it."

"That we did. Now let's get the hell out of here. Actually, give me a second."

I pull up the notifications from the battle with the Lich.

You have defeated Paltras Ruins. *Claim dungeon prize.*

Congratulations! You have reached level 15. +1 stat point to distribute. +1 Strength and Constitution racial bonus. +1 ability point to distribute.

Awesome! I can finally unlock a new ability, but first, we should claim our rewards.

We walk back over to where the tattered remains of the lich lie spread across the ground. Her obsidian scepter catches the sun and I reach down to pick it up.

Item. Forlorn Scepter. *Increases the range of summoned creatures by 50%. +5 Intelligence.*

Item. Cloak of Ruin. *Allows wearer to walk in the shadows undetected. +5 Dexterity.*

So that's how she was raising the dead from so far away. Those are some pretty good stats on the cloak as well. I know just who to give it to.

"Ismora, you didn't get a wyrm out of this dungeon, but I have no doubt your time is coming. For now, I think this belongs to you. It will make you unnoticeable at evening, night, and anytime we find ourselves in shadowy places."

She wraps the cloak over her shoulders. Even with the sun out, the shadows inside its creases seem to go on forever.

"I am here to serve the village. Yashi and Tormara have earned their wyrms. If it is seen fit that I earn one as well, then so be it, and if not, then I will carry on as I always have. The wyrms are not trophies, but members of our tribe."

Holding the Forlorn Scepter in my hand, it seems like a natural fit for my class, but the ranged attack of Petrified Staff has been invaluable so far. For now, I put the scepter in my bag.

"Chods, looks at this." Limery has his fingers buried in the dirt, pulling at a bone-white handle of what is obviously a chest. Gord reaches down to help him and the chest comes free.

The dark wood of the chest is speckled with dirt and the hinges are carved of bone.

It opens with a click. Inside, it is filled with bones, but when I look closer, I notice it is actually a set of magical armor.

Item. Bone Cuirass. *+3 Constitution. When all four pieces of bone armor are equipped, wearer takes 50% reduced damage from fire attacks.*

Item. Bone Greaves. *+3 Constitution. When all four pieces of bone armor are equipped, wearer takes 50% reduced damage from fire attacks.*

Item. Skull Helm. *+3 Constitution. When all four pieces of bone armor are equipped, wearer takes 50% reduced damage from fire attacks.*

Item. Bone Vambraces. *+3 Constitution. When all four pieces of bone armor are equipped, wearer takes 50% reduced damage from fire attacks.*

That's one hell of a set of armor, not to mention how intimidating it will look to go into battle against someone clad in bones. The bonus fire resistance will almost even out the weakness that trolls have to fire.

"Gord, this has your name written all over it. It's loose enough to not dampen your mobility."

He scowls at the armor as he takes out each individual piece. I know he doesn't like the idea of wearing armor, but the stats are too good to pass up. Twelve Constitution is insane. No wonder defeating this ruin was so difficult.

Gord carefully puts on the armor, each piece magically fitting to his giant body. When it is all equipped, he looks like a demonic warlord. The skull helm has an actual skull that covers the top half of his face, only revealing his nose-ring and massive tusks, one broken and shorter than the other. His emerald eyes are piercing through the mask. The giant ribcage wraps around his chest, while still allowing his mossy green skin to show through. The greaves and vambraces cover his forearms and shins in an assortment of welded bones.

Between the wyrms and assorted clothing and armor, we're starting to actually look like a formidable group.

While the others admire both Gord and Ismora's new looks, I take the time to sort through my ability and stat points. I have two stat points that I'm currently holding on to, but there's no point in waiting to use an ability point. I pull up both options for my summoning abilities. They are the only ones I have any real interest in at the moment.

Sacrifice. *Sacrifice X amount of horrors to receive a temporary buff. Horror of Power: +1 Strength. Horror of Vitality: +1 Constitution. Horror of Finesse: +1 Dexterity*

Kamikaze. *Sacrifice a horror to deal a burst of damage.*

Both are tempting. Sacrifice would make me a one-man wrecking crew if I happened to have a full army of horrors to sacrifice all at once. Plus, with a twenty Strength, Constitution, and Dexterity bonus all at once, I'd be godlike. Thinking back on the fights with the ghost and the specters, though, we need more than just Limery's magic damage. The wyrms are an added bonus, but right now, we need to keep them safe more than anything. I need to be able to deal magical damage myself.

I select Kamikaze and summon a Horror of Vitality. The plump orange and blue monster looks around, unaware of what is about to happen, staring at me with its big round eyes.

I use Kamikaze and the horror explodes in a burst of

orange light. There's no blood or gore, only the explosion, so I don't feel quite as bad about sacrificing it.

With no cooldown, the thought of an entire army exploding at once sets my hairs on end.

CHAPTER THIRTY-TWO

32. Seaside Strolls

Does it make me a sadist to have my horrors jump off the cliff and explode their bodies right as they hit the water just to see how big of a splash they can make?

I hope not, because even Gord is laughing as three horrors of vitality explode simultaneously, creating the biggest splash yet.

The two wyrms slither side by side between Yashi and Tormara. Far ahead, Ismora is but a blip along the cliff. Occasionally, a tree casts a shadow and she vanishes completely within it. Is it possible that she is truly as selfless as she proclaims, not caring whether she is bonded with a wyrm or not? In the short time I've known her, she has seemed pretty genuine to me. They all have. Sure, Gord and I were sworn enemies at first, but he has definitely dialed down his asshole antics, and I feel confident that he will have my back in every fight.

It makes me miss Taryn. With his personality, he would fit in well with the trolls. He's quiet and puts in the work, never complaining if he has to play support or fill in any roles that the rest of the team doesn't want to play. He's the embodiment of a good sport. I don't know how he put up with my antics for so long without punching me in the face. Hell, if he were in my position, he'd probably have handled things so much better. When he gets in the zone and his mind starts ticking, it's something to watch.

I lengthen my stride and fall in line with Tormara. She always has her eyes peeled, looking for anything out of the normal.

"Do you think you'll be able to ride them one day?" I ask.

The wyrms are as tall as me, but not yet sturdy enough to support the weight of a troll.

"I believe one day. The stories of old say that the trolls used to ride all manner of beasts. Wyrms, dragons, bears that could topple trees, but it has been a long while since our leatherworker has had occasion to make saddles. Perhaps the time is nearing." A few wisps of red hair that escape her braid twirl in the coastal breeze. I wonder if her temper will be more controlled by bonding with the wyrm or if her own tenacity will bleed into her bond? "You've done a great thing, Chod, securing the wyrms for our people. We will be forever in your debt."

I didn't do it for their gratitude. I did it because I felt they deserved more than they have been given. They are good people, regardless of what the outside world thinks.

One day, the rest of the world will see them as I do, but I fear there will be bloodshed before that happens. I remember from my history classes that revolutions rarely happen without violence.

There are two smaller magical sources between us and the forest, though neither one as promising as Paltras Ruins. However, there's really no way of knowing until we actually get there. One lies by the coast and the other several miles inland. We will hit the coast first and then work our way back inland toward the forest.

My herbalism skill increases again as I learn new plants associated with the coastal climate. We pick sea ivy and bay juniper, then strip the bark from the sunburst palm.

"There are also very powerful plants that live underwater," says Yashi, pointing to the ocean. "If we find an area where the cliffs fade off and are able to make it to the beach, I will show you." Now that we have secured two wyrms, we can also focus on stocking the village with rarer potion ingredients.

"How is it you know so much about the plants outside of the forest if you've never left it?"

"My mother made potions, and her mother before her. And her mother before that. The knowledge has been passed down for many generations. Trolls may not be known as great scribes, but we do preserve what is important to us."

Most of the day is spent traveling. Seagulls and other large birds patrol the coastline, filling the air with squawks while the salty air pervades every breath we take. Eventually, the rocky hillside fades off into a ravine, exposing the sandy white beaches below. As we descend, I am startled when Ismora emerges from the shadows.

"Wow, that cloak really does work. We would have walked right past you."

She just smiles as we walk past, her black cloak billowing in the breeze.

Waves crash against the shore, filling the air with salt spray. A variety of different sized crabs scatter along the beach. Limery hits the larger ones with fireballs while Gord gathers them up. The two wyrms lay straight as arrows against the sand, sunbathing.

Several hundred yards out at sea, there are many small islands with lush vegetation. No doubt it will be a great place to increase my herbalism skill even further. But first, Yashi mentions that there are certain plants we can find under water.

"Looks like Yashi and I are going for a dip. The rest of you can rest or explore."

The warm water is welcoming as Yashi and I dip our taloned toes. The water is a brilliant blue, not that different from my own skin. Tiny fish nibble at my toes and farther out, I can see through to the ocean floor as brilliantly-colored rays soar across the sandy bottom.

Yashi takes a breath of air and submerges underwater. Her stroke is elegant, perhaps from swimming in the lake near the village, and she darts through the water like a giant frog. The sandy bottom stirs and she comes up with a handful of green seaweed.

"Dragon seaweed." She hands the slimy plant to me and I understand why it has that name. The leafy structure looks like it is covered in scales. "It can be used in potions that temporarily raise Constitution. Now, grab as much as you can while I go catch us some fish for dinner."

Crab and fish. It'll be a nice change of pace.

I spend the next half-hour, delving deeper into the ocean as I pick seaweed and stuff it in my belt. It doesn't take long for me to look like I am wearing a hula skirt. Before I realize it, I'm all the way out towards the islands, so I decide to take a moment to rest on the shore.

The feeling of the sun on my shoulders is something I could get used to. Maybe one day, I'll journey back here just to take it easy for a few days. Almost like a real vacation.

The trees shake overhead as birds fly through the canopy, escaping something inside the forest.

My time in the sun is over when I feel a pointy object poking me in the back.

"Who are you and what business do you have on our islands?" The voice is raspy, like someone who has spent their entire life screaming at the sea.

A short but stout baby blue troll stares me down from the other end of the spear. He's no taller than Yashi, but his muscular proportions are no different than my own. Gray speckles cover his shoulders, tattooed from years spent on sunny beaches. A dense but short white beard covers his face and two thick tusks rise to the length of his nose. His braided white hair is adorned with seashells that clatter when he moves.

He holds the spear with purpose, webbed fingers wrapped around the tan wood.

"I mean you no harm. My party and I are just passing through. We stopped to gather herbs for the village."

He doesn't speak, but the spear tip lessens its pressure against my back.

"You have blue skin, but it is not the skin of a seaside troll. Explain."

"I'm from the forest. There was an accident. Too much magic turned me this way."

"You are from the forest? Then you should have known better than to step on our lands." He shoves the spear harder into my back. "Follow me and you will meet your judgment."

Great, Gord 2.0 has entered the fight. I stand up and the momentary widening of his eyes doesn't slip past me. He's but a dwarf compared to me. Even though he's level sixteen, I'm certain I could defeat him one on one. Regardless, these are my people and I don't want to start out on the wrong foot, so I take the lead and allow him to steer me by carefully-placed jabs in my backside. Is there a hidden rule that the first male troll I meet has to be an asshole to me?

"What's your name?" I try to be as friendly as possible.

"I am Imoko, son of Molma."

"You know my friends are going to come looking for me, right?"

"Do not worry, they will be handled."

I can't help but smile at the thought of someone telling Gord what to do. Or Tormara for that matter, especially with our new slithering companions.

Imoko leads me down a forest trail with dense vegetation. Brightly-colored birds chirp from high in the trees. There are no male trolls on guard in this forest. Why would there be? I bet they are all swimming in the ocean, hunting for fish or whatever else it is that these trolls do.

We travel all the way across the island and I don't see anything even remotely resembling a village. I want to ask where they live, but I keep my mouth shut and let the web-footed blue hobbit poke me forward.

My jaw drops when we exit the far side of the forest and step onto the beach. A floating village spreads out across the water with dozens of huts with green fronds covering the roofs. It's not as big as the troll village, but it is a sight to behold. A raft-like structure runs between the huts all the way from the beach to farther out in the ocean where I see many trolls standing on rafts, pushing themselves along with giant poles. One dives off a raft and comes up with a fish impaled on the end of his spear.

Children play in the water while the females watch them.

As soon as Imoko and I step onto the beach, several more seaside trolls rush to his aid, spears pointed at my throat.

"Imoko, what is the meaning of this?" one asks. He's younger and less weathered than Imoko, with many long brown dreads pulled together and tied with a leather thong at the top of his head.

"I found him on our lands. He says there are more across the channel. Take some of the others and see that they are brought here. I will take this one to the chief."

The others exchange glances before disappearing into the forest. They have no idea what they are in for.

A poke in the back tells me to go forward. Several pergolas are scattered along the beach where female trolls tend to various tasks. Fish roast over an open fire in one. The cooked fish hang along a rope that stretches from one support to another. Next to it, a bamboo shoot sticks out of the earth, spouting what I assume is clean drinking water into a massive clamshell the size of a bathtub. In another, spears are being dipped in a glowing purple substance. Several jellyfish-like creatures sit in baskets beside the table. Poison-tipped spears, maybe?

Another stab forces me to abandon my view and step forward onto the structure that floats in the ocean. The roots of whatever plant is being used disappear into the sand. This entire structure was created by mana-infusion, I'm certain.

When I bring up the map the chief gave me, I see that a small magical vein runs out to the island. Nothing major, but big enough to support this.

The pathway is surprisingly stable, even for my big size. I'm guided down the dock, past the huts to the open deck at the far end. The village is remarkably well hidden, not visible at all from the cliffside. When the female trolls notice me, they all stand in a defensive posture, backs towards their children. One of them steps forward. She has navy dreads that look fierce against her baby blue skin. Loose fabrics adorned with shells clatter as she approaches. A blade wrapped in leather hangs from her side. A shell necklace dangles around her neck, and eyes as blue as the sea give me a questioning look.

"Imoko, explain yourself."

"He crossed into our lands." Imoko looks at his feet.

Evidently, he is sensing something in the situation that I am not, but what? It's clear her tone is not what he was expecting.

"And this is how you think to treat him? Can you not see that he is our kin? You bring him here with a spear in his back. Do you know how long it has been since a land troll has stepped on our grounds? Too many years." She sighs and looks to me. "I am sorry for the inconvenience. We are a peaceful tribe. We do our best to stay away from the eyes of men and do not go looking for fights we cannot win. Now, tell me—"

"Chod." I fill in the blank.

"Now, tell me, Chod. How did you find yourself on our little island?"

"Well, it's a bi—"

Before I have an opportunity to explain, there's a loud crack of branches from the forest, causing many of the other trolls to gasp in horror. I turn to see the seaside trolls that were sent to find the others kneeling in the sand weaponless. Gord stands behind them, clad in his skeleton armor, roaring with defiance. The two wyrms flank his sides and the rest of the party emerges behind him.

CHAPTER THIRTY-THREE

33. Dinner and a Show

Imoko thrusts the tip of his spear against my throat. I don't blame him. Right now, I'm the only insurance policy that he has against my companions.

"Release our brother!" Gord shouts from the tree line, his deep voice carrying across the waves. I find it kind of sweet that he called me brother. I guess I'm growing on him.

"Imoko, drop your weapon," scolds the chief.

"Chief Lida, they have our brothers," Imoko protests.

"And we have theirs. Release him now so that we can move forward from this nonsense. Chod, I trust that you will make peace with your brothers and explain that this was all a misunderstanding. We are not fighters. We want no quarrels but the fight for our own survival."

Imoko removes the spear from my throat and I raise a hand towards the shore to let them know I am okay.

"Allow me to go talk to them. And then perhaps we can all speak together."

She nods, and I take off down the dock.

The seaside trolls that kneel in the sand look apprehensive when I approach.

"Gather your weapons and go. You have nothing to fear from us." Ismora tosses their spears in the sand and the trolls gather them, joining their chief at the end of the dock.

Limery flies up to my shoulder and takes his perch. "Chods, don't you disappears like that again."

"Yeah, he was about ready to kill every last one of them," says Yashi. "Gord, too. What the hell happened to you, anyways? I leave you alone for five seconds and you get captured." She rolls her eyes at me.

"It's okay. I'm actually glad we found them. Imoko is a little trigger-happy. Not that different from someone we know." I nod at Gord. "But their chief seems to have a pretty good head on her shoulders. At least as far as I can tell."

"They are so small." Tormara gawks at the seaside trolls. "I've heard stories, but I've never actually met a seaside troll myself. It's hard to believe we're the same species."

"I would like to sit down with the chief to talk. Maybe they will be valuable allies in the future."

The chief waits at the end of the dock. Several more trolls have returned from their rafts and stand beside her. The warriors Gord and company defeated stand by her side, the ends of their spears buried in the sand. Every face has the same look of wonder as we approach. Perhaps from seeing the wyrms that stick close like well-trained pets or maybe it's our very presence that awes them.

"Chief Lida, allow me to introduce my companions." I go through the line, acknowledging each in turn, telling their skills and talents.

She smiles when I finish. "It reminds me of the tales of old, back when the trolls used to travel the world in search of adventure. Nowadays, we are lucky to simply endure. I'm sure you are famished from your travels. Would you care to join us for dinner where we can talk more freely?"

"That would be nice."

We stand to the side of the dock as everyone prepares for dinner. Several of the female trolls go back to the massive platform at the other end of the dock and place their hands on its surface. Channeling the mana that runs through the living floor, they raise up many long tables. Others carry fish and pails of water from the pergolas. Once they are finished, the tables are filled with platters of roasted fish of half a dozen varieties, roasted crab, and even bowls of fish eggs and what looks like snails.

We all take a seat at the newformed tables, sitting on the bare floor of the dock. Our table consists of our party as well as the chief and several other female trolls.

The fish is delicious, much better than any seafood I've eaten in real life. Limery eats like an imp possessed, shredding the small fish he holds in his tiny hands. He scoops handfuls of fish eggs up at a time and swallows the snails whole. Everyone seems to be enjoying their meal, but Tormara looks at the snails with a questioning eye.

"It's not that bad," I tell her. "Don't chew it, just swallow."

"So, tell me, how is it you find yourself so far from the forest?" The chief bites into a massive roasted fish the size of my hand and its bones crunch in her mouth.

I go on to tell her about the attacks on the village, and after witnessing Chief Rizza bonding with her own wyrm, I had the idea to try and track down the others. "We need to show them that attacking the village will have consequences."

"It is a noble pursuit. We do our best to stay far away from the troubles of men. We are lucky to be so well hidden. It has been many years since unwanted eyes have stumbled upon us. Once again, I hope you will forgive Imoko's overzealous approach. He was only trying to preserve what little we have."

Looking over their tribe, it's evident just how close to obliteration they are. They have less than half the population of the forest trolls. One false step could erase them from history.

"What if you didn't have to hide away?" The other females at the table cut their eyes at me, but the chief looks on with a blossoming curiosity. "What if you could have more than just this little set of islands?' I may have overstepped my bounds on that last one, because I hear whispers, not just at my table but at those that surround us as well.

"What exactly are you saying, Chod?" she asks, no longer touching her food.

"I want you to join us. Side by side, we can stand up for ourselves. Wouldn't you like to be able to travel freely, to trade and expand, to adventure like the days of old? We could make a place for the trolls in this world again. I know you feel it, all of you, that burning desire inside of you to face greatness and grab it by the horns."

She stares at me for a long moment while her people murmur.

"The trolls have a place in this world, Chod, and it is right here. We are still a great and powerful tribe. In the water, our fighting is unequaled, but on land, we are not great warriors. I don't know how you do things in the forest, but I will not risk the lives of my people just because you happen to have a few wyrms and wear armor."

The sea splashes against the dock, the only sound in the otherwise silence. No one argues with the chief's words, not even me. How could I expect someone I barely know to send her people away for a cause they know nothing about? The seaside trolls live a good life here, even if it's not the one I would have for them.

"We don't just have the wyrms," Yashi interrupts. "We have magic. The imp can cast fire, our shaman has the phoenix as his totem, and Chod here, well, he's practically a one-troll army. Go on, Chod, show her."

"Magic, hah. Magic will not save you." She stands up and walks over to the edge of the dock, gazing into the clear blue water. Her navy braids sway in the breeze.

After a moment, she turns back towards us and spreads her arms wide. A fish jumps out of the water and wiggles through the air before splashing back into the sea. Then another does the same thing. After a few seconds, dozens of fish are diving out of the water in a beautiful arc.

"Tell me, girl, what good will this magic do on the

battlefield? If we are attacked, then the seaside trolls will defend themselves, but we will not go marching to our doom. I will hear no more of it."

"But he's a hero. Chod, just show her your power. Once she see—"

"I said enough!" roars Chief Lida, and for the first time, I see the power that dwells within her. The power that makes her chief. Then and there, I know that the seaside trolls will have no part in whatever comes our way. "I have heard enough. When you are finished eating, take your belongings and be on your way. If you remain on our lands past nightfall, it will not be Imoko who comes for you this time."

CHAPTER THIRTY-FOUR

34. Blood Spills

"Why were you so adamant about convincing the chief to join our cause?" I ask Yashi as we walk along the coastline once more.

There was something about the way she pleaded with the chief that I just can't shake. I've never seen her look so desperate.

The small troll twists the end of her black braid as we walk, her bow strapped across her back. Her wyrm stays close by, sensing her unrest. I am amazed at the change that they go through after bonding. There's no training period or acclimation, almost like they can read each other's thoughts. Maybe they can.

"I can see what is coming." She stops walking, and so do I. "Everyone can see what is coming. Blood will be spilled before we are left in peace. If more of the undying ones come, how can we possibly stand a chance?"

I don't know what to say. Am I going about this all wrong? Even though everything here feels real, I've still been treating this like a game in a lot of ways. Death doesn't come for me the way it does for them. The trolls are so powerful, so strong, that I didn't think for a minute that they might be afraid of dying. Maybe death isn't what they are afraid of, but losing everything, their way of life. Chief Lida didn't hesitate to protect her people. I could be leading them all to certain death, for all I know. If only there were another way, but with our reputations, there will be no option for peace unless we take it by force.

The only way to attain peace is by bloodshed. The irony isn't lost on me.

"I'm sorry, Yashi. I know it's unfair. At the end of the day, it's you and the others who will pay the steepest price if this all goes south. I wish I could guarantee that everything will work out, that when the time comes, we will crush whoever opposes us and things will be far better than they were when I met you all, but I can't do that. All I can promise is that I will do my best to make sure that no lives are needlessly lost. I'll die a hundred times over if it means I can spare one troll."

"That is more than enough," says Gord.

Limery rides on his shoulder, conjuring tiny fireballs and flicking them into the air until they dissipate. Clad in his skeletal armor with the small red imp on his shoulder, Gord truly looks like a being from hell. "When you first came to the forest, on that night we were attacked, you offered to risk your own life in exchange for mine against the undying one. In that moment, I was too proud to accept your help. You were an outsider, and I had no reason to trust you. But now, I will gladly let you die for me." Gord places his powerful hand on my shoulder.

Did he just crack an incredibly dry joke? There may be hope for him yet.

"I'm sorry, Chod." Yashi straightens her back and puts her chin up. "I know we are doing what needs to be done, for the good of our future tribe, but we have not known a real war in a long time. Not in any of our lifetimes. Small battles, yes, but not the horrors of war."

I pray it doesn't come to that, but if it does, we must be ready.

Regional Event Alert! *Richard Hummel, Ethan French, and Otis Wiggins have slain a mana-infused wyrm. 13/20 remaining. 11 days remaining.*

That's the first time three people have teamed up together. I don't know if that means they are starting to work together more or if it is just coincidence. No doubt every one of them wants their shot at the regional event and the loot it provides. Even though the notification says thirteen, in reality, there are only ten wyrms still left in the wild. If the humans found out we had three wyrms, nothing would stop them from attacking the village.

We make camp for the night among a copse of trees. Right now, remaining hidden is the most important thing. While us trolls have Camouflage, the wyrms do not, so I have Tormara and Yashi order their pets to burrow underground for the night just in case anyone happens to stumble upon us. Ismora disappears in the shadows of night underneath her cloak, invisible to even our heightened senses.

I wake to another notification.

Regional Event Alert! *Pressley Allen has slain a mana-infused wyrm. 12/20 remaining. 10 days remaining.*

No one speaks a word when we wake up. Two more wyrms have been slain in the course of about eight hours, and I can't help but think of how many adventuring parties must be out there. Eight have been slain by other heroes and not a single name has been repeated. Some of them must be traveling around with a group of NPCs like myself, but there is evidence that others have begun forming alliances. All the more reason to get to the next dungeon faster.

Even Limery can sense the unrest between us, because for once, he flies in silence overhead. The slain wyrms, combined with Yashi's worries and the interaction with the seaside trolls, have put a heavy cloud over our party. I hope that clearing a dungeon may put it to rest.

By midday, we are near the next cluster of magical veins. If we find a wyrm here, then we can head back to the village without checking the last magical area.

The mountainous coastline morphs into more docile and friendly beaches that stretch on for miles. Crashing waves are replaced by a gentle purr. A mixture of palm trees and oaks with swooping branches line the forest where brightly-colored birds flutter through the canopy. Long strands of moss hang from the trees like cobwebs.

We make our way through the wooded area until a hand appears out of nowhere and Ismora emerges from the shadows, telling us to stop.

"Someone is here," she whispers. "The dungeon must be close because I heard talking and then it just vanished."

"How many people?" I ask.

"I don't know. At least two, maybe more."

"Okay, spread out. We need to find the entrance before they emerge."

Ismora disappears into the shadows, Limery goes with Gord, and Tormara and Yashi stay together with their wyrms. I cast several horrors as quick as I can and set out in search of the entrance.

The forest is alive with sound, which is good for concealing our movement. Bugs chirp and birds caw. Nearby, something slithers through the tall thicket of grass. I wish we had a few more perception potions, but we haven't resupplied since leaving Paltras Ruins.

As I do my best to sneak through the humid underbelly, there's nothing that even remotely resembles a dungeon. Only trees, bushes, and more trees. Could Ismora have been wrong? It wouldn't be the first time the forest has played tricks on the ears. I continue to cast horrors regardless, and soon, I have a small army at my disposal. I'm thankful for the cacophony of sound to muffle their murmuring. Far away, I can see the blue glistening skin of one of the wyrms as they search as well. If Ismora did hear voices, then the entrance has to be close.

A shrill shriek cuts through the forest, silencing the wildlife, and a bright beam of light explodes beneath the shady canopy. It takes me a moment before I realize it is Limery's flare! Ismora must be in trouble. The blinding light burns white hot as I rush to see what the commotion is. Branches and limbs break off against my trampling body. I run with reckless abandon, panic throbbing with each powerful beat within my chest.

The flare fades and I find Ismora surrounded by a group of men, a dagger held to her throat. I count six well-armed men. Two of them clearly heroes by their garb. I focus on them and the names Jason Montoya and Lester Hobbes display. A wizard and a ranger, both level eighteen.

The names sound familiar. Pulling up my notification history, I see that they were the first group to slay a wyrm before Limery and I returned to the forest. They've been busy.

Ismora shouts as the men hold her captive, telling the rest of us to stay back, that we should take the wyrms and flee.

One of the foot soldiers has his dagger pressed to her throat. The blade of the dagger is black as night and a small skull adorns the pommel. Ismora towers over his body, causing him to have to reach up to apply pressure.

"Hey!" shouts the wizard. "If you don't shut up, Raymond here is going to stick his knife all the way through your throat."

Jason, the wizard, is clad in light green cloth armor with a red hood pulled over his head. Next to him, the ranger, Lester, wears similarly-colored attire. His armor is heavier, consisting of silver greaves and bracers, both shimmer with a green hue, and a studded leather vest. A cowl covers most of his face. He holds his bow at the ready, an arrow pointed out into the forest.

Beside the two heroes, there are three other soldiers, two clad in heavy armor holding shields, and another with light chainmail much like the one holding a knife to Ismora's neck.

"She doesn't understand what you are saying." I try to remain as calm as I can as I say it. One, to hopefully keep them from doing anything stupid, and two, to keep any of my party members from escalating an already volatile situation.

The wizard licks his lips. "We've heard about you, Mister Troll. Yes, we have. A troll that can speak the common tongue is a rare find indeed. Even rarer, a hero troll. You've made quite the name for yourself with your regional events and murder and whatnot. Hasn't he, Lester?"

"Oh, he definitely has, Jason. Definitely has. And now we find out that he not only started this whole thing, but he's also collecting the wyrms for his own private collection. If we would have known it was possible, we wouldn't have killed the first one." He changes the position of his arrow toward where the others are standing, and fiery red tendrils extend down his fingers and wrap around the arrow. "Don't be scared, honey. We see you. You and your little blue wyrms can come right on out. We've been watching you approach all day long, so no surprises."

They must have some sort of buff or potion that is allowing them to see us in the forest.

"What is it you want?" I ask, casting another horror behind me so that they can't see it.

"Experience, gold, women..." The wizard smirks at his comment and both men laugh. "Give us the wyrms, and we'll let you go in peace."

"We can't do that. The wyrms are bonded." Not that I trust a word they are saying.

"I don't care if they're bloody brother and sister. You give us the wyrms or the troll dies. And then you all die."

My blood boils at their audacity. Ismora's eyes are locked on me.

"They want us to give up the wyrms," I know that the men can't understand me when I talk to the other trolls. "Tormara and Yashi, they know you're there. I don't know what kind of abilities these men have, but they are higher level than us and they won't hesitate to kill."

"Take them and go!" roars Ismora. "For the good of our people. The wyrms are our tribe's only hope."

"There is no way we are leaving without you," I counter, but I can see on her face that she has already given in. She doesn't believe she will make it out of here alive.

"Enough of that gobbledygook," says the wizard, licking his lips again. "Tell them to bring the wyrms."

"They won't obey you. They are bonded."

"Let me handle that." The way the ranger says it makes me feel like he has something up his sleeve. In other games, rangers sometimes have the ability to make pets or control low-intellect animals. Wyrms aren't common forest creatures, though. "And while you're at it, tell Mister Big Scary Skeleton and the others to drop their weapons."

"They want you to drop your weapons," I tell them. A few seconds later, I hear the sound of their weapons falling to the ground.

"You too, Mister Big Shot. Weapon on the ground."

I drop my staff. Luckily, I don't need it to cast. I have nearly fifty horrors tucked in tight behind me, each new horror crouching lower than the last in an effort to not be seen. The mental connection we share is invaluable right now. Even if they have been watching us all day, they don't know how many horrors I am capable of casting.

Still, I have no idea how we get out of this with everyone in one piece.

"Now, the wyrms. I won't ask again."

"Send the wyrms." The look on Tormara's face is one of absolute betrayal. Nevertheless, she does as I say and both wyrms slowly slither towards the group of men.

Their eyes light up with greed as the wyrms approach and the ranger lowers his bow, the red tendrils of energy retracting into his hand.

"Kill her!" the ranger orders his soldier and I'm drowned in the roars of my party as the blade digs into Ismora's skin, spilling her blood. She collapses to the ground and all hell breaks loose.

Blue energy sparks out from wizard's hands, wrapping the wyrms in arcane chains from head to tail. The ranger bends down over one of the wyrms, his hands glowing a vibrant emerald as he passes them across the body of one of the bound wyrms.

I don't know what he's doing, but I have to stop it. Grabbing a Horror of Vitality by the horn, I toss it with all the force I can muster straight at the ranger, exploding it right as it hits his body. It knocks the ranger off balance, disrupting whatever spell he is casting.

Chaos unfolds all around me as we gather our weapons and rush towards the evil bastards that murdered our sister.

Absolute terror paints the faces of the NPC soldiers as we descend on them. The wizard conjures a cube of energy around him and the ranger as they continue their ritual against the chained wyrms, leaving their companions to die.

We take care of the foot soldiers first. With my horrors

and the furious rage of my party, they don't stand a chance.

With the foot soldiers dead, Gord swings Peacemaker with all his might at the cube shield to no avail. Limery pelts it with fireballs, but still nothing. The wizard must be charging a hell of a lot of energy to keep it in place.

"We need to break it!" shouts Tormara. The ranger presses his hand to the wyrm's body and Tormara seizes in pain. She bends over, screaming, barely able to move as emerald energy penetrates the wyrms scales.

The wizard has his arms extended, reinforcing the magical energy of his shield. I have a suspicion that the ranger is trying to make the wyrm his own pet, and it looks like the process will kill Tormara if he succeeds.

We've already lost one member of our party. I can't let them take another.

"Everybody, step back."

Gord lifts Tormara and carries her a dozen or so yards from the shield.

My horrors surround the cube, standing one on top of another until every side of the box is blocked from view.

"Yashi, ready your arrows."

I cast Kamikaze and every horror explodes simultaneously. The shield shatters and the wizard falls to the ground, knocked out from the backlash of energy. An arrow zips across the forest, hitting the ranger in the shoulder. He stumbles and the energy connection breaks for a moment. Without looking up, he presses his hand against the wyrm, focused on his task. Another arrow rips through the side of his neck and blood sprays in a sickening stream onto the wyrm. He grimaces in pain but keeps his hand pressed. He must know he'll never escape.

His only hope is in bonding the wyrm and using it to defend himself. A third arrow connects with the side of his head and he falls to the ground.

The chains that bind the wyrms are still active as the wizard groggily comes to. I ready my staff to finish him off, but Tormara stops me.

"This one is mine." She bends down over the blood-covered wizard and their eyes lock as he finally recalls where he is. She buries the blade of her dagger in his throat and rips it out with enough force to sever his throat down to his spine. The chains vanish from the wyrms' bodies, and they rush to their masters.

I receive a notification telling me I've hit level sixteen, as well as a -2399 reputation, but I brush it away. There's no celebration to be had in the victory. Instead, we all sit in stunned silence.

I'm the first to break the quiet. "I don't understand how she got caught. She had her Cloak of Ruin. It should have kept her hidden."

"Rangers have higher perception than most." Yashi wipes a tear from her eye.

I stand and walk over to Ismora's body, her chest covered in dirt and blood. Her scarred arms spill out from her cloak and I can't help but think that after so many battles, I am the reason for her most fatal wound. Did I make a mistake bringing them down here?

Bending down, I take her hands in mine. They're still warm to the touch.

"I'm sorry." As I wipe a stray hair from her brow, there's a slight gurgle in her throat.

CHAPTER THIRTY-FIVE

35. Death March

"She's not dead," I say it but no one comes. The words linger in the air for what feels like an eternity. Ismora's hands are too warm for there to be so much blood. I've never seen this much blood in my life.

As I watch the blood trickle out of her open wound, my mind drifts for a moment. Back to the day when I knew for certain that I would have to take care of myself in life. At eight years old, home alone, I was hungry. Mom and Dad had left the credit card for me to order takeout, but I wanted to cook for myself, to show them that I was a big boy. I sliced my finger opening a can of ravioli and blood went everywhere. It covered my clothes, the marble counter, the hardwood floors. Thinking back on it now, I don't know why I didn't panic. Maybe because I knew there was no one to help. I soaked an entire towel mopping up the blood and when Mom and Dad finally made it home, the kitchen looked as if it never happened. There had been so much blood, but not like this.

How could we be so careless not to check her body? "She's not dead!" I repeat, louder this time. I hold Ismora's hand in mine, but I'm not sure what else to do. She's still alive for now, but that could change at any moment. Should I lift her head or will that just make her bleed out more? I don't know how she survived and frankly, I don't care, but we need to figure out how to get her help fast.

Our group surrounds me. I'm so focused on Ismora that I didn't even notice them approaching. "Yashi, can you make us more potions?"

"I don't have the ingredients." Urgency coats her voice.

"Can you not find them?" I say it as more of an accusation than I mean to.

Yashi flinches at the harshness of my words.

"Maybe, but I could also spend all day searching and not find anything. I don't know this area. We need to get her back to the village. If we can stop the bleeding, then her natural healing will take over enough for us to travel."

I hope that's true. She's lost so much blood already that it pools around my knees.

I use Ismora's cloak to try and stop the bloodflow, but it does little more than soak it up. It looks like the knife missed its intended target. Her throat is intact, but a gash runs down the side of her neck. That will mean little if she bleeds out.

"Limery, I need you to cauterize the wound. Can you do that?"

"What's that means?" he asks me with wide eyes.

"Burn her skin until it closes the gash. It's the only way to stop the bleeding."

He nods at me apprehensively and moves in close. A tiny fireball crackles in his palm and he molds it until it is a thin layer of flat, radiating heat that fits him like a glove.

Limery presses his hand to her neck and the blood sizzles. The smell of cooked meat fills the air and something primal in me causes my mouth to salivate uncontrollably. Ismora thrashes for a moment before falling still once again. When Limery removes his hand, a white handprint is burned into Ismora's skin. If she makes it through this, she will carry Limery's mark for the rest of her life.

"Reach in my bag, there should be a strip of leather. I need you to hand it to me."

The satchel on my back shuffles and then a strip of leather dangles in front of me. Tormara takes hold of Ismora's hand. I rip off a piece of her cloak and fold it. Placing the cloth against her wound, I tie it securely around her neck.

She lays there unmoving.

"What now?" I ask.

"I think it is time we cut our journey short, Chod." Tormara's face is strained. "The undying ones know we have bonded with the wyrms. They will be coming for us. We must warn the village and do what we can to prepare. We still have two more wyrms than we started with and if we save Ismora, I will count us as truly blessed."

She's right. I know she's right.

"Okay. Gord, chop us some wood. I'm going to build a stretcher to carry Ismora on."

A few minutes later, Gord returns with two branches

about eight feet long. Using some of the leftover leather, I strap it across the two pieces of wood. With my nails, I poke several holes and run small strips of leather to secure it in place. When it's finished, we have a primitive stretcher. Lightweight, but strong enough to hold her body.

Congratulations! You have unlocked the skill 'Inventor.' You are now a level 1 Inventor (Novice). Increase your skill and learn techniques for advanced inventions by finding an advanced inventor (Apprentice or above). Ranks: Novice, Apprentice, Journeyman, Expert, Artisan, Master, Grandmaster.

I focus the notification away. The last thing I care about right now is leveling up my skills.

"Help me move her onto here." Gord grabs Ismora by her feet and I take her underneath her armpits and we lift her from the blood-soaked earth and onto the stretcher. "Now, let's get moving."

It's already evening as we set out towards the village. Judging by the map, it will take us nearly two days to get there. I fear Ismora doesn't have that much time. She's still unconscious and her health has not started to replenish at all. Could the weapon she was attacked with have been poisoned? I would give her my Tiger's Eye Pendant to remove any potential poison she may have, but she has to be awake to use it. Right now, our only hope is to get her back to the village so that she can be healed.

We walk with purpose, constantly on alert. Without Ismora to scout ahead, Yashi keeps her bow strung with an arrow and Tormara has a dagger in both hands. Gord and I march as fast as we can without jostling Ismora, until eventually, night descends upon the land.

Our night vision kicks in, allowing us to see for miles under the starry sky. No one mentions taking a break and we continue well past dusk.

Eventually, I'm hit with a notification telling me it's time to rest.

Warning! *Your body needs rest. If you do not sleep within the next two hours, your stamina, strength, and health regeneration will be greatly reduced. Recommended sleep: 6 hours.*

Two hours comes and goes.

Warning! *Your body needs rest. Your stamina, strength, and health regeneration have been reduced until you sleep. The longer you go without rest, the more depleted you will become.*

My Strength and Constitution reduce by nearly a quarter and I have to stop for a moment to catch my breath. I just lost the equivalent of four levels of stats and I feel it in my bones. I can tell Gord is experiencing the same thing by the way he readjusts his grip on the stretcher's handles. It seems heavier and my body feels weaker.

"We must push through." No one argues.

I shrug off the fatigue and we continue. Each step comes with increased effort and I can't help but notice the heavy breathing of everyone as we walk. Everyone except for Limery and the wyrms. I have a feeling the imp could go all night without sleep and not miss a beat.

By morning, my stats have decreased by fifty percent. Every step is a slog as the sun rises. We stop briefly to eat, but it does nothing to raise our stats. Not until we sleep.

I lose myself again in my own thoughts, robotically putting one foot in front of another. It's the only thing that keeps me going as I wonder how I got myself into this situation. A few weeks ago, I didn't really care about anyone. My parents were practically non-existent, and the only joy I got was from belittling strangers on the internet. Now, here I am, voluntarily going through hell to try to save someone I barely know.

It's interesting… I viewed my sentence to play this game as a bit of a joke at first. Just another challenge to overcome or castle to beat. The judge said it wasn't a punishment though, but a new form of behavioral therapy. Looking back on my actions, I'm beginning to wonder if that's true. Has this game influenced my actions or has this always been the person I am when I have people depending on me?

Kind of a chicken or the egg scenario since I've never had anyone depending on me.

Before I know it, we cross into the forest. Only a few more hours until we arrive at the village. Ismora hasn't stirred in a while, but each time Tormara presses the back of her hand against Ismora's forehead, it's still warm.

Our stats continue to drop, forcing Gord to leave his shield and the rest of us to strip down to our bare essentials. I leave a mark on the map so that we can return to claim our items at another time.

With nothing but pure determination, we push forward, nearing exhaustion. Some of the creatures sense our weakness and try to attack. Limery and the two wyrms defend us from what would be certain death multiple times over.

"It's okays, Chods. We's almost there." He offers encouragement and once again, I'm thankful for the little guy. I'm thankful for all of this.

We burst through the magical barrier of the village,

and I've never been so happy to see the translucent bodies of guardian trolls in the distance. They rush to our aid, sounding roars of alarm throughout the forest.

"Ismora needs healing," I manage to say before collapsing.

CHAPTER THIRTY-SIX

36. The Calm before the Storm

Incense fills my lungs when I wake. Somewhere nearby, birds chirp, welcoming in the morning. I open my eyes and the familiar living roof of the troll hut calms me. Good to know they didn't just leave me lying in the forest. I sit up, fully expecting the fatigue from the journey to hit me like a ton of bricks, but I feel fine. My stats have returned to normal, and I am none the worse for the wear.

The hut I'm in is mostly empty but for a few pieces of furniture and a bowl of smoking incense. I'm pretty sure it's the same hut I stayed in on the first night, all traces of the previous inhabitant gone. A couple of notifications beg for my attention.

Regional Event Alert! *Tommy Sullivan has slain a mana-infused wyrm. 11/20 remaining. 8 days remaining.*

Regional Event Alert! *Troy Malloy has slain a mana-infused wyrm. 10/20 remaining. 7 days remaining.*

Seven days remaining? How long was I out?

I step out into the courtyard and receive several warm smiles as trolls move to and fro on their morning routines. Several children hit a stone ball with a club across the ground. The action stirs some laden thought inside of me.

Ismora!

"Excuse me." I pull one of the children aside and his eyes go as wide as saucers. "Have you seen Ismora? Where have they taken her?" I'll search out the others later, but for now, I need to find her first. She has to be alive.

"She is with Jira and Chief Rizza." The small troll points at another hut on the other side of the courtyard, and I spot Chief Rizza's wyrm coiled up around the entrance.

The wyrm allows me to pass without incident and I find Jira sitting on the floor, legs crossed, as he chants and waves a burning piece of brush over Ismora's face. Ismora's forehead and cheeks are covered in ash.

"What is he doing?" I ask.

Chief Rizza signals for me to be quiet and motions me over.

"Ismora was injured with a cursed blade," she whispers, her face grave. "You were right to bring her here. She would not have survived for much longer had you not."

I can't quite place the look on her face. Is it worry or something else entirely?

"What kind of curse is it? Will she be okay?"

"Jira is doing all he can to remove the curse, but it is not so simple. Every bit of health she regenerates is being absorbed by the curse." Jira's white-tipped dreads sway back and forth as smoke rises from the burning herb.

"Is there anything I can do to help?"

"For now, all we can do is wait. I would like to have a council meeting once the others return. Bring Gord with you this time, I think he has earned it." She smiles.

"What do you mean return? Where's Limery and the others?" I would have thought he would be right by my side when I woke.

"The imp left, something about his mother. He seemed to be in a frenzy. I'm sorry, I wish I knew more. As for the others, they woke yesterday and mentioned something about gathering gear."

"Yesterday? Wait, exactly how long was I out for?" It must have been some time if Limery left and the others went back for our weapons. The little guy has stuck by my side like glue since I met him.

"This is the second day." Two entire days of sleep for depleting my stamina. Is it possible the game forced me unconscious after going so long without rest or was that the punishment for completely depleting my stamina? If it was the second, then why were the others not affected the same way? "We will talk more when the others return." Her dismissal is firm. There's not much that I can do here anyway.

What the hell am I supposed to do while I wait for the others to come back? And why could Limery possibly need to see his mother at a time like this? Maybe I'll go for a swim in the lake or take a walk in the forest. On second thought, I think I've walked enough.

The cold water of the lake is calming. It's a strange

feeling, being able to actually relax for once. I don't think I have truly taken a moment just to breathe since entering this world. It all started with an angry ogre, then an angry troll, then an even angrier wyrm and her demon-spawned babies. Sprinkle in a couple human interactions and attempted kidnapping by tiny blue trolls and it has been quite the adventure. More excitement than I've had playing a game in my entire life. I'm kind of sad to know it is all going to come to an end. I just hope I can really help the trolls before my time comes.

After a dip in the lake, I make my way around the village and attempt to learn more about the people who actually live there. I meet Kea, who always has a pot of soup boiling, and then Makali, who boils the leather and uses it to make clothing and whatever else the village needs. Bunu and Tayo nurse the youngest trolls today, but all females help raise them, or even feed them if need be. Zelia has filled in for Ismora while she has been away, teaching the children in the ways of combat. Jojin, Watu, and Malak guard the southern side of the village.

There are so many more that I don't have the opportunity to talk with. Each with their own lives, their own personalities. I burn their names into my chest as I try to envision what's next. War is coming to the village. To the other heroes, we aren't people. We're monsters, and they are doing the righteous thing by destroying us. For all I know, they think that we are bonding with the wyrms to try and sabotage the rest of the island.

When I meet with the council, I need to have some sort of plan. Honestly, I don't know what to do other than wait. We can reinforce the boundaries, setting up spikes and defensive measures, but we can't go on the offensive. We don't have the numbers, and marching away from the village leaves it at risk for attack.

Maybe the others will have better ideas at the council meeting.

I'm talking with some of the villagers, telling them of how we battled our way through Paltras Ruins, when I hear a cavernous voice calling to me.

"About time he woke up."

"Don't pretend you weren't worried about him, Gord," teases Tormara. She hands me my satchel and staff. "We weren't sure when you would wake so we went out for our items. Gord couldn't bear to go another day without Peacemaker."

"Thank you. Really, thank you all. There's no way we could have saved Ismora unless we all pushed through. And both of you, too." I reach out and pet the top of both wyrms' heads and they nuzzle against me.

"We're not quite out of the woods yet." Yashi twists her braid between her fingers. "The weapon that cut Ismora was cursed."

"I know, I've already spoken with the chief. Jira is doing the best he can, and she wants to have a council meeting this evening, Gord included." I can't help but smile at the look of surprise and then pride that crosses his face. "How much does she know about what happened?"

"We've filled her in on just about everything," says Tormara.

. . .

SENTENCED TO TROLL

A half an hour later, we gather at the council area. Chief Rizza, Tormara, Guilda, Kina, Sonji, and I take our seats while Yashi and Gord stand before us. With the three wyrms coiled up at the feet of half of our council, the area is beginning to feel a little crowded.

"Jira will not be joining us this evening. His talents are needed elsewhere." She pauses and her wyrm lifts up to touch her fingertips. "I have called this meeting to discuss our future. Based on your reports and interactions with the humans, I fear an attack is imminent. We do not yet know if all of the undying ones are working together. There could be one massive attack or several small ones, but we need to be prepared. I welcome advice on how we should proceed. Those of you who have dealt with them have an advantage over the rest of us, which is why you are here as well." She motions to Gord and Yashi before sitting back against her throne and giving us the floor.

I don't know what I expect from them, but silence is not it. Every council meeting I have been to so far has been hot-tempered and full of action. Even Tormara keeps her vipered tongue at bay.

Gord clears his throat. "These men are like none we have faced previously. The undying one we faced before may be the weakest among them. I fear we cannot win against them in open combat."

"I think we should start by increasing our defenses." Their eyes fall on me as I offer what little help I can. I'm a fighter, decent in small battles, but I'm not a commander. I say the simplest things that come to mind. "Spikes, thorns, vines that choke. Make use of your mana-infusion before they ever get close to the village. We know they will come with fire, so we'll need to infuse the trees. I'd also send our scouts out further. We want time to gather our forces before they are beating on the door."

"And what of the wyrms?" asks the chief.

I don't know. I've never planned an actual battle before. I don't know the first thing about battle formations or how to win against a superior foe. All I know how to do is play video games. I've skated by this far, but if they keep following me, I'm going to get them all killed.

I can't focus. They're bringing clubs and tough skin against magical abilities. They're all scared, afraid of what will happen if they fight fair.

"Chod?" She must sense my consternation.

Maybe that's the thing, though. We're the bad guys… We don't have to fight fair. A movie scene flashes across my mind where a small village is under attack by invading forces. They're coming onto our lands. That's something we can use against them.

"If we are camouflaged, how close do they have to be to see us with a perception potion or anything that modifies their awareness?"

"I was asking about the—"

"How close?" I cut the chief off. "Yashi?"

"It would depend on their skill?" She glances at the chief and then back to me. "Perception potions only increase awareness for what you are looking for, they don't point it out for you."

"Then I think I might have a plan."

The rest of the evening is spent infusing the areas at the magical barrier with as much defensive power as possible.

Every troll is put to use, carrying raw mana from the well to the edge of the forest. It's slow, laborious work, but it might just make the difference between life and death. For anyone who attacks us, I want it to be a hell of a lot of work just to get past the barriers. There will be more work to be done tomorrow, but once night falls, I do my best to explain my plan to everyone who is available and then have the others tell the plan to the guardians.

By evening, Jira still hasn't left his hut. I pray that he has a breakthrough soon, because we're going to need his power if we hope to have a shot.

"I don't know if there is anything more nerve-wracking than waiting for an attack that you know is coming." Chief Rizza steps beside me. The toxic ooze from her wyrm catches the moonlight in a beautiful way. It already seems bigger than when I first saw it. "I never had the chance to properly say thank you. We'd fight tooth and nail until there were none of us left if it came to it, but with everything you have done, I feel like we are finally embracing who we are again."

Proud warriors fighting for their lives.

"I don't know if I made a mistake going after the wyrms. I was so angry at everything happening here, at the lack of respect. I just wanted you to have something, and I don't know that I ever really thought about what could happen if we were caught. Or what my actions might bring upon the village." This is the first time I've been truly honest with myself about it. Part of me was channeling my own insecurities through the trolls. I thought that if I could save them, then maybe I could save a small part of myself too.

She pats me on the shoulder. "Don't beat yourself up

about it. We were dying out long before you showed up. More likely than not, we would have faded out with a blip. Now, if nothing else, we'll go out with a bang. Hell, we might just have a shot at winning. Now get some sleep. Tomorrow I'm sending scouts to the edge of the forest."

CHAPTER THIRTY-SEVEN

37. Healers are Overrated

My mana-infusion increases another level as I focus on the vine in front of me. The goal is for the vine to wrap around the foot of any human that steps on it, lifting them high into the air. When the plant accepts the mana, I give the vine a tug. It feels strong. At worse, it trips the person, and at best, they'll be dangling in the air, ready for Yashi or another archer to take them out.

We're making steady progress on the barrier, but it is slow going.

"Someone is approaching," one of the guardians calls out.

My body immediately tenses as I reach for my staff. Two small, red humanoid figures flutter through the air towards us.

"Limery? Where the hell have you been?" My heart

feels a million times lighter now that he is back.

"I had to goes home. Gets Mommy to helps fix Ismora." He wraps his tiny arms around my neck, giving me a hug.

Right behind Limery, his mother hovers, carrying a bag of what looks like junk parts.

"Limery tells me you had quite the adventure and that one of your party members has been cursed."

"Yeah, but what are you doing here? And what's in the bag?"

Limery flashes me a big toothy grin, his eyes bulging even bigger than normal with…excitement?

"I makes it, Mommy helped. Long time ago. Now lets goes. Lets goes." He pulls me by the arm and I take the bag from his mother as we walk back towards the village.

"You want to fill me in on what's happening?"

"And ruin the surprise? Never." She smirks and bats her long eyelashes at me, making her look all the more devilish.

Chief Rizza and Jira are already in the hut when we arrive. She stands next to Ismora, protesting our entrance.

"What is the meaning of this? Jira needs peace to work his magic."

"We's here to helps," offers Limery.

Chief Rizza looks at me questioningly and I nod for her to let them proceed. Limery hasn't led me wrong yet.

Jira opens his eyes, and they are as red as the heart of a rose. He sets the burning herbs aside and allows Limery to take his place. Limery pulls piece after piece from the bag and carefully begins assembling them together.

"Long times ago, Leo was very sick. He tooks an item from a mans. An items he shouldn't haves. It was cursed.

For three whole days, Leo doesn't moves. Mommy thinks he's going to die. Daddy thinks so, too. They pays all our moneys for healer to come see Leo. Healer says Leo needs clean bloods. Healer says needs more moneys to helps Leo. Daddy sells himself to the healer for moneys but the healer doesn't help Leo. The healer says Leo can die."

As Limery fits his pieces together, I wonder how I never knew about Limery's father. Out of all the words he spoke, he never once talked about him. I wonder if he's still alive or where he might be.

"Mommy gets real sads when Daddy is gone. Says soon Leo will be gone too. But Limmy doesn't want to lets that happens, so he builds this."

Limery stands up, proudly displaying the finished product. I honestly have no idea what I'm looking at. It's all a mess of tubing and coils, a couple of bellows, and a container on the bottom. Two of the coils have needles attached at the ends of them.

"Wait. Is that a blood transfusor?" I ask.

"Limmy doesn't know what that is. This makes the bloods clean. I just needs the magics. Will you gets some, Chods?"

Limery hands me a small metal cup and I take it to the well and fill it with raw mana. The substance glows brilliantly and I'm careful not to spill any as I walk. When I return, I hand the cup to Limery, and he places it into the container. Limery's mother takes one of the needles and inserts it into Ismora's arm. She stretches the second tube out and does the same thing in her other arm. When Limery shuts the door to the container, the machine whirs to life. The bellows start pumping, forming pressure inside the device. The tubes are not transparent, so it is hard to see what is happening, but I can hear suction and blood dripping into one of the beakers. When it sounds like it is filling up, Limery places his hands on the beaker and I can see the heat radiating from its edges. He's literally boiling the blood to recycle it back through Ismora.

For a second, I'm reminded of Berserker Rage. When its active, our skin grows hot and steam rises from our bodies. Maybe that's why we can't be slowed or poisoned or cursed while its active.

"How long does this take?" I ask Limery's mom.

"A few hours. She has a lot of blood within her. It will all need to pass through."

"I'll leave you to it. There is still work to be done."

On the eastern barrier of the forest, I'm forming a fence of thornbushes when trampling feet catch my attention. Several of the scouts Chief Rizza sent out run towards me. When they arrive, they're out of breath and panting like dogs.

"They're coming. The undying one has returned."

"Are there others with him? Other undying ones?"

"Not that we saw. They'll be here within the hour."

"Warn the chief. Then I want everyone who can fight out here as soon as possible."

I cast my first horror and it appears in a puff of smoke. I hope like hell this works.

Within minutes, trolls flock to my location. It's the most trolls I have seen since the party before I left to clear the mana obstruction. Each face tells a different story.

Some, like Gord, are angry. Others are worried, apprehensive, or downright afraid. Not of dying, but of losing everything. Then there are those who simply love the art of battle. Ismora would have been one of those.

Chief Rizza takes center stage, her wyrm rising to full height beside her. Its tongue licks at the air and it sways back and forth like a snake ready to strike.

"A great deal has changed in these past few weeks. Magic has returned to the forest. We have been blessed with three new protectors." At this, her wyrm spits fire into the air. "And a hero. For the first time in a very long time, it feels like we are on the path to greatness once again." Several trolls beat their chests at those words. "But there are still those who want nothing more than to destroy everything we have built. The undying one has marched on us many times. Each time, we have defeated him and pushed him back. We have lost many troll lives in the process. Today, we have a chance to defeat him once and for all, and to show the rest of the island that trolls are not to be trifled with. Even now, other armies march on us from the south, aiming not only to take your lives, but the very essence of the forest trolls. Tonight, we will show the world of men that the biggest mistake they ever made was entering this forest!"

Chief Rizza smashes her fist to her chest and every other troll repeats the gesture. A deep, thunderous pound resonates in the air. "Take your positions."

I stand alone in the forest, an eerie silence stretching on forever, almost like it knows what's coming. It's true what

Chief Rizza said before: there is nothing worse than waiting for an attack you know is coming. I'd much rather be on the offensive than waiting. The end of the Forlorn Scepter glows green as I cast another horror. I need its increased cast range for what comes next. As each horror fades away, its health depleted, I summon another in its place. Once Glenn crosses into our lands, I will be able to summon a greater number, but for now, they are capped at sixty before one completely decays.

The fiery tips of our enemies' torches blink into existence like fireflies. With each step forward, the dots grow bigger. My heart pounds in my chest, a mixture of excitement and nerves.

Glenn has upgraded his armor since I last saw him. The hodgepodge of armor he lost in the first battle has been replaced with golden plate. A yellow aura surrounds him and the men closest to him as he marches. He even has a fancy red cape that billows behind him. Not to mention he's now level eighteen.

His army is much larger than last time too. I don't know how he managed to find soldiers, especially after his repeated attempts ended in failure, but nevertheless, here we are.

Several rows of foot soldiers armed with swords and spears follow behind Glenn. They lack the plate armor of their leader, but many are clad in chainmail or boiled leather. Further back, rows of archers follow.

They cross the barrier into the forest and several men are stuck by thorns and sharpened limbs before their eyes adjust to their new surroundings. Many more are tripped or trapped and hang in the air from vines. Glenn's golden armor leaves him unscathed.

The second row of men quickly assess the situation and chop the wild plants down, but not before we draw first blood.

Glenn's eyes light up when he sees me from a hundred yards away.

"You." He smiles. "I've been looking forward to you." He continues to talk as his men regroup and march forward. "You plan to stop me and my army all by yourself?" He laughs a cold, calculating laugh. "They say you're strong, but I don't think you're that strong."

He's a talker, but for once, I have nothing to say.

"Where are the others? Are they afraid to fight their own battles?" He pauses. "Never mind it. I'll kill you, and then I'll kill the rest of them for good this time. We can hang your head in the town square."

Glenn's army comes to a halt and I can sense the internal struggle going on in his mind as I stand here alone. I just hope he takes the bait.

"What do you say we do this old school, just you and me?" I try to goad him, though I know it won't work. He's here for blood, not glory.

"As fun as that sounds, I think I'll just take the village."

"Don't say I didn't give you the chance."

"Kill him!" Glenn orders. He unsheathes his sword and it glows with lightning that arcs down the blade.

Before he has a chance to attack, I raise my fist high into the air, signaling the camouflaged guardian trolls in the trees high above the archers to attack. They fall from the canopy like meteors, smashing archers and ripping them to pieces before they even have time to nock their arrows.

With the momentary distraction, I cast Kamikaze,

exploding the wyrm tunnels filled with horrors beneath Glenn and his army, creating a crater big enough for a small pond. Soldiers are buried in the rubble and many die from the explosion. Glenn stares up at me, his face contorted with rage.

"You will pay for this!" he shouts.

"No, it is you who will finally pay for all you've done."

The wyrms emerge from their tunnels on the outer edge and blue flames ignite the battlefield. Chief Rizza and the rest of the female trolls rush from their hiding places to join the wyrms on the rocky terrain. Their job is to handle the soldiers. Jira's punches land with the power of the phoenix, and Limery soars through the air, raining fireballs from above.

Glenn struggles to his feet, his heavy armor making it hard for him to move. I can't risk anyone else dying to him, and I made sure everyone knew that before the battle began. His reign of terror ends with me.

I cast Berserker Rage as he climbs up from the rubble. I attack with Claw, my nails scratching against his golden chest and shrieking across the battle. He counters with a slash to my arm that's fueled by lightning. The electricity flows through me, but it does nothing to calm my rage. I pry back his pauldron, snapping the leather that holds it in place and exposing his shoulder. My tusks sink into his skin and warm blood floods my mouth. He screams in pain, but I don't release. Instead, I cast a Horror of Power with my free hand and the lion-like demon rips off Glenn's armor, prying it from his body with razor-sharp talons. I cast two more horrors, and they help me pin him to the ground. With his helmet removed, my claws rake across his face until he looks more demon than man.

He tries to say something, but it comes out a broken mumble. With my horrors pinning him to the ground, I stand up and let their explosion send him to his next life.

All around me, the trolls finish up the battle. Tormara stands over a man pinned in the rubble, dagger raised, when I call to her.

"Wait! I need to ask him something."

The man's jaw shakes violently as I approach.

"If you tell me where he will be reborn, then I will show you mercy."

"L—lynchton," the man stutters. "Now, p—please, help me out of here."

"Make it a clean death," I tell Tormara. That is the only mercy he deserves.

"No, wait! You said you would show merc—" His words trail off as I search out the chief.

I find her back by the fallen archers as they pull armor and weapons from the bodies. She smiles at me as I approach.

"We did it. Without losing a single troll. We did it!" She embraces me in a firm hug, her excitement palpable.

"It's not over yet. We need to finish this once and for all."

My reputation has plummeted even further since the battle, almost doubling, but I did gain a new level, putting me at seventeen and giving me another ability point. I spend it on Sacrifice.

Sacrifice. *Sacrifice X amount of horrors to receive a temporary buff. Horror of Power: +1 Strength. Horror of Vitality: +1 Constitution. Horror of Finesse: +1 Dexterity.*

"Limery, stay behind and burn the dead. The rest of you, we're going to Lynchton."

CHAPTER THIRTY-EIGHT

38. Politics of War

From the forest's edge, Lynchton looks almost peaceful. A soft glow radiates from the lanterns that light the gate and just by looking at it, you would never know that they just marched on a troll village intent on exterminating an entire race. I'm hesitant for the precedent I'm setting, but what comes next must be done for not only the good of the village, but for trolls everywhere.

The half-asleep soldier on gate duty almost shits himself when an army of over one hundred trolls, sixty horrors, an imp, and three wyrms casually strolls up.

"You have two options. Either you open this gate and allow us to find the man we are looking for, or we tear the whole thing to the ground."

"Fuck me," he mutters before unlatching the gate. "I knew I should have called in sick today."

The gate swings open, revealing the first town I've seen since entering the game. Even at night, it's everything I love about fantasy worlds. Several buildings line the road as soon as we enter the town. There's a blacksmith, a tailor, and an apothecary all on one side. On the other are the stables, an inn, and a market. Several other buildings line the street farther down that sell everything from pottery to spices. In the center of town is the church, its steeple rising high into the sky. All of the houses are on the other side of the town.

"Where is Glenn?" I set my mind on what must be done next.

We need to end this as quickly as possible.

"He stays at The Dancing Donkey." The guard points to the inn down the street. "Please, don't kill us. I have a family."

"Give us what we want and no one will be hurt. Now follow me, you're going to convince Glenn to join us outside."

The streets are mostly empty, but the vagabonds and night owls that roam at this hour quickly scurry away from our approach. The guard tells them that everything is okay, that there is no need to worry. I'm certain he is scared out of his mind right now, but people will go to great lengths to protect the ones they love.

We come to a stop in front of the inn. A donkey wearing a dress and standing on its hindquarters is carved overhead of the entrance.

"What's your name?" I ask the guard.

"Jameson."

"Well, Jameson, it's your time to shine."

He wipes the sweat from his head and opens the door to the inn.

"Are you sure we can trust him?" asks Chief Rizza.

"I trust that he wants to protect his family," I tell her. This man has a life he wants to protect, and I'm sure he wants us out of town as soon as possible.

Gord and Malak, another guardian troll, wait beside the door as Jameson leads Glenn outside. Glenn wears nothing but a gray tunic and socks when he emerges.

"Now, what's this you said about a talking donkey?" asks Glenn just before Gord and Malak grab him by the arms.

"You!" He struggles against their grip. When he realizes they aren't letting go, he spits in my direction. "And you, guard, you'll pay for this too. I promise you that."

Jameson looks fearful of Glenn's threats as he backs away.

"Don't worry about him, Jameson. I need one more thing of you and then you are free. Ring the town bells. I want everyone here for what happens next." The only way for them to know the truth is for them to witness it with their own eyes.

He disappears from sight and several minutes later, the church bells ring out. There are gasps of horror as people spill out of the inn and from their homes. Some run back in for weapons, but return too afraid to use them. I'm sure many of these people have never seen actual trolls before, having only heard of them from stories. The rogue and the wizard heroes that I recognize from my encounter in the field exit the inn, ready to fight, but when they see so many trolls standing before them, they simply watch from the porch. Jameson does his best to calm people as they enter the town center, where Glenn is forced to his knees.

A man in frilly pajamas and wearing slippers rushes through the crowd. "Jameson, what is the meaning of this?!" His face is beet red as his head twists between us and Jameson like a sprinkler.

"They don't want us. They want him." Jameson points at Glenn.

"This is an outrage!" the man shouts. "There will be consequences!" He puffs out his chest and points an old wrinkled finger in my direction.

"You are sure this is the spot?" I ask Jameson.

"We have witnessed it several times," he confirms.

By the time people quit filing into the courtyard, several hundred wide eyes search for answers. I wonder how many of Glenn's army came from this very town. It's as big of a shock for the trolls to see how the other half lives as it is for the humans to wake to the stuff of their nightmares. Whispers snake through the crowd on both sides.

"I'm sure you are surprised to find us here." Many faces wince at the roar of my trollish voice. "If there was another way, we would not be here. You all have been taught to fear the trolls, told that we are nothing more than murderous monsters dead set on destroying everything you know and love. I am here to tell you that is a lie. We live, have families, grow old, and die, just like you. The heroes of old have returned to this world, many of them human, but I am also a hero and I have set it upon myself to right the wrongs against my people. The man standing before us is a murderer. He has led raid after raid on my village, killing my people and terrorizing their way of life." I pause to let that sink in. "Long ago, the trolls were a mighty race. They traded and adventured beside man and dwarf alike. I hope that one day, they do so again.

"As with man and troll alike, there are those who do good and those who do evil. The same is true for heroes. The man before you is not a true hero. He takes pleasure in the pain of others. Therefore, it is my duty to make sure he hurts no one again. Tamora."

She hands me a dagger.

"You will pay for this, you son of a—" The dagger slices through Glenn's throat, draining his HP and decreasing my reputation yet again.

He vanishes from existence, leaving Gord grasping at nothing before reappearing a few feet away, this time level sixteen.

"Someone help me!" he shouts just before I rip through his throat a second time. The crowd stirs, but no one moves to his aid.

This time when he respawns, his eyes are full of madness. "Help me or I'll kill you all!" he rages at the crowd. I kill him again, but this time, my reputation only decreases by half.

"I'll burn this whole town to the ground!" At level fourteen, my reputation stays the same. It seems they are finally seeing him for the monster he is.

"…your children, your children's children, for as long as I live!" Level thirteen.

By level five, Glenn has broken down to tears. When he hits level one, he drools at the mouth and just mumbles to himself.

"This is a dangerous man. If I were you, I would lock

him up before he has a chance to hurt someone you care about."

"What now?" asks someone from the crowd.

"Now, we will go back to our village. We wish you no harm, but if we are attacked, we will respond in kind. My people do not speak the common tongue, so it will be hard for them to communicate with you for now. We will leave you in peace and pray that you will do the same for us." I turn to the trolls. "It is time to return home."

Glenn crawls on all fours as we walk away, mumbling to himself with drool dripping down his chin and madness raging in his eyes. I know this isn't the end of him. In a world where heroes never die, how could it be? I just hope the townspeople keep him locked up long enough for me to finish the final stages of my plan.

Ismora waits for us next to Limery's mother when we return. Aside from a new scar in the shape of Limery's hand, she looks back to normal.

"How did it go?" she asks.

"Time will tell, but I think I may have changed some minds. If nothing else, it will be a while before Glenn troubles you again."

"What do you mean 'you,'" asks Chief Rizza. "Are you leaving us?"

"My time here is nearly up. While I will do my best to try and come back, I don't know how long I will be away or if I will even be able to return. I want to do everything that I can in what little time I have left to make sure that I set you up for success after I am gone. I think we have gained the respect of one town, but the island is large and there are many others who will attack simply for the wyrms."

"And how exactly do you plan to stop that from happening?" she asks.

"By going straight to the source. Lillith, may I speak to you in private for a moment?"

Limery's mother smirks. "Why, Chod, I thought you'd never ask."

She sits on the table in my hut and I take a seat on the bed.

"What's on your mind, big blue?" she asks.

"I need to get a message to the king."

She sits in silence for a moment. "The king? As in—"

"Yes, *the* king. It's life and death important. Can you do it?"

"Chod, imps aren't the preferred messenger of the crown anymore. Not since everything happened with the wizard."

"Just tell me, can you do it or not?"

She runs the tips of her talons over her bottom teeth. "I may have a few favors I'm still owed from the old days."

"Good. How fast can you get there?"

"If I don't stop to rest, I can have it there by tomorrow."

"Then we have no time to waste."

Lillith reaches in a small pouch and pulls out a quill and some paper. "What? Some habits die hard. Now, what should your message say?"

"Hold on." I find my own satchel and pull out the crown I looted from Paltras Ruins.

Item. *Kingly Crown. +10 Charisma.*

I put the crown on and my head spins for a moment. Confidence rushes through my body, and I feel like I could run the world if I wanted to. Why don't I? I'd make a pretty good king.

"Chod?" Lillith vies for my attention. What is it we were doing?

"Right, the message." I remember my goal and let the increased Charisma guide my every word as I tell her what I want to say to the king. The words flow out of my mouth so easily that I wonder why I never went into politics. I'd be a great king. The thought crosses my mind again. I just need a bigger army and I could conquer this entire island. Why didn't I wear the crown when I spoke to the seaside trolls? If I had, they certainly would have joined our cause.

Lillith pulls the crown from my head and it feels like a weight has been lifted. My mind clears and I'm glad to be returned to my lowly six Charisma.

"Would you like me to read the message back to you?" she asks.

"No, just make sure it finds the king." I trust that the Charisma did its job. "Thank you, Lillith. For everything."

With a wink, she disappears out the door.

CHAPTER THIRTY-NINE

39. Game Over

The blue haze distorts Valery's face as she leans over the pod. The nanite level decreases and the door to the pod opens, allowing me to sit up. I cough up some of the nanite gel and my lungs take in a breath of air they haven't experienced in a month. My body feels fine, better than fine, actually. Like I could run a marathon if I wanted.

I lay there for a minute. It's not easy knowing that I might never see my friends again. Limery loved me more than any real person. Gord became like a brother to me before it was all said and done. Tormara, Chief Rizza, Yashi, and all the others hold a special place in my heart as well. To me, they'll always be more than video game characters, even if I never see them again.

The blue gel filled with nanites rolls off my arms and

back as I sit up in the pod. The other twenty-four white pods are closed, their occupants still logged in the game. Video feeds are mounted over their pods, displaying their in-game actions in third person view. Monitors surround each pod with their vitals and in-game stats side by side.

I'm shocked when I see several dozen new pods against the far wall. Black pods like mine. They're empty, but for how long?

"Well, what did you think?" asks Valery. She wears a red dress that hugs her body just like I remember. It's still perplexing to me how someone that looks like that works in a place like this.

"It was amazing. It actually felt like I was a troll. After my body adjusted to the difference in size, it was like I was a six-hundred-pound beast of pure muscle. And the NPCs, they were indistinguishable from you and me."

"That's weird." One of the technicians goes over to the monitor displaying lines of code.

"What's weird?" Valery asks.

"Thompson, come over here," the tech calls another. "You see this?"

"Yeah, that's...strange."

"Will you two nerds tell me what the hell it is you're rambling about?" Valery scolds them.

The first technician runs his fingers through his balding hair. "Something is up with the AI. It's behaving...abnormally."

"Yeah," Thompson echoes. "It's behaving sporadically, almost like it's missing something. You see this?" He points to the screen, showing Valery something I can't see. "This line of code keeps repeating itself. It's like it's searching for something that isn't there."

"What does that mean exactly?" she asks.

"I'm not sure. It's interrupting certain processes. Spawn timers are off for animals, for starters. There are gaps in the mana flow, too."

"What has changed that would explain the sudden chaos?"

"Nothing. We haven't changed anything. We logged Chad out, but he's not a part of the system."

"Okay, well, keep an eye on it and let me know if anything else comes up."

The technicians take a seat and begin typing commands into their tablets. I hope everything is fine for those still in the game.

"Mister Johnson, we have your clothes ready if you would like to change into something less revealing." Valery winks.

In the bathroom, my clothes are neatly pressed and folded on the counter. I slip out of the spandex-style underwear I wore for the last thirty days and quickly dress. I thought I would feel like I needed a shower, but the nanites kept me so well groomed that I feel cleaner than I ever have.

When I exit the bathroom, Valery is waiting for me, tablet in hand.

"We have an exit interview for you to complete. Once you're finished with that, you'll be free to leave."

"Just like that?"

"Just like that. You served your time, now you are ready to become a productive, and hopefully less trollish, member of society. You did a lot of good things while you were in *Isle of Mythos*, Mister Johnson. Imagine if you had that kind of resolve outside the game. You could really make something of yourself."

I've heard those words a million times from my parents. "If you only applied yourself, you could do anything." As if playing games for a living isn't exactly what I wanted to be doing with my life.

"Do you know if my parents are coming to pick me up?"

"We haven't heard anything. We'll be happy to drop you off at your home if you need."

They missed my trial. They missed my sentencing. Thirty days locked away in a game and they haven't made the effort to secure me arrangements. What could be more important than their own child?

She hands me the tablet and I start answering the questionnaire. Questions about my in-game experiences such as "How were the taste and smell receptors?" "Were there moments where you were keenly aware that you were in a game?" It's nearly a hundred questions asking for my input on ways to improve specific instances in-game.

"Can I ask you something?"

"Shoot."

"Glenn, what's his deal?"

"He's a special case. You know, most criminals are still just normal people. Even for those who commit violent crimes, it usually happens in a fit of rage. They're triggered by something and have a reaction. Not to say they are all nice, because many of them are not, but they are just people. Glenn may be the only true psychopath of the bunch. The things we have watched him do... He's more charismatic than you would believe. No one else besides you and him were able to gather a force of hundreds of NPCs to fight for them. He did it multiple times, even after suffering defeat. You may have knocked him down a peg with the shenanigans you pulled, but I have no doubt he'll be back."

"Don't you think it's dangerous, having someone like that in a game where he can actually hurt people?"

"Until you, he was only ever hurting NPCs. He actually seemed to be functioning better for a while there, so we let it continue. The name of the game is rehabilitative therapy after all. If he can take out his aggression and psychopathic tendencies in-game and live a normal life out of it, I'd call that a win."

I don't know if I buy that. Especially in a game this realistic.

I hand Valery the tablet when I'm done, and she escorts me into a waiting room.

"We'll come find you when your ride is ready."

It feels like hours have passed when Valery burst into the room. "Come with me." She practically pulls me out of the chair. She talks as we speed-walk down the hallway. "Our guys have been going over the coding for hours now, trying to figure out what could be causing the malfunction in the AI. It's grasping for something that's not there. It took a while, but we finally narrowed it down."

"What is it?"

Her dark brown eyes stare into my own. "You."

"Me?" How is that even possible?

"Yes, we don't know how, but the AI thinks that you are part of the system. Something must have happened when you started a regional event, or either all your influence on the game caused the AI to think you were part of the system. We don't really know. All we know is that unless you get back in the game, it is going to crash."

My sentence is up, though. It's finally time for me to go home.

"Can't you just restart it?"

"You don't understand. If the game crashes, it doesn't get rebuilt. It would start over as something new. There's no backup for NPCs when they behave like real people. Players would be booted, and every town, city, and NPC that is currently in the game would cease to exist. Forever."

I want to go home, order some pizza, and team up with Taryn for a good smash-fest. I haven't talked to him in a month.

But then, Limery's face flashes through my mind along with every other member of the troll village. They trusted me with their lives. If I leave, they would all be gone in the blink of an eye as if they never existed. Everything I did would be for nothing.

"What do you need me to do?"

"Log back in. Give us a chance to fix this."

"And if you can't?"

"Then you get to decide when it all comes crashing down."

"I'll do it on one condition."

A smile spreads across Valery's face. "What is it?"

"My friend Taryn, I want him to join me in-game. If I'm doing this of my own free will, then I want my partner in crime for whatever comes next."

I strip down into the nanite receptive underwear and take my position in the pod. I thought I would be going home today. Back to an unfulfilling life of talking down to other gamers on the internet. For the past thirty days, I never really missed my old life. I missed Taryn occasionally, but everything else didn't seem to matter much. The minute I logged out of this game, I missed the people I met there. That tells me all I need to know.

Thirty days ago, I was sentenced to troll.

If Valery's people can't fix the problem, if me being in the game is the only way for my people to keep living, then I'll take a life sentence.

ACKNOWLEDGMENTS

Thank you for reading my book! I hope you had as much fun reading about Chod and his adventures as I did writing them. If so, please leave a wonderful review. Reviews are the lifeblood of indie authors like myself, and the more positive reviews I have, the more likely it is that others will read my books as well.

There are so many wonderful people that played an integral part in the creation of this book. You all have my sincerest thanks. Rick Scott, for helping with the ending when I couldn't see the forest for the trees. Blaise Corvin and Lars M., for helping a friend in need out of the goodness of your hearts without asking for anything in return. My Patrons: Michael Didato, Taj El, Richard Hummel, and Tim Krason. You all really go the extra mile. Caroline, for encouraging me to think outside the box. My amazing team of beta readers: Kegan Hall, Ian Mitchell, Michael Spizzirri, Cindy Koepp, Ezben Gerardo, and Jake Goodrich.

If you're looking for more books similar to my own, check out the Gamelit Society and LitRPG Books, two of the best places for all things Gamelit and LitRPG.

And check out the LitRPG Store on Amazon for all the newest genre releases.

ABOUT THE AUTHOR

S.L. Rowland is a nomad. He loves traveling and has road-tripped coast to coast three times over with his Shiba Inu, Lawson. When not writing, he enjoys hiking, reading, weightlifting, playing video games, and having his heart broken by various Atlanta sports teams.

SLRowland.com

Patreon-For signed paperbacks, advanced chapters, exclusive short stories, art, merch, and more. This is a great way to show your support between releases.

Newsletter: For updates on new releases and all things Pangea Online related! Click the link at the end of the book to download *Path to Villainy* for free.

Email: slrowland@slrowland.com

ALSO BY S.L. ROWLAND

Pangea Online

Pangea Online: Death and Axes

Pangea Online 2: Magic and Mayhem

Pangea Online 3: Vials and Tribulations

Sentenced to Troll

Sentenced to Troll

Sentenced to Troll 2

Sentenced to Troll 3

Sentenced to Troll 4

Sentenced to Troll 5

Path to Villainy: An NPC Kobold's Tale

Vestiges: Portal to the Apocalypse

Collected Editions

Pangea Online: The Complete Trilogy

Sentenced to Troll Compendium: Books 1-3

Printed in Great Britain
by Amazon